LOVE AND WAR

With thanks to:

Keith Topping – the creator of Johnny Chess.
Martin Day – much patience.
The MSCT – fraternity.
Jonathan Head – research.
Penny List – moral support.

And to all my friends, for their love and patience.
And thanks to Mum and Dad, for Bread and Butter and Honey.

For

Julia Houghton

&

Lisa Wardle

THE NEW
Doctor Who
ADVENTURES

LOVE AND WAR

Paul Cornell

First published in Great Britain in 1992 by
Doctor Who Books
an imprint of Virgin Publishing Ltd
338 Ladbroke Grove
London W10 5AH

ISBN 0 426 20385 2

A catalogue record for this title is available from the British Library

Cover illustration by Lee Sullivan
Printed and bound in Great Britain by
Cox & Wyman Ltd, Reading, Berks.
Typeset by Type Out, London SW16

The Prologues:
Deaths

Two birds circled each other in the sky above the Lincolnshire marshes. They were owls in love, as much as owls could love. They were two predators, spinning past each other through the night. Their thoughts were animal concerns of nest and prey, and the moon shone bright on their outstretched wings.

Owls in love notice little, but they know more than humans might think they do. Under the full moon, in the wind that breathed over the midnight marshland, they heard a noise. To you or I, it would be the noise of a car. The owls swept past each other again, and shared the thought in their pass that the noise was a dark thing, darker than they were.

The noise was a memory-to-be, a little piece of tragedy. The owls looked down, and their eyes fastened, in and in, searching out the heart of the noise.

They provided words for what they saw too, in the semi-language of owls. The words were a kind of poem, a long song, and the poem began like this:

Long ago, when love was real, an orange Allegro screeched around a corner, throwing up gravel on the single-track road. Its headlights caught a rabbit on the verge, and the animal hopped back into cover.

In front of the car the road split into three, and there was no signpost. Wavering slightly, the speeding car shot up the middle path.

'How did you know that was the right one?' shouted the woman.

'I didn't!' called Julian, laughing. 'What's on your map, Ace?'

'A load of nothing.'

'We're getting there then!'

There had been this road on the map that headed out towards

the sea, and then stopped. Not in a town or anything, just stopped dead. Julian had shown up outside the school gates that morning, and thrown his L-plates at Ace. She was Ace by then, of course, developing that Ace frown that was starting to push her friends into two groups: the ones who wanted to walk over the line and the ones who wanted to walk away. She was fifteen.

Julian was a lot older. He'd been over quite a few lines and walked both ways. Ace liked him loads, like he was an older brother. They'd shoved on a Bowie tape and driven north, eating at a motorway service station, and wandering around Lincoln Cathedral, talking.

When Ace was on the point of wondering if they'd be calling the police at home, or if they'd notice she'd gone, she'd spotted the road to nowhere. It stopped, out in the middle of a void on the map.

Of course, she had to see what was out there.

The flatlands sped past the windows, September winds whipping into the car. Standing on top of a bluff near Scrane End, Ace had smelt a terrible approaching cold in that wind and shivered.

She was too young to feel so bad, she thought. If you ran at that cold, if you ran and ran at it, holding your arms wide like you were a leaf launching into autumn, then maybe you could turn the horror into some kind of experience. You didn't have to be sad about the seasons.

Lights were approaching in the distance. Julian glanced at Ace and scrunched up his face in that way of his. 'Whatever's out here, it's very bright.'

'Maybe it's a spaceship!'

'You wish. Let's find out.'

'You always do that, don't you? Jump in and have a go.'

Julian shrugged. 'You have to live before you die.'

The first clump of earth dropped on to the coffin lid.

Ace blinked in the summer sunlight. She'd been thinking about that old Allegro. Julian had had only one more car before he'd died. Ace had only seen him one more time. He hadn't been ill, but he'd had that distracted expression that suggested he might have known.

Known that he only had two years of life left.

Ace looked up at the sky as the soil covered the name plaque. She wasn't listening to what the vicar was saying. There was quite a crowd around the grave, mainly the young men that Julian had known in London. While his relatives wept and shuddered, they stood with a sorrow that was kind of fraternal, like what Julian had been would continue as part of them.

Ace thought that was good. She hadn't wanted to weep herself, because, dear as he'd been, she hadn't seen Julian for years. Recent experiences had taught her about the pain of nostalgia. Maybe she'd think about it a while later, shed a few tears when she'd got the memories sorted out. You had to be careful with tears. Ace sometimes wished that that wasn't true.

A boy glanced up at her, and their eyes met. He was very beautiful. After a second, he nodded in greeting, and Ace felt a little parting of time. If it had gone another way, long ago, she might have been with Julian. Loved him.

Parting two: then they might both be dead.

Ace gave the boy a gentle smile.

The sun was getting lower over Perivale, splitting through the trees as they trooped out of the cemetery to the waiting cars. Autumn was rushing in hungrily, a cold breeze in every three warm ones.

'I thought you said you weren't coming back.' Shreela had taken Ace's arm. 'Are you staying?'

'No. I can come back anytime I want. How're you doing, anyway?'

'Oh . . . ' The Asian woman sighed, looking at her feet. 'Okay. We all are. Trying to make sense of what happened to us.'

'Wouldn't bother if I were you. I haven't managed.'

'Come and have a pint at least.'

Ace squeezed her friend's arm. 'I wish I could. But I have a lift waiting . . . '

Shreela grinned as she saw the twinkle in Ace's eye.

The walked up Horsenden Hill, talking about the Christmas cards that Chad Boyle had suddenly sent everybody last year, after years of silence, and about poor dead Midge and poor dead Julian. Shreela had actually called Chad up and got a job on his newspaper, doing odd jobs in the office, learning the trade.

Shreela was about to mention Mum, Ace could tell. She didn't know that Ace had actually walked up to her old front door that morning, looked through the letterbox. She'd asked the gang not to mention that they'd met her recently. Maybe Mum thought she was dead. After all, the time storm that pulled her away from Earth had left things in a mess. If she'd mourned and got over it all, Ace sometimes thought that there was no point in going back and opening all Mum's old wounds.

But, and this was odd, as Ace got older she was thinking more and more of just popping in, having a cuppa. Hugging her Mum and just saying, No, that was just a stupid childish daydream. That couldn't happen, so there was no use thinking about it.

She put a finger over Shreela's lips. They hugged, made their goodbyes, and Ace was left alone to climb the hill.

She was feeling sadder than at the funeral. Must be the cold, stinging her through her jacket's fraying seams. Damn, maybe she was going to cry after all. Well, if that was gonna happen, she'd stay here and get rid of it. Julian had been such a happy man, why do people like that always have to go? What's the point in that? But the walk was hard, and that kept her emotions in check.

Besides, in Ace's life, there was something that worked against sadness every time.

On top of Horsenden Hill stood a police box that was not a police box.

Outside it lay an odd little man, his hands behind his head. His eyes were closed, and the low sunlight sparkled off the dark gem in his ring. He didn't seem cold at all.

Ace smiled. How could she be sad when the Doctor was in the world?

She'd been surprised when he'd woken her up that morning, looking rather uncomfortable. He'd told her that there was a sad event she ought to attend. Of course, he hadn't told her what it was, but that was because he had real trouble with spiky feelings sometimes.

Getting here at all must have been difficult. The TARDIS,

the Doctor's multidimensional police-box craft, had been behaving erratically lately. One time, Ace had been wandering along a corridor for what seemed ages, only to realise that she was never going to get to the other end. She'd turned around and sprinted in the other direction, and actually watched as a door sped away from her, the corridor becoming an endless loop. Finally, she'd slammed the wall in frustration, and a new door had appeared.

When she'd told the Doctor, he'd just raised an eyebrow, and put it down to the age of the ship. But then, the Doctor was getting strange these days too, a bit distant, like he was plotting again. Another big game hunt, another war against the monsters. Hadn't that attitude got him into enough trouble already?

Ace crept forward across the grass, her fake leather gloves just above the surface. She hadn't know what to wear to a funeral, but at least it was all black. Should have been orange, like Julian's hair.

She reached out a hand to flick the Doctor's chin, but one eye opened, and he grinned.

'How did it go?'

Ace rolled on to the grass and nestled her head next to his. 'Mate of mine died, they put him in a hole, end of story. Wish I'd known he was going. I'd really like to have been there for him.'

'If I'd have been able to get you there –'

'I know.' Ace put a hand under her chin and looked into the Doctor's eyes. The Doctor wasn't a man, although he looked like one. Shreela had joked about Ace looking for a father figure, and Ace had replied that it was more like an ancestor figure, since the Doctor was 783 years old, give or take a year. He was a Time Lord, more than a Time Lord, from the ancient world of Gallifrey. He navigated time-space in a police box. He fought evil and did good. And he was Ace's best friend.

'I've nothing to do . . . ' the Doctor frowned. 'Nowhere to go.'

'No monsters to finish off?'

'All the dragons are dead. Little Jimmy Piper isn't pleased. Do you fancy going to do something trivial?'

'Fine. I'm still a bit shook up by the funeral. Hasn't really hurt yet.'

'It will. When it does, I'll slip away into a library, to find a book that I've been thinking about . . . ' The Doctor raised a finger, and bounced it up and down, watching Ace's gaze follow it. 'Shall we go?'

'Let's go,' said Ace.

Silently, the insectlike forms of three Peggcorp swift-response fighters streaked through the cometary debris on the fringe of a binary star system.

'The edge of human space . . . ' Captain Mark Diski wandered between stations on the bridge of his ship, stroking his beard. 'Here be Daleks . . . '

Brewer looked up from the sensor desk nervously. She knew that Diski had the ear of the Managing Director, and was hoping for a full Sword and Colours if he could find the missing Dalek fleet. The War was still blazing away in other quadrants, but Earth wasn't itself under threat at the moment. So, an individual captain with an urge to travel . . . well, he could go far.

Rumours persisted that during the battle of Alpha Centauri, when a small squadron of Silurian – Brewer checked herself, they liked to be called Earth Reptiles now – vessels had seen off the main Dalek force, a whole fleet of the tin monsters had vanished into hyperspace. They were almost a legend now. It was a mark of Diski's reputation that he had been given such resources to locate them. Personally, Brewer hoped that he wouldn't.

'Full sweep reveals nothing, sir. May I point out that at this range we are in danger of Sontaran interest.'

'Nonsense, Kate! They're busy in the Magellanic Cloud. I just hope the Daleks have fallen foul of them. We'll do a reconnaissance on the solid worlds here, then . . . Benson, we'll warp out two more systems, so have a course ready.' Diski settled back at his command post, and flipped open the heavily bound leather volume that was his log. Pulling the quill from his belt, he made a note. Half those notes, thought Brewer, were just dashes, a nervous habit made into an official pose. The book had been a gift from the MD, of course. Diski thumped the book closed, and stood again, his eyes gazing wildly into the darkness.

His eyes found that suddenly something was there.

'Massive body emerging from hyperspace!' Brewer was shouting, suddenly. 'Weapons systems reacting –'

'Stop them,' Diski cut in. 'That's not a Dalek design.'

It was a vast sphere, almost the size of a small moon. Its surface shone a glossy brown, and any features on it were tiny. A thin tracery of mottled lines ran over the body of the sphere. It was rolling through space, the glistening exterior reflecting the orange hue of the twin suns, and it was right in front of the patrol.

Something about the sphere made Diski feel nauseous. 'Battle stations anyhow ... ' he murmured. 'Give me a run-down on what that thing's made of.'

'Not responding to our messages,' the com officer called. 'It's not emitting at all.'

'It's made of ... organic material!' Brewer glanced up at Diski.

'Alive?' The Captain frowned. 'Not possible.'

'Not alive, sir. There are standard life processes going on inside, but the surface ... ' Brewer bit her lip. 'That's dead skin.'

Diski spun to ask the science station if anything like this had ever been encountered by humans before. The answer would have been in the negative, but before the question could be asked, a shout came from the navigator. 'Sir! Look at this!'

The woman had punched up the display on the main screen. Billions of pixels were approaching the dots that represented the three patrol ships. 'It's small, sir, but there's lots of it.'

'Visual.'

A great white spume was billowing across space from the sphere, towards the patrol ships.

'Evasive action!' barked Diski, but it was too late. They were inside the cloud. The vision screens blazed and gave out as the external sensor pods failed.

'We're covered sir, there's –'

A low concussion sounded from deep in the ship. For a moment, a silent horror swept the faces of the bridge crew. Then they grabbed for emergency oxygen lines. Clasping his to his face, Diski shouted, 'Which lock?'

‘Science pod lock . . . ’ A helmsman was frantically running a systems check. ‘Vital signs down for . . . od’s blood, six engineers! The whole lower deck is out!’

‘Any leakage here?’

‘Wait . . . no. No.’ The crew dropped the masks, and started running through emergency routines.

‘All sensors dead,’ Brewer reported.

‘Full reverse, we’ll run away. Tell the other ships if you can, Hussain . . . ’

At the rear of the bridge, the airlock panel bleeped. Diski spun round. The sound meant that someone was coming through to the bridge. ‘Shug, we’ve got this wrong! Small arms, we’re being boarded!’

The crew snatched up their hand weapons, Diski himself jumped behind the com to take up a position aiming at the door. Brewer glanced at her panel. ‘Sir, this isn’t possible, the hull has contact monitors and they’re still working. We’re swamped with the stuff, but –’

‘Hush!’

The lock slid open. A spacesuited figure entered, staggering. The nameplate on the suit said ‘Carter’. The bridge crew relaxed, some giving out laughs of relief. Carter was the chief engineer. The helmsman shouted that he was supposed to be dead.

Diski stood up, feeling rather foolish, and tucked his blaster back in his sash.

Carter grabbed his own pistol and blew Diski’s head off.

The corpse was catapulted into the com, and the crewmen dived aside, small explosions spurting on their desks.

Brewer fired twice, heart and abdomen. So did the rest of the armed crew. Carter’s body stumbled backwards as bursts of high-energy light sliced through it, flesh blasting off it in clumps. An arm spiralled off in a burst of ash and heat.

And then he fired back.

The weapon was set to automatic. An arc of blue fire danced along the control boards, slicing officers where it touched them, severing limbs and heads, boiling away blood and muscle. Shots still hitting him, Carter carefully mowed down the opposition. Clouds of steam and body fluid filled the cabin.

Brewer was the last, huddling behind her post. She believed in Allah, and cared about her species, and she was proud that she felt no fear at her approaching death. As Carter's blasts reduced her instruments to molten slag, she shot away his joints, his face plate, his genitals, his chest . . .

The fatal shot took her straight between the eyes, and for a tiny second she was glad. Then her corpse slapped backwards into the panel and lay still.

The thing that had been Carter paused for a moment, inhaling the slaughter. Then it staggered to the weapons post, its body's synapses failing. Jerkily, it reached out for a control.

The missiles struck the second ship in the fleet, blind as it was, without warning. The explosion bloomed for a moment in the silence, and the ship was gone.

Diski's ship turned slowly, and faced the remaining craft. Its engines flared, for an instant, and then the two vessels touched.

The second explosion lasted an instant longer than the first had.

The sphere, alone once more, paused to consider the situation.

Then, with a sense of pleasure, it began to roll slowly through space again.

1:
Heaven's Gate

The world was Heaven. Shirankha Hall had called it that when his deep-space incursion squadron had sheltered there from the pursuing Draconian fleet. The place was way off line, in a system halfway between the ever-growing Dragon and Human protectorates. It was a place to hide.

His crews had wandered through the grassy plains, marvelled that there were no large predators, made themselves comfortable under the grand arches of some long-lost race.

It had, actually, reminded Hall of a book he'd read a long time ago. He thought of calling the place Senacharib, except that would have been a private joke and Hall, having wandered long and alone in the meadows himself, wanted everybody to know about them.

So, he called it Heaven in Common Tongue, which meant that the translation fitted with whatever your own particular vision of bliss was. The High Command hadn't liked that much. They hadn't liked it either when Hall, once the Dragon Wars had ended and the two species were united against the Daleks, walked into the Draconian Embassy and told the Ambassador about Heaven too.

The Ambassador was old Ishkavaarr, the Great Peacemaker, Pride of a Thousand Eggs. He and the President of Earth were working on a deal then, as they always were, and Ishkavaarr was worrying about it. One night, he woke from a dream, because Dragons do dream, and realised what the missing element was.

He called Madam President in the middle of the night, actually woke her up, and, laughing in his hissing Draconian way, told her that he knew what they both could do. The key was a world called Heaven.

Heaven was to be the Edge Of Empire, the Peacemaker

explained, a place that both sides would love to be able to visit, but neither really needed very much. It had no mineral wealth, no actual tactical value. Not even the Daleks would want it. It was, simply, beautiful. What if the two great powers were to take joint possession, declare Heaven an open world, and use the place to bury their dead?

The President was amused.

Years later, during a lull in the fighting, the leaders of the two powers met one glistening summer morning on Heaven. The grass was blowing lightly in the warm breeze, and small herbivores were gently chewing the cud. The Emperor and President signed several agreements, she wearing the ceremonial robes of an Honorary Prince. Members of their entourages sighed and sneaked off to lie in the sun and fall in love. War made any calm planet into Heaven, but this one seemed suitable for the name.

Before he died, Ishkavaarr wrote: 'If I may be allowed to be a prophet, I believe that Heaven was given to both our peoples deliberately. There is a purpose in the giving, and a purpose that we may not discover for many years. I believe that purpose is a good and just one.'

In a typically Draconian manner, Ishkavaarr was both right and very wrong.

Ace wandered through the corridors of the TARDIS, more carefully than she once would have done, staying in the areas that she knew well. It was night, the TARDIS was travelling towards its new destination, and the low lighting of the walls would occasionally give way to patches of darkness.

It was still good dark, at least. Under-the-bedclothes dark, somewhere to feel safe. Sometimes when she had felt bad in the past, she had come upon a room full of books, or the gym out of place, as if the time-craft had known what she needed and put it there.

Well, it was no surprise that it didn't seem to know this time. Ace wasn't sure what she was after, either. It was just one of those nights, the tail end of the wrong time of the month, when there was nothing to do but walk.

Ace stopped, and leaned against the wall, feeling the warmth of it with the palm of her hand. The roundels meant something like home, now. When you thought about it, that wasn't great. Just the other day she'd wanted to ask the Doctor to take her back in time to see Julian again. She hadn't asked, because she'd know what he would have said: that you can't go back, that things have to be said in the here and now.

He'd once told her that the First Law of Time was a moral law as well as a legal one. The Doctor broke it all the time, of course, stage-managing his battles with monsters.

But still . . . Ace thought she could have done it nicely. She would just have had a day out with Jules, gone to the seaside or something. It would have been a bit sad, but okay. She could at least have kissed him and said a proper goodbye.

Kissing Julian had been great. It had happened once, outside Ace's house. It had started off as a brotherly peck and turned into a full-blown snog. Julian had run off, pretending that he'd seen the curtain twitching. The truth was that he'd already decided what he wanted.

Ace sighed, and ran a hand down her face angrily. What was the point in knowing about grief if it didn't help you get rid of it? And why couldn't she just sit down and remember it all, and let it all flood past?

Still, it was a long time since Ace had been kissed. The thought gave her a small smile.

Professor Bernice Summerfield awoke with a start, sat up in bed, and laughed her head off.

She quickly slapped a hand to her mouth. She'd better not wake up Kyla and Clive in the next tent. They'd been working flat out for days, bless them.

Bernice's hand snaked out from her sleeping bag, and located the clock. Well, it was six-ish. Still on Earth time, after all these years out here. Mind you, on Heaven, Earth time was fine, because the planet had a twenty-three-hour day.

She allowed her head to drop back to the pillow and sighed. She didn't feel like sleeping. An Ellerycorp archaeology grant got you only so far, and time was running out on this one. Clive and the gang would have to be off to their various universities, and she . . . well, she'd have to find somewhere else to go.

Somewhere far out . . . somewhere where she might find . . .

Bernice killed the thought. That way lay madness.

Right.

Benny unzipped the bag, and pulled on some sturdy trousers and a pullover. Tipping a few paper credits out of her boots, she quickly started to lace them.

She opened the tent, and strode out into dawn rising over Heaven.

Benny was thirty. Much humour there, she remembered; oh yes, this team of hers had fondly taken the piss. Thing is, she didn't feel much different. Still a girl, still drinking too much wine and sighing a lot and keeping that stupid diary.

She stretched her arms over her head and yawned. The endless downland all around was green and quiet and lovely. It was still on the edge of dark, the green a sort of hint under waves of retreating black. In the distance, a forest loomed on the horizon. The night creatures would be slowly retreating there, Benny reflected, curling up in burrows to avoid the dawn. The air was cool and crisp, and dew had formed on the grass. The first birds were chirruping from their woodland nests, and, against the deep blue of the sky, a pair of owls were slowly flapping their way home.

Humans had brought owls to Heaven, and they liked it here as much as the people did.

The tents were garish orange against the bulk of the hillside, but they weren't the biggest shock in the landscape. Benny was staring at that, as amazed by it now as she had been the first time.

The Arch.

It stood, shining silver, flaring with the first touches of the sun. It looked newly poured, a vertical arc, ten storeys tall. Below it was the pit, the site of the dig, a hole dug out by the team, now supported by wooden slats and accessed by ladder.

Benny was sad that such beauty had to be spoiled to learn more about it. But to learn about anything you have to break it.

She smoothed back her short dark hair. 'Nothing bad here,' she murmured. 'You only get good dreams on Heaven.'

The TARDIS ground into existence in a muddy market square, causing a flock of chickens to scatter, squawking.

Ace stepped out first, pulling on her jacket and sniffing the air. Gorgeous. Lots of ozone, and a warm purity that made you think of mineral water and new cotton sheets. 'Come on out, Professor,' she called back into the police box, 'we're in a shampoo advert.'

Well, that wasn't really true. The square itself was muddy, and filled with tents and stalls and tethered animals. It was only the sky above the place that made it look so fabulous. The sky was very blue, empty of all clouds and celebrating the rise of a big sun.

The people of the market had reacted only slightly to the materialisation of the TARDIS. They had turned their heads, shrugged, laughed and moved on. That, Ace knew, was an unusual reaction. The arrival of the Doctor's timecraft usually instigated panic, anger, and the approach of arresting officers.

The Doctor stepped out, locking the door behind him and jamming his hat on his head. 'Chickens,' he said. He peered down at the birds as they scattered, smiling his halfway smile. That smile always made Ace nervous, 'cos it wasn't his cartoon grin, or his secret freak-the-enemy smile. It was a smile like the arrow on a decorative barometer. One Doctor was going in with the sun, another one was coming out, ready for the storm. The Time Lord squatted suddenly, took a handful of earth, and sniffed it heartily.

'Yeah.' Ace glanced around the square. Ancient stone walls surrounded it, and electric trailers buzzed out through an oddly shaped arch. Women in large white tricorns were carrying sacks of heavy produce over their shoulders. 'What's this place called then?'

'Heaven,' replied the Doctor, frowning. He stood up, dropping the soil from his hand. 'It's pastoral. A small community of settlers, lots of people passing through.' He swung his umbrella up over one shoulder and strode forward. 'Lots of people staying. There would be tourists, but we're in the middle of decades of war. Messy war, all over the place, front changing continually. Daleks, mainly . . . '

'Daleks? Are they here, do you reckon?'

The Doctor sniffed the breeze. 'No. Why do you always assume the worst?'

'Must be the life I lead.'

The Doctor frowned at her. 'People here are poor. But there's one thing that makes Heaven special, something I'll explain later . . . '

'Why?'

'I like to illustrate my explanations. I'm here because of the library. A library of forbidden texts . . . they come here for the same reason the people do. They're not wanted on Earth.'

Ace was about to ask what the book the Doctor was after was, but a sound had wafted across the square. It was so familiar that, at first, it hadn't registered. She'd heard it only this morning while she was washing her hair. 'Hey,' she grabbed the Doctor's sleeve. 'That's "Golden Green".'

'Ah . . . ' the Doctor nodded sagely. 'Yes. I see . . . '

'A song,' Ace explained, sighing. 'I've got it on a tape in the TARDIS. What are they doing playing it here? Won't be a second . . . '

She turned and started to walk in the opposite direction.

The Doctor stopped and turned to look after her. For a moment, his face clouded, as though he was thinking about roads. Roads taken and roads ignored. Then, with hesitant step, he followed his friend.

Ace was listening to the music. It was stopping and starting like a band was rehearsing. If somebody was busking, they weren't gonna make much cash. Pushing her way past a stall of colourful fabrics, she caught sight of the people making the noise.

'Crusties in space!' she grinned. There were five of them, dreadlocked and scruffy, heavy coats and solid boots over elegant tattoos. They wore heavy wool for warmth, and dogs clustered around them for protection. Ace knew them from the city centres of her childhood, travellers from the convoy, moving about Britain, barely surviving on what they could busk, beg or steal. Ace had no romantic image of them. While she'd been talking to one guy that year at Glastonbury, another had tried to snatch her jacket. She'd bust his nose, and the gang had had to drag her away from a gathering knot of the travellers, who, as always, clustered together to defend each other.

Still, it was a blast to see that they were still going, all these years into the future. The symbols weren't quite the same. This group wore pentagram medallions, but the A of Anarchy had, over the years, melded in with the starlike pattern of the design.

There were three men and two women in the group, who had just started up the song again. They had a basket in front of them, and were looking up expectantly at the morning shoppers, hoping for coins. One of the women had dark, cropped hair, too short for dreads; the other had a whole mass of them, tied tight to her head. She carried a very visible gun in her belt, and beside it hung three long, pipelike objects that Ace recognized but couldn't place. The women were playing small finger drums, alternating to build up a complex beat. Thumping away at a larger drum was a stocky man, his shoulder muscles visible even through his heavy coat. His short beard was straggly like he hadn't shaved for months. Behind the group stood a thin figure in a cloak, staring out at the passers-by almost accusingly. Ace was sure that that wasn't going to do the band any favours. She'd thought that the figure was a man, because he had a male chin and cheeks, but the eyes and shaved head were almost feminine. Ace found herself unsure, and fascinated.

'Got any money, then?' The voice had come from beneath her gaze. Ace realised that she'd wandered almost up to the group, looking up at the strange figure that stood above them. Yeah, that was the idea, right? She glanced down, and found herself looking at the most beautiful man she'd seen this side of Kirith.

No, he was ugly. Well, he was both. He was thin, sure, with a wolfish edge to his clean-shaven jaw, but there was something lopsided about his face, just on the edge of perception, like he'd got a real bad side. A real bad side. His eyes were bright blue, the sort that you could really get hung up about if you let yourself. He played a sort of guitarlike instrument, and had just stopped to scratch his neck and look at her. He wasn't smiling, quite. He saw her as just another customer, something to keep him alive.

So Ace didn't answer. She turned away, and walked straight into the Doctor, who had been carefully examining an old egg-timer on a stall of someone's dead possessions. 'So, where's this library?' she asked.

'This way,' the Doctor muttered, not quite looking her in the eye. They started back the way they had come, and walked for a while, the sun rising steadily over the mottled buildings. After some time, Ace slowed down.

'No, Professor, this isn't right.'

'Isn't it?'

'Long time ago, I told myself that if I had enough, I'd always give money to people that needed it. That lot back there looked as if they did. I just got scared by that guy in front –'

'They shouldn't scare you,' the Doctor murmured, interrupting her. 'That doesn't help.'

Ace frowned. 'Well, maybe it works sometimes. Anyway, I'm just gonna nip back and give them something, okay?'

'Yes. That's the Library, over there.' The Doctor pointed with his umbrella to a fluted spire that rose above the cluster of buildings that they were approaching. 'Can you find it?'

' 'Course I can. See you in a minute.' Ace dashed off back into the market.

The Doctor shook his head, peering after her. For a moment, he seemed very sad. He turned towards the Library, then, with a wince, he turned back, and followed his companion.

The wolflike man was counting coins from the basket into a pouch when Ace got back to their pitch. He carefully left a few in there to make it look like nobody was giving the musicians much.

Ace strode up confidently this time, wondering what the hell had scared her. She didn't understand herself, sometimes. Getting old. She grinned at the guy with the guitar, and was about to say something, but he looked up at her suddenly.

And Ace was scared all over again.

It was like time was tapping on her shoulder. The morning breeze sent a shiver down Ace's spine that lit her up from her cheeks to the small of her back.

'Oh, no, wait!' The man stood up, his long coat flapping against his guitar as he placed it aside. 'What's wrong? Are you lost?'

Whatever had got inside Ace found itself beaten against the wall of her skull by a sudden swell of anger. He was talking to her like she was a lost child!

'No. I was just gonna give you some cash, that's all. What're you staring at?'

'Sorry.' He lowered his eyes to the ground and smiled gently. 'I stare, I know. We need the credits and I don't want you to feel worried. It's just that you seemed to run away. I was only asking.' He seemed to be a little angry with himself, like a man who had dropped a favourite ornament. He had a strange accent, halfway between Irish and something colonial. He seemed . . . lost.

The woman with the cropped hair glanced up at the sky and sighed theatrically. 'Do anything for money, Jan will, like. It's one of his better features.'

Jan, without looking up, muttered something that Ace realised she wasn't supposed to understand, a curse in another language. Being with the Doctor allowed Ace to understand anything, which was way cool.

'No problem,' Ace laughed in Palare. 'How much d'you want?'

'She speaks the Palare!' hooted the bearded man on the drum. 'Now you should marry her, Jan!'

Jan reached across and tugged the man's beard. Hard.

Ace reached into her jacket and threw three Decacredits into the basket. Jan's hand was on them instantly, and his eyes flew up to meet Ace's again. 'You Palare Roman but you're rich. Want to join us?'

'I'm not rich.' Ace had never really thought about it, but the Doctor carried with him a vast supply of wealth in different currencies. All Ace had ever really wanted money for was clothes, gigs and a ticket on the last train out. Now she had all she wanted, and the priorities hadn't really changed. 'I'm Ace. Where did you learn "Golden Green"?'

'From Cathlan here,' Jan jerked his head to indicate the bearded man. 'It's a traditional song, passed on down all along the Convoy.'

Ace didn't argue. 'Know any Johnny Chess?'

Jan picked up his guitar and strummed the first few chords of 'Baby, The Rain Must Fall'. His eyes never left Ace's. His pupils were huge.

'Wonderful!' The Doctor walked up the group, smiling. 'I'm the Doctor, and this is my friend Ace.'

'Professor!' Ace turned to him, startled away from the lovely blue. 'Don't get in the way of a good song!'

'Oh, I can't sing it.' Jan grinned. 'I'm not a good singer.'

'So what are you good at?' Ace asked, finding that her eyes had met those of the woman with cropped hair.

'Playing music and blagging . . . oh, and there's one more thing I'm good at.'

At the same instant, three things happened. The Doctor, who had been counting out three coins into the basket, began to say something. The woman with the cropped hair whacked Jan lightly with her drum. And the tall being at the back of the group shouted. This was what got Ace's attention.

'There are troopers coming!' The being had closed its eyes.

'How long, Christopher?' asked the dreadlocked woman, flicking a catch on her pistol.

The being considered, and Ace made the mental note that he must be a man. 'They will be here in . . . oh. Now.'

A plasma charge blew a chicken into a ball of expanding feathers. Ace automatically rolled aside into the cover of a stall, but Jan had dived with her, and was shouting to his people to run away.

A group of soldiers, dressed in blue uniforms, were running into the square. A man began to yell about his chickens. The leader of the squad pointed at the scattering Travellers. Blue blasts of light hissed through the air, turning pots and pans to ionised gas as they dove past a metalwork stall.

'That's Kale!' Jan snarled into Ace's ear. 'The mad spaleen, he'll take anyone's cash!'

He grabbed her hand as if to run, but Ace wrenched it away again. 'So what have you done?'

'Nothing! He just wants to turn us over, maybe get friendly with Roisa, I don't know. Find us, lass, I want to see you again!' Biting his lip, Jan jumped from cover and weaved his way through the market. Peering up from under the stall, Ace could see that the market traders were shouting at the troops. Barrows full of vegetables had been overturned as the militia barged their way in.

Ace caught a glimpse of the two women jogging, bent at the waist, away towards a side exit. The one with the gun had it pointed at an angle from her, ready to blast at anyone who got in the way. Christopher was walking imperiously towards the front gate, his robes and tall strength marking him out. Still, the guards didn't seem to notice, one even tripping over the being's foot, then jumping up and looking around in surprise.

Jan was making his way along the wall, behind a rack of furs. Suddenly, the guard called Kale caught sight of him, and aimed his rifle.

Ace shouted out a warning. But it was going to be too late.

The guard aimed and was about to squeeze the trigger.

Suddenly, his gun was jerked skywards.

'You don't want to do that!' said the Doctor. 'You haven't followed due process . . . '

Kale whirled, pulling his weapon from the Doctor. 'I could kill you right now!' he shouted.

'No. You couldn't. Not in front of so many witnesses. Who do you work for?'

'Operative Miller, you little –'

'Who do you really work for? IMC? The Spinward Corporation? The BBC? Can you remember?' The Doctor stepped forward, walking straight into Kale. He noticed that a patch on the man's arm identified him as an IMC man. Guards were already clustering around, anticipating trouble. 'Let me through,' he told them, advancing. 'I'm the Doctor.'

'How do you –?' Kale was blustering, afraid to meet the steely glare of the Time Lord. He'd stepped back, and found himself retreating as the Doctor kept on walking. He raised his gun to chest height.

'You can't shoot me, you can't arrest me. You're hollow. Run away.'

Kale opened his mouth, looking as if he was about to cry. Then he turned on his heel and strutted off. The other guards looked between him and the Doctor, wonderingly.

After a moment, Kale turned back and shouted. 'I'll let you off this time, but you better be careful in future!'

'I always am,' the Doctor said, smiling to himself. The guards wandered off. The Travellers had vanished.

Ace emerged from hiding and leant on the Doctor's shoulder. 'Well confrontational,' she grinned. 'Thanks.'

'Yes.' The Doctor frowned. 'Now, shall we find that book?'

As they wandered towards the gate of the market, listening to the laughter and cheers of the stallkeepers, Ace found an apple in her pocket. Maybe Jan had grabbed it from where they were hiding and stuffed it there.

She remembered that he'd bit his lip when he left.

That had to be because he was about to risk his life, right? Not about what he'd just said to her?

Ace bit into the apple thoughtfully.

The old man moved a book from one shelf to another, and back. He stared at the spines, and closed his eyes, raising a nervous hand to his mouth. It was as if some thought, far back in the dark of his mind, kept coming back to him.

The sudden noise made him spin round, gasping.

The Doctor picked up the slim volume of Marlowe that he had dropped, and raised his hat in greeting. 'Hello, I'm the Doctor. This is my friend Ace. I'm after a certain volume . . . perhaps you could help.'

'Oh!' the librarian put a hand to his chest. 'You startled me. I don't get many visitors here . . . '

Ace had been looking around the building. The shelves themselves were metal, reminding her of some civil service office. They were out of place in a building like this, she thought. The walls were smooth and grand, and arched up to a round skylight that was surrounded by abstract carvings.

'Because this is a Terran repository,' the Doctor murmured, glancing up at the smooth white curves of the vaulted ceiling. 'The Terran Parchment Library in fact. Funded by six corporations. And we're trespassing. The architecture . . . very dramatic. A suitable place for literature . . . especially literature that has to be stored away from prying eyes. What's your name?'

The librarian blinked at the abrupt turn the Doctor's train of thought had taken. 'Why, I'm Trench. Fyan Trench. Why do you want to know?'

'I like to know who I'm dealing with,' the Doctor said, glancing around at the high shelves of books. 'This place was built by the Heavenites, wasn't it?'

'Yes, so they say. Well, I suppose it must have been. It was here, along with quite a few other buildings, when the first humans arrived here.'

'You what?' Ace grinned at the Doctor. 'This is all alien, then?'

The Doctor was about to hush his companion, but Trench seemed eager to talk to Ace.

'Oh yes, my dear! The colonists used the buildings as administration centres, and, since this place seemed vaguely like a library . . . ' The old man shrugged.

'Bit empty, innit?' Ace smiled at Trench. 'D'you work here all alone?'

'Indeed I do. I have no great need for sleep in my old age, so I do what has to be done, only gradually. You might visit me and have a cup of chocolate, if you'd like . . . '

Normally, Ace would have found such a direct offer a bit off-putting, but the loneliness in the old man's voice was obvious, and the poor guy seemed really scared of the Professor.

'Sure. Yeah.'

A bit strengthened, Trench turned to the Doctor. 'Have you recently arrived here, sir? Or are you perhaps with the archaeologists?'

'Archaeologists?'

'Yes, Professor Summerfield's party, excavating in Yeatsland. They hope to find some bodies, it is said, because of the nature of the ground.'

'I might nip over for a visit,' the Doctor smiled. 'But for the moment, I'm more interested in a book. It's called *The Papers of Felsecar*, an ancient text of Felsecar Abbey. They're a little worried about it on Felsecar, put it in the Out tray instead of the In, you know.'

The librarian's eyes widened, in fear or surprise. 'But that text is over a thousand years old!'

'You can see why they're worried. Anyhow, could I have a look?'

The librarian took a step back, looking up at the light that filtered in through the high windows in the ceiling. He shook his head. 'No! No, that is . . . impossible. The text vanished a long time ago, doubtless the Travellers have used it as kindling. I'm sorry that your journey has been wasted . . . '

'Not at all.' The Doctor slowly replaced his hat on his head. 'I'll have to make my own enquiries,' he grinned. 'Come on, Ace!'

The two companions walked to the door. Ace turned back briefly. 'Catch you later!' she called.

The librarian waved, weakly. After they had left, he leaned on a bookcase, and gave a low moan of relief.

Piers Gavenal stared at the sun until he had to look away. He took a deep breath, feeling the cold of the air in his lungs. He was shivering in the robe that Phaedrus had given him. Perhaps it was because of the weather.

The tower of the Church Of Vacuum looked out over the settlement of Joycetown. In the market square, Piers could just make out the blue shape of the TARDIS, but it didn't interest him. Very little did.

'It's time.' Phaedrus stopped at the top of the spiral stairs and sighed. He was a thin, bearded man, his face weather-wrinkled and kindly. The robes of the Church hung on him like a flag, his eyes full of faith. 'Oh Piers, if I could spare you some of this . . . '

'There's no need.' Piers lay a hand on his old friend's shoulder. 'I'm determined, Phaedrus. I've made my peace with this world.'

'Then come with me. There's nobody else here, I've cleared the room of all distractions.' He let Piers walk before him down the stairs. 'I've been thinking about anaesthetics . . . '

Piers shook his head. 'Please don't . . . don't make this harder than it is. We've talked about this, we know what has to be done.'

'Very well.' Phaedrus pursed his lips and steeled himself. They walked down into the main hall of the Church, and then through the door into the basement, where the big old wooden table was. Phaedrus and Piers had often argued over it when they had first arrived on Heaven, building the church with the help of their first converts. There was a final door then, the one to the cellar, where the frame was. Phaedrus paused at it.

'Step through the door, brother.'

The room at the bottom of the stairs was completely black, its only feature the upright metal frame. Beneath the frame was a shallow trough.

Piers walked slowly towards the frame, and dropped the robe to the floor. His hands were shaking.

'Will you need the restraints?' asked Phaedrus, his tone level and controlled.

'I . . . No, I will not need them.' Piers climbed on to the frame, and gripped the metal supports. 'I'm keeping my eyes open. I make this sacrifice gladly.'

Phaedrus fought down a spasm of fear. He had expected his comrade to talk of old times, to meander and go sweetly. It took great courage to launch straight into the ceremony. Or perhaps it was the bravery of a warrior, leaping straight into the unknown before he could think about it.

'Have you considered the world and all that it is?' Phaedrus asked it as a real question, half hoping that Piers would relent, would climb down and . . . no, that was blasphemy.

'I have,' Piers gasped.

'You know that nothing awaits you but endless darkness, that there is nothing beyond death?'

'I do!'

'Do you give your body to the Vacuum now?' Phaedrus took a quick step forward, making himself look straight into Piers's eyes.

Piers paused. Sweat had appeared on his forehead. His eyes were full of pain. 'Yes!' he shouted.

Phaedrus slammed the blade into his friend's stomach and twisted it once, expertly, before slashing it sideways. Piers screamed, high and short, but his eyes never left Phaedrus's gaze.

The sound, and the body, died together. The corpse fell back on the frame, the blood flowing into the trough below.

Phaedrus stepped back, shaking. He dropped the knife. It had never before been someone he knew, never such a friend as poor, dedicated Piers had been.

He muttered the invocations quickly, staring at the corpse.

In the trough, there was activity.

Fluffy filaments were reaching up into the air, following the continuing gush of blood back to its source. Swiftly, the white fibres grew vertically, burrowing into the wound.

The flesh began to bulge and shift, dark shadows moving under it. The muscles jerked.

When it happened, it happened suddenly. The human flesh seemed to stretch and lose its colour. A fine mist of genetic material hissed out of the pores. Then, explosively, grey masses erupted from inside the body.

What was standing in the frame was no longer human. It swayed gently against the metal bars, filaments bobbing, a huge grey fungoid mass, the shape now unrecognizable.

A hole opened in what had been Piers's stomach, thin fibres vibrating across it. Phaedrus fell to his knees.

'We are here . . . ' the fungus hissed. 'Piers Gavenal has been absorbed into our consciousness . . . Now you will obey our orders.'

'I will,' nodded Brother Phaedrus gravely. 'I will.'

2:

Wild Horses

Ace wandered away from the Library, thinking about sex and death. She glanced up at the Doctor, deep in thought. He wasn't really into either, she figured. If he died, he'd just regenerate, and although he sometimes let slip things about a family, he never seemed to fancy anybody.

Which was 'cos he wasn't human, let's face it. But she was. And she was starting to shiver both ways in this cold morning. Poor Julian, in his grave now for five centuries. At least he was warm.

A baby broke from its mother and dashed across the muddy street into Ace's legs, falling over. It looked up at her, surprised, and opened its mouth to howl.

So Ace picked it up before it did. It, he, glared up at the new face, the frown wrinkling every line on his forehead.

'You're lucky, mate,' Ace told the little boy. 'You've got years left before you need to start worrying . . . '

The Doctor leaned over the baby and grinned at it. The baby grinned back.

A laughing mother in a linen tricorn reached into Ace's arms and retrieved her child. They exchanged greetings, but Ace didn't feel like she wanted to do her usual bit and make a new friend so she took the Doctor by the arm and they went on their way.

On Earth, she hadn't been particularly chatty. Okay, so if somebody got introduced to you, you'd talk about the music or your new boots or something, but she'd never just gone up to somebody and said hello. Being flung across time and space made you into a real party animal. You could either talk to anybody with food or a job or a squat, or you could be shy and dead.

And love got to be like that too. On Earth, Ace had always

hoped to meet somebody and have a long, horrible romance. Not tacky, but real. She'd got a little way with a couple of people, and always had Midge chasing her, the poor dead lad. It was all getting on well cool.

Then something huge and raging and brightly coloured grabbed her and a sackful of clothes she'd hidden away for a week out with Julian. It had pulled her through a wall and thrown her out across the disc of the Milky Way. She'd watched the disc spin, stars flashing past, until suddenly she was lying on the floor of Sabalom Glitz's spaceship in the Iceworld dockyards. Ordinary little girl, a long way from home.

But damn, she'd proved she wasn't ordinary. Okay, so she'd taken what warmth she could find on that planet, and it was painful and tawdry and sodding meaningless . . . Ace shook her head and smiled. She'd done it because she'd wanted to do it.

Love had been so odd, after meeting the Doctor. They'd land somewhere, she'd get a real crush on some flash guy and they would always – another grin – always get the idea, and then, just as she was going to suggest that maybe a day or two in this time zone would be great for her nerves, the Doctor would want to move on again.

She looked up at him. This time, Ace decided, she was going to stick around.

Bernice had walked a mile, counting her paces, before setting off back to the camp. The grass was moist and added a spring to her step. In the distance, above the gentle rustling of the grassy autumnal plain, came the sound of horses' hooves. Bernice grinned, and searched in her belt pouch as the riders came into sight.

They were racing each other, galloping, and Roisa was, of course, in the lead. Jan was trying to keep up, shouting after her, and Cathlan was laughing his head off. As if shouting could stop a horse.

'Hoi!' Benny shouted. 'Over here!'

Jan glanced up and suddenly spurred his horse towards her, out of the race. Benny closed her eyes, and stood straight and relaxed, one arm out in front of her. In her fist, she clenched a wilted flower.

A sudden concussion, a quick leap, and she was riding behind Jan, the flower stuck behind his ear.

'One day . . . ' she muttered, tapping the boy's shoulder, 'you are going to get that extremely wrong.'

'And what'll happen to you then, Professor?' Jan laughed.

Benny pretended to consider. 'I shall die,' she said, 'having thrown myself under a horse. That's what you'll tell them I did, anyway, and history's written by the winning side. Take me back to your tent and fill me with mead.'

'Isn't that what we did the night before last?'

'Really? I don't remember. You must be right. How are you and Roisa?'

Jan was silent for a moment, and Benny hugged him a little closer. Finally he said: 'I think we'd better try and catch up with her . . . 'He whacked the flanks of the horse again and they angled back towards the other riders. 'And no, there'll be no mead for you this morning, you have to work!'

'Well,' muttered Benny, 'there's a hole in the ground, and I put spades outside my workers' tents. I think they'll understand what I'm getting at for an hour or two at least.'

The Doctor and Ace had wandered to the edge of the small settlement. Beyond the gates of the town, a vast landscape of green downland lay, a rutted dirt track leading off into the distance. The sun was higher now, and the day was becoming a little warmer.

'Do you want to hear all about the planet Heaven?' asked the Doctor.

'Yeah, 'course I do,' frowned Ace. 'I'm interested.'

The Doctor smiled, a sad old smile that Ace didn't see often. 'Good. Let's stretch our legs . . . '

They walked across the grasslands to a small copse that stood atop a hill. As they did so, the Doctor told his story.

'Heaven is a wonderful world, a glorious place. It has a tiny population for such a colony, because it's on the edge of human space.' The Doctor did a quick pirouette, his finger raised, as if figuring out a direction. Finally he pointed straight down. 'That way lies the Draconian Empire!'

'Not a very liberal empire that one, eh?'

'Not at all. They don't think females can think. You wouldn't like them. But otherwise they're quite civilized.'

'That's cool then.'

'The Earth and Draconia were at war for a very short time, but managed to wipe out large numbers of each other. The Daleks were influencing the war. Finally, the two races joined forces against the Daleks. Bad times. Billions of people died.'

'And lots of Daleks, too?'

'Yes . . . too many. In the end they started coming up with other schemes. We're at a point where humanity is trying to get on with its neighbours. That's the good thing about Daleks. They make you realise that there's always something worse than what you've got at the moment.'

'And is there anything worse than the Daleks?'

The Doctor stopped for a moment, and considered. 'Oh yes . . . ' he said, after a moment. 'There are much worse things.'

Ace didn't like the way he said it, so she let the matter drop. 'So how do people survive here?'

'Farming, which is heavily subsidized by the Earth corporations. There are special interests here, such as the Library, and the archaeologists. Which brings me to my illustration . . . '

They had reached the top of the hill. Ace leaned on a tree, and gazed out over the landscape.

A vast grassy plain, the sun picking out the occasional river and lake. Mountains rose on the far horizon, their peaks shining silver. But the sun picked out other things too. Crystal spheres and silver needles, little rings of gleaming metal pyramids, and sculpted tangles of liquid glass. The objects were dotted about the landscape, they must have been buildings. The largest of them would be the size of an office block.

'The locals,' nodded Ace. 'Smart kit!'

'Not any more. When the humans and Draconians arrived here, they noticed the architecture. Very well made. Could be millennia old. Everything else has gone. No roads, no books . . . no survivors.'

'So the Heavenites died out. Happens all the time.'

'Yes. Indeed the archaeologists have found roads, and perhaps one day they'll find books. But nobody has ever found a

Heavenite body.'

'That's 'cos they were amoebas or something else blobby.'

'But there are very few remains of any animals of the period. There are native creatures here now, and the ecosystem is changing, with all the Earth and Draconian animals added. But there's no fossil record for any recent era. Time has shut up the book of all this planet's days . . . '

Ace recognized something in his tone. Something hidden. It was the sound of a hunter, contemplating his prey. She walked between the Doctor and the landscape, and looked him in the eye. 'Is something bad going to happen here? Do you know what?'

'No.' His gaze was steady.

Ace decided to ask. 'How long are we staying here?'

'I'm not sure . . . ' The Time Lord frowned. 'I want to find the book. Are you going to explore?'

'Kind of. I just want a bit of time here. Want to stick around for a bit. Is it okay if I wander off?'

'Where are you going?'

'Don't know,' Ace lied.

'Be careful if you're going to meet the Travellers again. They're rough people. Very dangerous.'

That hurt a bit more than it should have. Ace paused, and answered calmly. 'I'm dangerous too, Professor. That's why I'm here, right? Yeah, I probably will go and see them. Meet you back at the TARDIS. I hope you find what you're looking for.' She squeezed his shoulder quickly and set off.

This time, the Doctor didn't follow Ace. He just stared after her. After a moment he sighed. 'You too . . . '

Ace ran back to Joycetown. For the exercise, right? It wasn't as if she was used to the Doctor respecting her feelings, after all. This was a bit of a treat. Lately, he'd stopped explaining everything, stopped sighing and showing her that he was hurting too. He was like a sheet of placid water, hardening into ice. At least he didn't know about her fantasies. Well, she hoped he didn't.

Still, it would be good if just once . . . Maybe this time the Doctor could face down the Zargoids on his own, or they wouldn't need her. She could just hide in a shelter somewhere with Jan and come out and congratulate the Time Lord when it was all over. Nice one, Professor. You really showed those Zargoids a thing or two. You don't need me at all.

Christ. You don't need me at all.

Ace stopped, and leaned heavily on the gateway into Joycetown. She remembered Julian, staring into those lights, like a rabbit in the road.

And she knew that she wanted to be loved.

Standing up again, she walked determinedly into the town.

Brother Phaedrus was on his way to the market to buy provisions. He was thinking that he was a good man, that nobody ever understood why good men did bad things. You could be as guilty as you like, but the guilt didn't change what you did.

Of course it didn't. All was all. If he did something, it was because he did it. As always, the words of Phaedrus's scriptures soothed him.

Ace was as deep in thought as Phaedrus was. They hit each other at full speed around the corner, and Ace fell.

Phaedrus helped her up. 'I'm very sorry. What were you thinking about?'

Ace blinked at him as she got to her feet. 'Erm, nothing.'

'Good.'

Something about the priest's smile disturbed Ace. 'Hey, you look like you know this place. Where do I find the Travellers, the ones who were playing in the market this morning?'

'Well, I do know . . . ' Phaedrus stroke his beard thoughtfully. 'And I will tell you, but first I had better warn you about them. They're a lawless bunch of brigands, who would think nothing of stealing everything you own. Please do not approach them.'

'Nah, I'm not planning to approach them. I just need to be able to identify one of them.'

'For the troopers?'

'Yeah. Thin one, craggy face. Strange eyes.'

Phaedrus looked horror struck. 'My dear girl! That's Jan Rydd, the worst of them all. What has he done to you?'

Ace looked at her boots and glanced up at the priest coyly.

'Terrible things,' she whispered, her lower lip vibrating with the effort of not laughing. 'I need to find him so that my brothers can shoot him.' She'd expected a bit of hassle about this, but Phaedrus just grinned.

'It's not far,' he said. 'If you have the right transport.'

A wind was rising across the plains of Heaven, buffeting the tall grass into strange and luxurious shapes. It was autumn here in the planet's northern hemisphere, and soon there would be snow. Perfect, wonderful, snow.

Through the grasslands the Doctor strode, his hat in his pocket. He was approaching a squat concrete building, a low blockhouse with a dome on the roof. It was surrounded by a mesh fence, and the flashing lights of a helicopter landing pad indicated why no path led to its gate.

The man called Kale stood inside the fence, clad in flak armour. He looked up as the figure of the Doctor approached, and stepped forward to the fence. A plasma rifle hung from his shoulder.

'You again?' he shouted. 'What do you want?'

The Doctor didn't answer, and kept walking.

'Stay where you are!' the man yelled.

The Doctor was nearly up to the fence. Kale snatched his rifle and aimed.

'Stop or I fire!' he cried out.

The Doctor stopped. 'There's a fence between you and me. I'm unarmed,' he murmured. 'Touchy, aren't you?'

'I'll say I'm touchy!' snarled the sentry. 'And you're under arrest, you cocky bastard!'

'I should write a book on that subject,' the Doctor grinned.

Ace had found a horse, or rather she had bought one. A Draconian merchant in a flowing red robe had a chain of the animals for sale. He had only one of his native Shiskarshtas, an old beast which would bear him south to Irvingport where he would board ship. The winter frightened him, he confided in Ace, and he was looking forward to returning to the Draconian settlements near the equator.

Ace assumed that she was being ripped off, but she had the

cash and she doubted that the shivering reptilian wanted to haggle. She was sorry for him, too. Maybe he'd end up frozen on some bleak stretch of sand.

The horse took her out of Joycetown, and Ace began to feel more relaxed. She'd learnt to ride in Adelaide in 1967, trained by a man called Medge. Yeah, she could ride before she could walk.

It was a fine horse, a chestnut gelding. It had certainly been born here, swapped in some edgy Draconian deal along the temperate fringes. Eager to run free, it galloped over the downland, its hooves throwing up clods of mud.

It was early afternoon before Ace reached the Valley of the White Horse, as Phaedrus had described it. The sun was low in the sky, and a soft gloom was hovering about the forests that lay in the dells.

The camp in the valley was made of stiff tents, supported by struts. They formed a circle around a central bonfire, as yet unlit. Around the tents ran a circle of tall stones. Figures could be spotted moving from tent to tent, and the low skirl of music drifted up the valley.

Ace found herself sighing. Hell, what was she doing here? What was she after? It has been months since Robin Yeadon, months and years and centuries. But Robin Yeadon had been good, and very ordinary, and had taught her that nostalgia was worse than death.

So why did she miss him?

Bernice Summerfield inspected the earthenware cup carefully. 'Mycenian influences . . . Cathlan's been swotting up on his potted history.'

Jan was picking out clumps of soil from the heel of his boot with a blade. 'Drink up, Benny,' he advised. 'You're more interested in the cup than in the ale.'

'Now that,' Bernice nodded, 'neatly sums up my whole nature. Which is odd, because I am interested in the ale.'

She took a deep breath, jerked the cup to her lips, and threw back the whole pint.

They'd been talking and drinking since the early morning in the communal tent of the camp. Initially it had been warm mead, but a lunch of hot soup had convinced the two friends that ale would be the drink for the afternoon.

Roisa had arrived at one point, and sat leaning on Jan a mite suspiciously. Roisa kept her hair cut short and rough. She and Jan had their troubles, but Benny had taken her suspicion as a good sign. Benny and Jan had talked about the twentieth century, and how mythic content tends to seep into historical stories, and about Benny's restlessness. Gradually, as the ale found them all, the conversation became freer, and Roisa started to add the occasional word.

'Why are you here?' Jan asked Bernice at one point. 'Is getting pissed in the afternoon any way for a professor to behave?'

Benny paused, and lowered the cup, her eyes narrowing. 'What do you mean?'

Jan ran a hand through his hair and laughed, nervously. 'Well, I was just joking, like. Nothing's meant by it . . . '

'If I understand what you're saying,' said Benny, 'you mean that my behaviour isn't worthy of a real professor. Correct?'

'Oh, come on, Benny –'

'I will not come on. Outside!'

Jan stood up slowly, shaking his head. He plucked the blade from a block of wood, and reached into a chest to toss Bernice one, which she caught easily. 'If you must . . . ' he sighed.

Roisa swore loudly in Palare, and swung aside the tent flap. 'Tell me who kills who!' she shouted, and stalked off towards Máire's tent.

Benny brushed back her hair and exhaled, her breath visible in the cooling afternoon. Cathlan was carrying piles of kindling to the bonfire. Chemical light sources were being ignited inside the tents.

Damn it. Pride again. She felt the weight of the blade in her hands, a short sabre with a curved tip. She drew it up experimentally to her shoulder. Well balanced, probably home made. A few of the Traveller children were watching her, standing back a little in their fur-lined parkas.

When Jan came out of his tent, pulling on a woollen jumper, Benny spread her arms wide. 'I think you should kill me,' she confessed. 'This is an awful idea. My temper again. Sorry.'

Jan laughed, and swung his sword experimentally. 'You're just scared!'

'No,' Benny muttered. 'No, I'm not scared. I just don't want to hurt you.'

Jan wandered forward, scratching his chin. 'Well, I don't want to –'

And he slashed for Benny's stomach.

She parried instinctively, and hacked straight back, sending a series of blows at Jan's head until he had to retreat. Elegantly Jan began to swing his blade in a figure of eight, catching Benny's jabs easily.

Benny feigned a blow, and tossed her blade from her right hand to her left. In the same second, she slashed straight for Jan's sword hand.

Jan's blade spun into the air, and Benny leapt forward, shouldering him on to the ground. The Travellers who had gathered to watch clapped and cheered.

Bernice raised her sword above Jan's head.

And then a body slammed into her, sending her sprawling. As she fell, Benny wondered if it was one of the Travellers, perhaps Roisa, thinking that she really would have hurt their leader.

The two of them rolled over, and Benny's cheek slapped into the cool earth.

'Stay there!' Ace growled.

Benny had every intention of not moving. Something had caught her eye, inches from her face.

Laughing heartily, Jan wandered over and took Ace's hand, pulling her upright. 'Welcome,' he said. 'I'd say you saved my life, except you didn't.'

'Help me up too, won't you?' called Benny from the ground. She still hadn't moved. 'And while you're at it, get me a jam jar!'

Ace frowned at Jan. 'Who's she?'

Jan looked at his feet again. 'That's the Professor,' he explained. 'She's completely insane.'

The Doctor sipped his tea.

'This is the best arrest I've suffered in some time,' he smiled.

shyly. 'Lovely tea.'

Operative James Miller leaned back in his chair and adjusted his uniform jacket. He was a gaunt, middle-aged man, the lines of worry etched into his face. But his eyes held a twinkle, and when he spoke, his voice was full of humour.

'And you're an interesting prisoner. I must apologize for Kale's behaviour. It could have been worse, you could have been handed to my deputy, Howarth. My crew here are on loan from IMC, and most of them don't know their arse from their elbow. Now then, you told my guards that you're called the Doctor. Doctor who?'

'Ah, well, that's the question isn't it?'

Miller appeared to ignore the vagueness of the Doctor's reply. 'Some of my lot were down the market in Joycetown this morning, probably misbehaving themselves with the Travellers. They noticed a big blue box. Is that yours?'

'Yes.'

Miller was smiling like a man who was about to guess the right answer to a charade. 'And you know the Draconians quite well, am I right?'

The Doctor leaned back in his chair and grinned sheepishly. 'I'm not often recognized.'

'I've heard stories about you from an old Draconian business partner my father had. He called you Karshtakavaar, the on-coming storm. You appear only when there's terrible danger, he said.'

'Yes. I have a talent for being in the wrong place at the right time.'

'Why were you so keen to get shot this afternoon?'

'I wanted to see how nervous your staff were.'

'Well, lad, you found out. They pick it up from me.'

'You're not happy?'

'No. Heaven's a dull spot, but I keep seeing dangers around every corner. Getting paranoid in my old age, I thought. Until you arrived, that is.'

The Doctor leaned forward, appearing suddenly to take Miller into his confidence.

'I can't see why Earth has such a military presence here. You have the Library to guard, of course –'

'Hah!' Miller stood and began to pace his office, stopping to straighten the reproduction Van Gogh that hung on one wall. 'Embarrassing diaries, official records of the lunar penal colony ... couple of security men could do it.'

The Doctor silently took another sip from his cup.

'I work for the Directorate of External Ops, Doctor. I answer to Earth Central only. I used to be one of these corporate mercenaries, mind. A Dalek specialist opened me up with its claw. Then I opened it up. This is a dead-end planet, a place where things end up. And I'm here with a big squad of sararimen, trying to persuade them that I'm actually in charge and not their managers.' Miller settled back into his chair. 'You may well ask why.'

The Doctor paused, and then looked him in the eye. 'I am,' he smiled.

'Then I'd better tell you, hadn't I? said Miller, smiling back. 'More tea?'

Bernice and Roisa had been fascinated by whatever it was that Benny had caught, and Ace had been pretty interested too, until Jan took her arm.

'Let me show you around the place,' he whispered. 'Those two'll argue over the origins of an insect. They'll be at it for ages.'

'Yeah, great.' Ace had walked quickly off with him, and they'd scampered through the camp, past the crying babies in their pouches, the many dogs that jumped up and licked Jan's hand, the colourful tents and fluttering washing lines. They headed up on to the downs at the head of the valley.

A white horse had been cut out of the chalk, a Celtic etching of something that was wilder than a conventional horse, a bunch of flying lines with a ferocious mouth. The eye was formed out of melted crystal, cemented into the ground. It glinted in the low sun.

'We cut this ourselves ... ' Jan sighed, flopping onto the ground inside the horse's body. 'You can see the whole camp from here. What's your name?'

'I'm Ace. Dorothy if you like. Didn't used to like it, but I'm getting into it.' She'd sat down, at a little distance.

'I'm Jan Rydd. I have a secret name too, but I'm not brave enough to offer it up like you offer up Ace.'

'Nah, my real name's the secret one. And I just thought I could tell you it. Do I get to hear yours?'

'Eventually.' Jan smiled a knifey smile and Ace shivered again.

She found a question to keep the conversation going, 'cos otherwise he'd have just sat there staring until something happened. And something would happen. 'Where do you lot come from?'

'All over. Most of us were born in the Convoy. If you speak Palare, then you must know about us.'

'Not much. Tell me.'

Jan sighed, and brushed his hair back from his forehead. 'Well now. Way back in the twentieth century, anarchists and various other people who weren't happy with the way of life in Britain – oh, that was on Earth – they joined up with groups of travelling people who'd been around for centuries . . . '

Ace knew it all, but she was, quite quietly, looking at Jan. He had big hands, notched with hard work. His hair was tied back into a ponytail, knotted way down his back. There would be a lot of hair in that. He was muscular, but thin, a boy who'd been active all his life. He wore thick wool and leather, in black and purple.

'Now, the Convoy, as it came to be called, moved around the country, visiting various musical festivals, celebrating the solstices at really ancient megalithic temples. They were pagans too, as we are.'

'What do you worship?'

'The Goddess and her followers. I'm into the Trickster myself, the god of randomness. Does it worry you?'

'Nah. Whatever you want to do.'

'There's a ceremony tonight, if you want to stay.'

God, this guy was quick off the mark. Ace pretended to consider. 'I dunno. Is there anywhere where I could crash?'

'I'm sure somebody will find you space. We offer hospitality to everyone, even pissheads like the Professor. Now, back to the story –' Jan slithered up on to his knees, looking Ace straight in the eye. He was becoming more animated, obviously excited by the history of his people. And excited by her. Oh yeah. 'The Travellers suffered greatly under the governments of the Earth, begging and stealing and living in squats. They sheltered in camps in the winter, and came down to the cities in the summer. Over the centuries, they kept their culture going by oral tradition. The legends, the language, the songs. When the first great human expansion into space happened, a Traveller called Fox saw that his people could finally be free. They stole a ship that was in dock for repairs, and took it as far into hyperspace as they could . . . ' Jan laughed, imagining the scene. His hands were drawing pictures in the air, squeezing meaning out of the cold atmosphere. 'When Earth ships first met the Arcturans, the Earth ambassador was told that they'd met humans before. Fox and his crew had landed on Arcturus Six and busked for their supper!' Jan threw his head back and laughed, and Ace saw that he was tattooed, a snake eating its own tail, wrapped around his throat and down into his shirt. 'Anyhow, the colonies kept on expanding, and the Travellers found their places on the fringes, setting up megaliths, scratching a living on the frontier. Then the frontier closed in this direction. It closed on Heaven, the world between the Protectorates. This place is the real margins, a place where things are sent to be lost if the corporations don't like them, if they're against money. So we're here, because we're against money. We don't use it amongst ourselves, we barter where we can. Money malforms a civilization, makes it frigging obscene. We just want to live free, and Heaven's one of the last places where we can do it. It's a kind of home, until they come and take it from us again!'

Ace was impressed. She sat hugging her knees, wondering when she'd get to kiss him. He was just showing off, knowing that he could ask her back to his tent and she'd go. Bighead.

'You the leader of that lot, then?'

Jan shook his head, aghast. 'Anarchists don't have leaders. We talk everything over and decide what we all want to do.'

'Does that work?'

'Yes. There are about thirty of us in the camp, including six children. Everybody's got a voice, but we try to argue things out rather than vote, accommodate everyone. Christopher's the priest, he makes sure everybody gets heard. Máire's the priestess, she makes sure that what everybody says makes a difference. I've just got a big mouth, so people watch me. Hey, look down there!'

Bernice was standing in the middle of the tents, waving her arms above her head.

'She wants us to go back.' Ace got up. 'They must have decided what it is they've found.'

As they walked back down to the camp, Jan seemed to make a decision. 'Listen,' he said, a hint of concern creeping into his voice. 'I'd like to talk to you a lot and tell you stories, and, well, listen to you –'

That uncertainty again, like suddenly he looked down and wasn't half as brave as he thought he was. Did he know how cool that was? Was that part of his act? What the hell, it worked.

'Yeah. Yeah, I'd like that too ... '

'But my life's complex. Roisa's going to tell you how complex. All I want to say is, listen to my side afterwards, okay?'

'Okay,' Ace whispered.

Oh great, she thought, trudging towards the tents. The bastard's married.

When they got to Jan's tent, everybody was already there. Well, Roisa and the woman Bernice were. The large canopy was full of brightly coloured silks and bundles of cloth. Jan explained that he made clothes, sold them for good prices, put the money into the tribe.

Ace sat awkwardly on a beanbag, looking between Jan and Roisa.

Hell, she thought. Girlfriend at least. And she wasn't sure about Bernice, either. She was close enough to Jan to brawl with him, but she seemed almost like a mother, even if she was only thirty. Ace liked her instantly, and wanted to get to know her, but no way was she gonna let Jan out of her sight at the moment. Bernice was staring at the thing she'd captured in a jam jar, oblivious to the quiet conflict happening in the tent. She'd shared out some more of Jan's mead, and explained in a whisper to Ace that Roisa had been getting annoyed about them sitting up on the white horse, so she thought that she should call them in out of the cold. She didn't mention Ace's rugby tackle, but the look in her eyes suggested that she was amused.

Jan sat in the centre of the tent, at an equal distance between the three women, and from the way his gaze hopped back and forth, Ace could see that he was almost enjoying the situation.

'You can't just let tension eat away at you,' he explained. 'I'm glad that Benny and I fought. I think you have to fight if you want to, like you have to do whatever else you feel.'

Roisa frowned. 'There are tensions you don't talk about, you quinx wretch . . . ' She looked up at Ace. 'We're together, if you were wondering. We've got a contract, bound on the Great Wheel it was.' She ruffled Jan's hair, and Ace made herself smile indulgently. 'I have another friend, so Jan can spread his seed as far as he likes so long as he comes back to me. The thing is, he knows that anytime he wants to be with me, properly and forever, all he has to do is say so.'

Ace looked down at the thick rug on the floor, following its complex Celtic knotworks. She couldn't look Roisa in the eye. Was it that obvious? Had Jan said something to Roisa? Oh god, why did she get involved in things like this?

Bernice had heard the nervous silence, and spoke. 'I wouldn't have hurt Jan, you know. But there are certain things that I'm . . . touchy about. Now' – she offered the jar to Roisa. 'I've had a look. What do you think of this?'

The woman made to unscrew the jar, but Benny stopped her. 'No. I don't know what it is. That's why I used tweezers.'

Ace was surprised at how much this Professor reminded her of the Doctor. She was a real expert, even though she still seemed slightly pissed.

Roisa stared in at the thing in the jar. It was a tiny white filament, like a couple of strands of dog hair.

'Our Lizzie dog's been shedding again,' she sighed. 'So what?'

The thing in the jar twitched.

Roisa put the jar down. 'I thought I knew every plant and animal on Heaven,' she murmured. 'I'm the herbcutter for the tribe. Can I check it against my books?'

'Of course,' Bernice said. 'But I want it afterwards.'

Jan had turned his head in Ace's direction, and was looking at her, rather than at the jar. Staring. Ace forced herself to meet his gaze.

They looked at each other for a full minute. God, why did he have to be so blatant? He was so sure of himself, so confident. And he had a sell-by date of his own, which was good. She wouldn't be here forever.

It was a second before Ace realized that Bernice was looking at her too. The scientist had winked, almost imperceptibly, and Ace suppressed a laugh.

Roisa was still staring at the jar. Poor woman. Damn it, her life was gonna get so much worse. Ace frowned when she realized how hard she was having to try to be sympathetic.

'I need to get back to my dig,' Benny sighed, standing up. 'Anybody fancy walking me back?'

Ace looked once more at Jan, and then back to Benny. The man looked far too expectant. You can't always get what you want.

'You're on,' Ace grinned, and picked up her backpack.

The look on Jan's face was wonderful. 'Will you be back for the ceremony tonight?' he asked, like a kicked puppy. 'We're going to the Great Wheel.'

'Oh, I dunno.' Ace smiled maliciously. 'Let's see how tired I am, eh?'

'You're very interesting,' Benny said as they wandered out into the dusk, Ace leading the horse behind her.

'Cheers.'

'Mainly because of the badges on your jacket. Those are really odd, because they're all from one of the eras I specialize in, early space age. They must have cost you a fortune.'

'Nah.' Ace grinned. 'I'm a time traveller from the nineteen-eighties.'

Benny giggled in a surprisingly girlish way. 'That is less possible than something very impossible indeed. That is really crukking impossible.'

'Lots of people do it. Even Daleks have time travel.'

'Do they? Do they really?'

Ace caught the slight hint of something lost in Benny's voice. She suddenly felt the need to be serious. She stopped walking. 'It's true. I used to live in Perivale, London. Ask me anything you like.'

So Benny asked her about the design of tube trains, the Italia '90 England squad and the destruction of Blackpool Tower.

'That must have happened after I left,' Ace said.

'No it didn't. I was trying to bluff you. Either you're as expert as I am or you're telling the truth. Well banging, me old cock sparrer.'

'You what?'

'Aha! You don't recognize the speech patterns of the time.'

'Yes I do! That was nothing like the way we used to talk! Where did you –' Ace realized that Benny was laughing again. 'Oh, right.'

'I believe you,' Bernice smiled, patting the younger woman's shoulder. 'You move like you're telling the truth, all relaxed, no tension about the shoulders. And you've been looking at me all the time.'

Ace groaned. 'Aw, no, you're one of these body-language people?!'

'Quite a bit. Sorry. I won't do it to you again.'

'Good. I hate it!'

'It isn't just that, though. I'm a bit like Jan in some ways. When magic comes along, we ought to just accept it. If you were also into Martian culture and body language, I'd think you were some sort of gift from above. How did you get here?'

'I travel in a police box.'

'How baroque of you.'

'The bloke who owns it is into the whole bit. The Doctor. He might be able to tell you how it all works.' Ace decided to ask her question. 'Have you and Jan ever . . . '

Bernice looked up at the sky ruefully. An ocean of stars was starting to appear in the deep blue. 'Well, we tried. But I'm not really built for that sort of relationship, and we decided that it was a bad idea and why didn't we have some more mead instead. I've only ever had three boyfriends, and . . . I'm sorry, what's your name?'

'Ace,' said Ace, extending her hand.

'It suits you. I'm Professor Bernice Summerfield. Benny, if you want.' They walked on for a while in silence, then Benny suddenly said: 'He's not a very safe man to be around, and he's my friend, but so is Roisa, and maybe . . . well, no. Whatever.'

Ace smiled. 'I'm after danger, I don't want to hurt Roisa, and I'm here for the weekend, okay?'

'Okay. Now that is the right idiom. Jan uses it all the time, but then he's obsessed with your time as well. Oh look, here's Christopher.'

The tall being was looking up into the sky, his robes dark against the greeny grey of the hillside. Ace looked at Benny questioningly. 'Is he a bloke, then?'

'He's neither. He and Jan were in the military together. There were some experiments done. Christopher's given up his gender in favour of his mental powers. I think that's a good deal, sometimes.'

'I don't . . . ' Ace shivered. 'Hey, is Jan –?'

'Despite the efforts of a hundred angry husbands . . . yes he is. Ahoy, Christopher, what are you looking for?'

'Hush!' the voice boomed back.

The two women and the horse drew level with the gaunt figure. Ace noticed that, now the hood of his robe was down, Christopher's scalp was covered in delicate tattoos. They decorated an ugly plug which jutted from the base of his skull. With a jolt of distaste, Ace realised what it was. A jack plug, like you might find on the back of a video recorder.

Christopher was looking up at a particular point in the sky, his eyes narrowing. 'I am looking into space . . . ' he whispered. 'I was preparing for the ceremony tonight. Then I noticed. There is something out there, just beyond my sight. Something evil. We have been warned on the Wheel about some danger. If I could only see it.' His voice took on a pained tone. 'Then I could spare us all such suffering . . . Oh.'

At the point where Christopher had been staring, a thousand shooting stars suddenly burst across the sky. Meteor trails whizzed outwards in a burst of light. After a few seconds, they had all faded away.

'That was great!' grinned Ace. 'What was it?'

'Death,' said Christopher. 'The re-entry trails are made by pods ejected from a spacecraft. They each contain one or two dead humans. Soldiers, colonists, people who lost their lives in this area of space.'

'But why here?'

'You are new here, aren't you?' Benny smiled. 'That's what Heaven is for, Ace. This is Club Dead. The Earth and Draconian peoples designated Heaven as a graveyard world. It's been declared sacred ground by every religion of both races. The place is kept lovely, and billions of corpses keep the ecosystem flourishing. This is one gigantic graveyard.'

'Great,' said Ace. 'Planet of the Corpses!'

Christopher turned to her, his eyes glowing slightly in the dusk. 'And there will be more . . . ' he whispered. 'There will be many more.'

3:

Twenty-Fifth-Century Boy

Roisa sat in her tent, in the big wicker chair that her mother had made. She was staring at the thing in the jar, trying not to think about where she'd be sleeping tonight.

Roisa had been born halfway between Arcturus and Rigel, in the hold of a cargo ship on which the Convoy had bought passage. She was the daughter of three generations of Travellers, and had so many skills, so many talents which Jan ignored. He could have anybody he wanted, and that was why he didn't want her as a permanent partner. Maybe soon she'd make him an ultimatum. At least that girl in the black jacket had thought better of him. Good for her.

There was a noise, something like a noise. Roisa glanced around the hangings and furs inside the tent. Then she realised.

The fibre was squealing. Right on the threshold of hearing. She put her ear to the jar.

And jumped back as the thing leapt against the glass.

The jar fell and smashed.

Luckily Roisa wasn't barefoot, as she often was. She found the worm on the floor and stamped down on it with her boot.

She stamped several times, and when she looked, it was gone. Roisa sighed. Oh well, at least Bernice wouldn't be able to patronize everybody about the thing. She considered doing some more work, preparing medicines, but her heart wasn't in it. There wasn't that long until the ceremony, after all.

Pulling on a shawl, Roisa threw aside the tent flap and stepped out into the frosty night air. The smells of cooking were blowing from various tents, and the mumble of low speech was everywhere.

She popped her head into Máire's tent. 'Busy?'

The dreadlocked woman looked up from her book. 'Not really. Just reading about Daak. The story so far . . . '

'Daak's dead.' Roisa dropped into the pile of cushions that her friend had thrown into a corner. While Roisa's tent was kept neat, diagrams and tables pinned to the fabric and everything folded away into pockets, Máire's was replete with hanging fabrics and hand-painted designs. Her clothes piled up in corners to be cleared away at intervals. Whenever the Travellers broke camp, it was a familiar joke that Máire would still be packing hours after everyone else was finished.

Máire smiled and shook her head quickly. 'We Exile DK agents don't die, we get exterminated. There's a big difference.'

'Ah yes, about ten stone in corpse weight. D'you fancy a walk?'

'Bit cold. I'm honoured by your presence. Will you be staying tonight?' Máire's gaze had strayed back to the page, but she gave Roisa a little smile, trying to pretend she was joking.

'If you want . . . '

'Not if you don't want to. Forget I asked. Enjoy your walk.' Pointedly, Máire turned the page of her book.

Roisa stared at her for a while, wanting to say something. Finally, she turned and strode away from camp, out towards the forest.

The creature that had been Piers Gavenal flicked its tendrils out, exploring its immediate environment.

A basement. The meat used this place to store things. Gavenal was part of the group memory now. What he knew, the fungus knew.

The meat at the core of the grey mass shrivelled as more sustenance was sucked from it. The minerals were instantly processed and used to build a long tendril, which the creature threw out towards the door. It lay in the shadows.

If any of Phaedrus's temple acolytes got curious, they would become a further source of energy for the fungoid mass.

Roisa had thought about going to Jan's tent, but had heard the sound of drumming, and the gruff laughter of Cathlan. He and Jan were probably trying to write some new melody for the evening, and discussing the weird little girl with the black jacket. Stupid male laughter.

Roisa enjoyed walking in the woods. The whisper of the wind in the trees always calmed her. The Travellers had been on Heaven for a year, and maybe it would be good if they never left. There wasn't going to be another place that suited them so well, that let them be so free in such great surroundings. She'd put that to the tribe on the Wheel tomorrow, ask them if they wanted to stay. Jan would go into a rage, probably go into a passionate speech about moving on, and sway everybody around to his point of view. Again. Or perhaps this time they'd listen to her, and the children could all grow up knowing where they were going to be living.

Maybe she could have Jan's child then.

And maybe the trees would answer her when she talked to them.

A light mist was rising from the valley. When she turned back to look, the lights of the camp were small and far away.

'Good evening, Roisa McIlnery.'

Roisa spun, pulling the long blade she carried from the sheath along her wrist. The owner of the voice stood silhouetted against the trees, his dark robes outlined in the vague light that diffused through the mist.

'Phaedrus.' Roisa was quite relieved. The man was boring, but hardly dangerous. 'Still complaining about that goblet Jan snatched, or are you after donations?'

The priest smiled sadly. 'I'm afraid things have become more serious recently, Roisa. Do you have a hole in your boot?'

Roisa had felt the leak as she'd walked up the hill. It hadn't mattered to her then, but now she felt a sudden dread in her stomach. Phaedrus sounded like he was about to anounce a death. 'Yes.'

'Then we must talk.' The priest held out his hand. 'I have some very bad news for you.'

Lights were shining all around the dig, chemical lamps that bathed the arch in a ghostly white glare. Figures moved in the light, carrying bags of earth up from the reinforced entrance.

Ace tied the horse to a post and followed Bernice to the site. She was staring up at the arch when a stocky young man strode forward and nodded to Benny.

'Where have you been, boss?' he laughed. 'We've broken through to a chamber. There's an entrance visible. We're just clearing the way now.'

'Please, Clive, I'm feeling guilty enough already. This is Ace, by the way. Let's have a look.' She turned to Ace. 'Want to come too?'

'Yeah, but then I'll have to get back to the camp.'

'You're going back? Yes, well I probably would too. Here, take a lamp. Don't touch anything, and don't fall over anything drunkenly in the dark, right? I'll be extremely angry if anybody does that . . . '

Ace shook her head. Benny's grin was, if anything, brighter than the lamp she had handed her.

Clive lead the way down a metal ladder. 'You're just in time . . . ' he told the two women as they emerged into a low tunnel. 'We're at the point where we can breach the chamber if we want to. Do we want to?'

A group of seven young archaeologists stood in the tunnel. Ace saw a kind of respect in their faces. They were waiting to see what Bernice wanted to do. They moved aside as she walked along the tunnel.

In an earthen wall, a door had been revealed. It was nine feet high, rounded, and the frame was carved in the manner that Ace was starting to associate with the Heavenites.

'Well,' said Bernice. 'We found it. No, no, wait a moment. Who did find this?'

A young man with a floppy centre parting stepped forward, looking abashed. 'Paul Magrs, boss . . . ' he said.

Benny stepped up to him and kissed the top of his head. 'Paul, I love you, and will name this door after you. This is the Paul Magrs Door. Enjoy it while you can, because after a night's careful excavation, we're going to smash the bugger in!' There was a cheer from the students, and Ace joined in the clapping. Paul was laughing too. 'And, in case anybody has been wondering, I shall be up all night myself. Working. Thank you all.'

Ace didn't want to interrupt the feeling of impending bustle. She tapped Benny on the shoulder, and whispered to her. 'I'm off. See you soon.'

'Yes,' Benny was pulling her sleeves up. 'Look, come on back tomorrow. I want to hear all about time travel, okay?'

'Okay,' Ace grinned. 'Hope there's something good in there.'

'Yes . . . ' Benny sighed, clapping one of her band on the back. 'So do I.'

Ace trotted the horse back across the downlands, enjoying the purity of the chill air. This place really was something. A large moon was rising over the meadows, full and shining, and thin high clouds scudded across it. The moon was mottled with craters and seas that were different, and this difference, the way that something familiar could be so strange, set Ace thinking of distance.

'You've come a long way,' she whispered to herself. Then, with a grin, she added in an Irish voice: 'So, Ace, when did you start thinking of yourself as a citizen of the universe?'

'Well, Terry,' she answered in her own voice. 'I think it was when I started talking to myself, because there was nobody else to talk to . . . ' The joke trailed off, and Ace continued to ride in silence. It took about an hour to reach the valley, and Ace was glad to see the glow in the distance. The central bonfire of the Travellers' camp had been lit, and the light from it shone over the fields, making the stone circle into a giant wheel of shadow spokes. The sound of drumming echoed down the valley, and Ace urged her horse into a gallop, thundering down the hillside.

She closed her eyes and raised her arms above her head, holding on with her legs.

So long ago, running into the wind at Scrane End. Julian laughing, the leaves being pulled from the trees by the cold wind. Even on Heaven, drifts of them had piled up, thrown aside by the horse's hooves.

The wheel grew closer, and Ace reluctantly took the reins again, opening her eyes. Maybe she'd wanted Jan to see her throwing herself forward: into the water, into the snow, into him. This time there was a huge leap to make, she could feel it. Something big was going to change, and to survive that change would take more than her own strength. This time the leap would be made for her.

And all Ace could think of was Julian, and the unsaid thoughts that he'd leapt with into his grave.

Jan ran forward, laughing, and helped her down from the saddle.

'I saw you, doing tricks!' he laughed. 'You can ride better than I can!'

'That's surprising, is it?' Ace held on for a moment as he lowered her to the ground. The whole camp was gathered around the fire, drinking and talking. The Travellers were wrapped in colourful wool robes, passing a cup between them and smoking long pipes. Cathlan and a group of three others were beating on large hide drums, the rhythm getting faster and faster. Behind them, two other musicians were blowing into didgeridoos, making a low warble. The night seemed full of magic, like Bonfire Night or Hallowe'en. Ace glanced around the crowd, and found only two people set apart. Máire was sitting alone, lost in thought. Christopher was standing on his own, watching as the embers from the fire whirled into the sky.

Roisa was nowhere to be seen.

'Yes, it's very surprising.' Jan laughed. 'I'm a great horseman.'

'So that's the other thing you're good at?' The drumming was getting faster.

Jan shook his head. They were still touching. 'No. I forgot the matter of horses. You'll find out.'

'What if I don't want to find out?' Kiss me now, in front of everyone. I won't stop you.

'Then . . . ' Jan looked down at his feet and then suddenly away. 'Why then you won't.'

Ace let go of his lapel. She would have said something really good, something that would have saved the situation, but Christopher had strode up to them, and put a hand on Ace's shoulder. Jan glared at the tall being, but was silent.

'You wish to join the tribe in ceremony tonight?'

'Yes.' Ace felt the seriousness of Christopher's gaze.

'Then you must talk to Máire. We will discuss matters of great import tonight, and she will instruct you on how your voice may be heard.'

'Well, I don't really want a vote or anything . . . '

'There are no votes. Go and talk to her.'

Without looking at Jan, Ace nodded and walked over to Máire.

The woman looked up from her meditations and smiled. 'Hello. You're Ace, aren't you?'

Ace had stopped, looking down at the pipelike objects that hung from Máire's belt. 'Those things . . . Sorry, I was trying to place them. They're Dalek eyestalks, aren't they?'

Máire nodded, and motioned for Ace to sit down on the rug she had spread in front of her. She unhitched an eye stalk from her belt and handed it to Ace. Something organic rolled around inside, and the dead eye washed from black to white as Ace rotated the stalk.

'I was a Dalek Killer,' Máire sighed. 'Exile DK. Political crimes. I planted some bombs in support of those imprisoned on the lunar penal colony. I survived on a Dalek world for three months until a Traveller ship miscalculated a hyperspace jump and crashlanded in the mountains near my base. I hitched a ride, helped them repair their engines.'

Ace was impressed by the quiet in Máire's voice. 'Why do you keep the eyestalks?' she asked.

'Bounty. These days a Dalek eyestalk is worth twenty deca-credits at an Imperial base. These are my last reserves of cash. They're here in case . . . in case anything happens that I can't control.'

Ace could feel the pain in the woman's soft words. 'Look, is there something wrong? I dunno, it just seems like you've survived so much, and this is such a great place –'

'Is it? It's full of death, Ace. I don't need to see any more killing. Neither do you, I think. I'm missing somebody, some-body who ought to be at the ceremony. I might have annoyed them earlier. Things will be better if . . . when they get here. Now, Christopher has told you to come to me for instructions.'

And Máire proceeded to tell Ace the lore of the ceremony. Ace listened as best she could, but she kept looking round.

Once, Jan looked back at her at the same time.

The helicopter flew low over the grassy plains, great flurries of leaves rushing in its wake.

James Miller looked up from the controls and glanced back at his passenger. The Doctor was reading a file of papers marked with a Black Secret seal. He had asked to be dropped off at the archaeological dig site, for reasons best known to himself.

'What do you make of it?' Miller asked, wondering again if his sudden confidence in the strange little man had been misplaced. Miller was old enough to know what he liked about somebody, and the Doctor had the manner of somebody who understood the military. Maybe the old soldier would be lucky enough to be there when the storm happened again, just once more.

'Random interceptions in nearby space, a mysterious object that shows up on tracking systems and then vanishes . . . I think the question is what do you make of it?'

'Well, we thought it was Daleks, of course,' Miller said. 'But the Draconians have been scouring the local systems for their energy wakes and they haven't found anything. Those lads are on a jihad, they don't miss owt. No, it's something else, summat new. And that scares me, Doctor.'

'It's not new.' The Doctor frowned. 'It's very old, if I'm right. Very dangerous. I thought that I could spend some time finding my book, but now . . . '

'Now you've got more important things to do?'

'No.' The Doctor looked up, his eyes glinting in the moonlight. 'Now I have to find the book as soon as possible.'

Christopher stepped forward, carrying a strange object on a black silk cloth. It was cylindrical, the matt black surface painted with gold designs. Many small jackholes studded the exterior. Christopher held the device aloft, and walked slowly round the bonfire three times, anticlockwise. The drumming reached a crescendo, and then stopped. All was silent.

'All those who wish to join the ceremony on the Great Wheel, stand forward.' Christopher's voice was loud and low, and Ace shivered at it. The Travellers all stood, and she stood too.

'What's that?' she asked Máire.

'It's a Puterspace deck,' the woman told her. 'Centuries ago, Travellers used chemical substances to enter different states of consciousness. They caused their bodies great harm. Instead, we enter a collective hallucination, a computer-generated virtual reality, programmed to meet our needs. This way is more honest, but it can be dangerous. That is why you'll be partnering Jan.'

'Well, I dunno . . . ' Ace found herself backing off, and then stopped. 'No, that's cool. If it isn't drugs, I'll do it.'

'It isn't drugs.' Jan had been standing behind her. Now he put his hand on Ace's ponytail and moved it gently aside. Ace found herself breathing harder and forcibly slowed it down. 'Ah, but you're going to need a beginner's terminal . . . '

'What d'you mean?' Ace asked. Máire had wandered off, and was talking to Christopher.

'No jackhole.' Jan turned his head and pulled aside his own braided locks. At the top of his spine was a jack plug, exactly like Christopher's.

Ace shuddered.

'We've all got them.'

'Well you're not drilling into my neck!'

Jan raised an eyebrow. 'That's why we've also got this.' He produced a thin wire headpiece. 'You put this on, it'll get you into the Matrix. We go into Puterspace piggyback. If you get into trouble, I'll pull you out.'

'Or I'll pull you out.'

'Why, yes, lass, if that's the way it turns out.' Jan licked his lips quickly and grinned.

Christopher called the whole tribe forwards, and began to hand them lengths of wire. They formed a dancing circle around the terminal that he had placed atop one of the stones, and plugged the wires into their own jackholes. Then they plugged the other end into the deck. They tossed their heads ecstatically as they did it, the wires tangling with each other. Ace wanted to join in, but didn't really know how. 'Sides, the crown was a bit more fragile.

Jan glanced at her and ran into the melée, flinging his head round, getting his line tangled with several others.

Máire was looking around, waiting for someone. 'Who will guard us when we have entered the Land Under The Hills?' she asked formally.

A man in an apron shouldered a plasma rifle and nodded. 'I will!' he called.

'Thank you, Cook William!' called Máire. Then her face broke into the sweetest smile that Ace had ever seen.

At the edge of the camp, hugging herself, stood Roisa. The look on her face was like the first breeze on the edge of the storm.

Ace looked back to Jan, who was fighting free of some female Travellers' lines. He staggered towards her, and handed her a length of wire. Ace checked the wire mesh across her brow, and walked towards the deck. As she reached up to insert the other end of the wire into the jackhole, she made a wish, the closest she had ever got to a prayer.

Protect us all, she thought. I don't know everything that's going on, and I don't like it. Let's all get through these times alive.

Something running along the wire and into her mind seemed to be about to answer her.

'Don't be scared,' Jan called. 'I'll be there with you in a –' A single strobe flashed lonely in some deserted club, and a great sigh of sweat broke from the stage, like an invisible audience was waiting for some huge band.

But Ace was the band. All alone on the big stage. The silence roared with electricity, and she found herself raving, like she'd got very pissed and was dissing everything in sight.

Some small bit of her heard it all, appalled.

'What's it all for?' she was yelling. 'When we die do we come back? Does death pull us out of the car at the end of the ghost train and say, hey la, what about another ride? Or is it dust time? What's the point of love if we're gonna die?'

Behind her, the curtain swished open, and the band came on.

It was death. The noise of death. Like My Bloody Valentine turned up to eleven. Ace never saw what it looked like.

The sound blew her forward, out across the cheap seats, flying curled into a ball, her mouth open in a final gasp.

The floor swung up to kill her.

She hit it, and dived under, bubbled under life, struggling and spinning in blood, trying to find a light inside her mother's womb.

Now there was a well dead thought. Why had she hated her Mum that much? She laughed at the distant hate, and blood filled her lungs.

She could see her body, back in the real world, jerking. Her heart was beating too fast, close to stopping. Under her lids, her eyes rolled and rolled. She was dreaming too quickly. She was going to die! Here in dreamland! And not enough was done, no love and no reconciliations and no final, final word about Mum or Glitz or the Doctor or Robin or –

'Stop.' Christopher reached out and touched her forehead, and they were alone again, in darkness. 'Who are you?' asked the slim being.

Ace was panting. 'Erm . . . dunno. Is it important?'

'Ace,' Christopher insisted. 'I can feel everything you are here. Let's see . . . Dorothy. Warrior chemist, Dalek killer, she who loved not wisely but well. The woman who never ran away, never betrayed anyone, never deserted a friend. She has sacrificed herself, stood up and shouted out against the world. She kicked and kicked and kicked –'

'– Until everything she hated was kicked out! And she's still kicking! One up at half time.' Ace clapped and rubbed her hands over her face. 'Freaked out or what?' She smiled up at Christopher, relieved that she'd found her personality again. 'You just saved my life, right? Cheers, big ears!'

They were standing now on a silver disc, in their real bodies, or so it felt. That had been a really dodgy moment, like death was breathing down her neck. Been there before, of course, didn't like it last time. In the sky were blocks of careful colour, like a kid's building kit. They were labelled with little signs: IMC, Heaven Defence Centre (big black one, that), Draconian Solarshnar. Clumps of data, she reckoned, the office blocks of the computer world. All around Ace and Christopher, across the plane of the disc, Travellers were appearing. Some of them looked quite different from how they were in real life. More muscular, heroic, voluptuous.

'What do I look like?' Ace was suddenly embarrassed. She could feel everybody sharing her head. She hoped that she hadn't got herself all dolled up.

'You look like you,' Christopher smiled. 'If that's what you wanted.'

Nah, slimmer, taller – Ace stopped herself. No way was she ever gonna look like anything apart from what she was. Still . . .

'Best kit,' she decided. 'Um, keep the Doc Martens. Purple leggings, Kingmaker shirt, do my hair up in beads, okay?'

Christopher nodded, watching as Ace's black funeral look was transformed before him. 'I am glad that you do not want to change yourself,' he said. 'That is the greatest strength a warrior can have. If I wished, I could be male or female here, and even take a lover. I choose not to, for this is but a dream. Dreams make the world, but we never can take anything from them into our waking lives.'

Ace gently touched Christopher's nose. 'That's beautiful.' She smiled. 'And you're beautiful too, whatever you are.'

The being gazed mournfully at her. 'If I am,' he murmured, 'it is just a cruel accident.'

Jan appeared. He was twice as muscular, done up in the harness of a Celtic warrior. His hair stuck out in rough spikes, and his body was painted with blue spirals.

He'd also evened his face out, the idiot, so it was twice as even but half as sexy. It was like Jim Morrison had got a facelift.

He was holding a golden cord that was suddenly attached to Ace's wrist. '– moment,' he grinned. 'Oh, I see that Christopher got here first.'

'Just as well,' Christopher muttered darkly.

'How do you feel?' Jan asked.

Ace shook her head. 'Awful. What's this cord for?'

'That's what I use to yank you out if there's trouble. Ah, we must all be here . . . '

Máire had appeared in the centre of the disc, naked but for a belt on which hung various belt pouches. She held on to Roisa, who looked lost and worried.

'What happened to her?' Jan whispered, the concern in his voice apparent.

'Go and see her, if you want,' Ace told him.

'No, we'll all meet on the Wheel. I have to look after you.'

Máire glanced around, checking numbers. 'Into the Dreaming!' she called. 'And be careful, the atmosphere's not good today.'

'Here we go!' Jan called, and jerked the line on Ace's wrist.

A block of green shot out of the sky and enveloped them all.

Ace and Jan were alone in a sunlit forest clearing.

'Where are we?' gasped Ace.

Jan leaned on a tree. 'Well, if you want to be ordinary,' he smiled. 'we, our minds, are in the computer unit of the Puterspace Deck. This is a virtual reality, formed on a communications net between all the computers on Heaven or in Heaven orbit. The big corporations, the governments and embassies, all have their data in this net. It's easier to get at by wandering about in it, so hackers have themselves biologically linked to the matrix via the jackholes. We Travellers made this particular place. We call it the Dreaming, or the Land Under The Hills.'

Two owls fluttered down to a low branch and stared at Jan. He smiled to them. 'Those owls, the trees, everything here is made of information. We pirated a little space, and made it into Fairyland. It's always summer here.'

'Why did you make it?' Ace could smell pine, and hear the crunch of twigs under her feet.

'For worship. This is where the gods live. They might be mass hallucinations, for everybody sees them in different forms, y'know. Or they might be real, living, thinking beings. In that case, they live here when we're not around. In the end, there's no real difference.'

'Like, if a tree falls when there's nobody to hear it . . . '

'I know it makes an almighty racket,' Jan grinned. 'That's magic. D'you want to be kissed yet, lass?'

Ace laughed and looked away. 'Not with you looking like that, mate!'

'What's wrong with it?' Jan looked down at his costume. 'I can change it if you'd like.'

'And who said I wanted to kiss you? Who said I didn't just think that you'd be fun to talk to?'

'Not the way you've been looking –'

'I look at a lot of things, and some of them are ugly. You're way too confident, you are.'

'No, not all the time, I –'

'Besides, you've got a girlfriend. Sorry, I mean you're on

timeshare. Not my style.'

'So you're not interested?'

Ace walked up to Jan and ran a finger down his brow, along his nose, across his lips. She let him kiss the finger for a moment, then took it gently away. 'Don't talk like you're selling me double-glazing. Now where are we going?'

Jan looked crestfallen at Ace's little grin. It took him a second to pull himself together. 'Ah, well, that's the hard bit. Obviously, to talk to the gods is a bit of an adventure. You can't just plug in and have a chat. All of us Travellers, on the way to the Great Wheel, where we'll have our debate, will meet some of them. You meet what's damaging you, what's playing with your insides. So when you get to making decisions, you've lost all your hang-ups.'

'Dunno if I like the sound of that. I like a lot of my problems.'

'So I noticed. Maybe what you've got is good then. It's not just the gods though. You get intruders from other datascapes, corporate hackers who want to know what this place is and if there's profit to be made. The last one of those who came here, a hotshot from IMC ... Artemis touched him. The Dark Goddess freaked him so much that when he woke up in the real world he chucked it all in and became a poet. Sometimes you get real monsters too, aliens from who knows where. There's a lot of weird stuff out here.'

'Don't I know it. Let's go and meet your problems then, eh?'

Jan looked at her worriedly as they made their way into the forest. 'You're a hard woman, you are.'

'Ta,' Ace smiled.

Jan lead by a few feet as they wandered, letting the cord drag along the forest floor. He'd taken care not to tug it, hadn't even acknowledged its presence. That was either kind or forgetful of him.

'How far have we got to go?' she asked after ten minutes. It was, after all, just like a real wood. No psychedelic stuff. Bit dull, really.

'No idea,' shrugged Jan. 'Depends where we are in our heads. Ah.' He'd stopped and was peering through a gap in the trees.

Ace ran up and looked over his shoulder. In the centre of a clearing was a desk, and on it stood a goblet, shining gold in the sunlight. A man sat behind the desk, a crooked grin on his face. He wore an old-fashioned blue suit, and had slicked-back black hair.

'You would not believe,' he said to the two adventurers, 'what's been going on around here.'

'The Trickster!' Jan breathed. 'Not this again! Why do I always have to go through this?'

Ace had recognized the figure instantly, and frowned at Jan's fearful face. 'Come on,' she muttered. 'He's nothing to be afraid of. That's –'

'Arlan Jardolz, the Betalan comedian, I know. But he's really the Trickster, the archetypal god of universal jokes. And this joke's on me, because he shows me that goblet every time . . . '

'Just the other day,' the Trickster continued, 'I saw that goddess Minerva down the swimming baths, and she was measuring field mice with an industrial micrometer. I told her, I said, you know that gives me indigestion . . . '

Jan stepped into the clearing. 'Why are you showing me that cup again?' he asked. 'What are you trying to tell me?'

'It's not your cup!' The Trickster did a double take, startled. 'It's my cup!'

'It's mine!' Jan shouted. 'Why do we keep having to go through this? This goblet is mine!' Ace was amazed at the anger in his shout. It had burst from nowhere, like a sudden fire.

'You could have just kept quiet about it.' The Trickster stood up, putting his hands on his hips. 'But you couldn't, could you? You wouldn't let it lie!'

Jan strode forward, and put his hand on the goblet. 'I stole the goblet from the chapel of the Church of Vacuum because of the ceremonies I saw performed there. The goblet was full of blood. I cleaned it and put it in my treasure chest. I purified it, and it's not something to be guilty about. This cup is no longer full of –'

He grabbed it, and pulled it from the desk.

Blood sloshed over the sides of the cup and covered him. It ran down his face and chest.

Jan howled like a baby, and threw the goblet aside. He ran, off into the woods. Ace followed, suddenly aching inside.

'Ace!' the Trickster yelled as she was about to leave the glade.

She turned back for a second, accusingly. 'What?'

'What's at the end of the race, Ace?' asked the god, and turned to wander off into the trees, swinging his arms extravagantly.

Ace caught up with Jan after a few minutes. He'd collapsed under an old oak tree, and was frantically trying to remove the blood with a bunch of dead leaves he'd scooped from the forest floor.

Ace sat down quietly beside him, and took a big rag from her pocket. She began to wipe the blood from Jan's chest and it vanished, erased like chalk on a blackboard. Jan looked at her, amazed.

'Tell me what's wrong,' she murmured. 'What was all that about?'

Jan ran a hand through his hair. 'I've got this thing about self-sacrifice . . . ' he muttered, looking aside. 'That's why I hate the Vacuum Church so much.'

'Why? What do they believe in?'

'Nothing.'

'What, they're atheists?'

'No. They think that the universe is an accident and that life is meaningless. They embrace death as a release from pain.'

'Okay, so they're goths. Are they dangerous?'

'No. Well, they have radical factions that sometimes support terrorists, but they do good works too, I suppose. They attract depressed people, especially those in mourning. Instead of telling them that everything's going to be fine, they help them to deal with it all in the real world. They recover. Then they usually leave the cult.'

'How do they keep going, then?'

Jan leaned back against the tree and sighed. 'Some followers get wrapped up in it. They donate themselves to the cause, allow themselves to be sacrificed. You can do that, under Earth law; it's like legal suicide.'

'That's horrible.'

'The church makes generous donations to the Imperial budget. All those wills, you see. Ah, damn them all. I only stole their bloody cup!'

Ace put down the rag and leaned gently on Jan, her shoulder

touching his. 'So who sacrificed themselves for you?' she asked.

Jan looked at her, startled, and Ace could see that she was right. 'Christopher . . . ' he sighed, screwing up his eyes tightly. 'You sure you want to hear about this?'

'Yeah, I really do.'

'We were in the same unit in the military, drafted . . . ' Jan looked up into the blue skies that shone about the forest canopy. 'We were going to fight the Daleks. But we were given the option to test some new drugs instead. They were supposed to give you psychic powers. They hadn't really got any idea what they did to people. I was really afraid of the war, y'know. It looked like a great mincing machine, chewing up lads like me and spitting out their bones.'

'That's what all wars are like.'

'Christopher knew that I was scared of going. And he knew that I was scared of taking those tablets, too. The boy loved me like a brother.'

'You don't seem so close now –' Ace bit her lip. 'No. Go on.'

'We were each given a different set of pills to ingest,' Jan sighed. 'They put both lots of them on a table, and we wandered up and down that little grey room, wondering who was going to go first. They were watching us on monitors. I was curled up in a little ball, weeping. I couldn't jump either way. We started to shout at each other, and finally Christopher, who was a mad bastard then, just grabs both bottles and starts throwing them down his throat. I managed to get them off him, and took about half my share. He was so brave. He just wanted to save me it, get it over with. They grabbed us and took us in for examination. They weren't really angry, more excited. They wanted to see what the effects were. They were sodding awful. I sat there over a week, watching as Christopher . . . lost his sex. His skin was like clay, it all just melted into nothing. He's just smooth now, like some bloody doll. Sounds like a joke, doesn't it?'

'No . . . oh god no, it doesn't.'

'It worked, mind you. He got some vast powers in exchange. Mrs Rydd's little boy just got a little something –'

'What?'

'Please, later . . . '

'Okay, hush . . . '

'And I didn't lose a bloody thing. You're thinking that all this isn't so bad, aren't you?'

'No, that's not –'

'We knew the same woman, lass, back at home. The same Traveller woman who hung around the spaceport and kept telling us that if we could stay on the planet one more day she'd get us out of there. Christopher and she were in love.'

Ace heard the passion in his voice. He'd kept this inside him for so long. 'Roisa?' she asked.

'Roisa.' Jan looked aside, ashamed of his tears. 'That's why I can't, quite . . . why I'm afraid to . . . '

Ace couldn't say anything. She reached out, and took Jan's chin in her hand, and turned his face to hers.

Then she kissed him.

After a moment, he kissed her back. The tears had made his breath hot, and his tongue met Ace's. His hand stroked her hair, and the kiss continued, both of them falling back against the tree.

A shadow fell over them. Suddenly, they were scrambling upright.

'It's all right . . . ' sighed Roisa, looking down at them with infinite pity. 'It doesn't matter now.'

And she walked away, leaving the two of them lying there. They looked at each other awkwardly.

Jan sprang up and ran after Roisa.

Ace sat there for a moment, wondering if she should follow. She was feeling well vulnerable. The man kissed like hot mead.

Another shadow obscured the computerized sun. A vast shadow. It was angular and utterly black. It swooped across the treetops silently, sweeping in the direction Jan had gone.

Ace jumped to her feet and sprinted after it.

They were far off along a dirt path, Roisa walking stiffly ahead, not listening. Jan was trying to convince her of something, probably that he bloody loved her, the fool. He didn't love her, it was just his own guilt keeping him interested. The cord that bound him to Ace lay slack on the ground, expanding with the distance between them.

Overhead, the boxlike craft was diving down at the two

figures. It looked like an attack run, straight out of the sun.

'Jan!' Ace bellowed, sprinting. 'Look out!'

He couldn't hear her. He hadn't noticed. Please don't let him die.

She killed that thought. This place wasn't real. Ace could do what she liked here. What would the Doctor do?

The Doctor would win.

Ace closed her eyes, and yelled: 'Everybody here gets out alive!'

The ground whipped away beneath her feet, Puterspace spinning with her effort of will. Mud scattered aside from the speed of her boots.

A moment later she was running at Jan, feet from him.

She hit him and Roisa full tilt, leaves flying. They fell into the bracken in a sprawling heap.

A blast of light rammed past their heads, turning a tree to vapour. Wood splintered like shrapnel.

The dark thing swooped back round for another try.

They were still untangling themselves, and Roisa was shouting some fervent prayer for forgiveness. Ace reached across to Jan and grasped his hand, struggling to get up.

The shadow swept across them.

And a brilliant light cut through it. The beam sliced straight into the black shape, and it exploded into an expanding ball of pixels.

When the noise died away, Ace looked up to Máire, puffing smoke off the end of a Dalek gunstick.

'I knew I kept this for a reason,' she said. 'I can even visualize it in here. Kills anything, even Dalek puterships.'

Ace helped Roisa to her feet. She seemed to shiver at her touch. 'The Daleks are in Puterspace?' Ace asked.

'Yes,' sighed Máire. 'They get everywhere. But they're not good at it yet. Their hackers are still vulnerable. Christopher and I must talk about improving the defences around the Dreaming. Now, we should get to the Wheel. Everybody else is waiting.'

Ace caught a glance that passed between Máire and Roisa, and realised that the Dalek Killer's easy tone concealed a world of concern.

Then she looked at Jan, and they shared a smile together. Still alive.

The Great Wheel was a vast round table, mounted on a single bearing. It spun slowly and continuously in the middle of a shady clearing. In its very centre, illuminated by the sun, was stuck a slim sword with a bejewelled hilt. The table was carved with a complex pentagram design.

'The sword's pulled out when we move on,' Jan told Ace. 'It's not a real sword, just our imagined version of one.'

Around the Wheel there was a chair for everyone, each seemingly appropriate to the Traveller who occupied it. Christopher's was a carved mixture of male and female symbols. Máire's was a Dalek casing, lined with plush satin. Jan's was made of wooden flames, curling up over the back. This surprised Ace, because she couldn't understand it. But what surprised her more was her own chair.

It was a stout, straight, wood-backed chair. The arms were carved with female motifs, and the back was inlaid with a carving of the globe of Earth. But on the arms, down the sides of the thing, there was something else. Every inch of the chair was carved with tiny graffitti. She read some: 'Free Alex', 'Higher Than The Sun', 'And David Seaman Will Be Very Disappointed With That'. Yeah. Ace sat down, chilled to the gills.

Máire watched as all the Travellers found a seat. Then she spoke. 'We will talk later of what happened on the way here. Firstly, I believe that Roisa has an idea concerning us all. Roisa?'

Roisa seemed to consider, watching the table rotate under her gaze. Then she stood up.

'I have decided to make my home here on Heaven.' Her voice was almost a whisper. 'And at one point I was going to ask you all to stay. But now ... I've reconsidered. You can't change your lifestyle for me. I think you should all move on. And soon. Can we please make this a quick goodbye?'

Máire stared at her, almost daring Roisa to meet her gaze. Ace realized that she hadn't been expecting this.

'That's all I have to say. Except ... I'm sorry. Forgive me.

I enjoyed being one of the tribe. I enjoyed it so much . . . ' Roisa sat down again, and was silent.

Despite herself, Máire was the first to speak. 'I thought you wanted us all to stay. Why –?'

'It's about me, isn't it?' Jan cried out, standing up. 'This is all some horrible . . . ' he wrung the air with his hands. 'Some horrible jealous game! I can't stand this any more!'

Christopher raised a hand. 'Sit down, old friend. Let us slowly, over a period of debate, find all the corners of this question. Now . . . '

Roisa began to weep.

Ace felt it first. A slow tingle at the back of her skull. She turned to Jan, who sat beside her. 'Something's wrong. Is that Dalek ship coming back?'

Jan shrugged, distracted. He was still absorbed in Roisa's outburst. 'No, of course it isn't. Nothing can hurt us on the Wheel. We're safe here.'

'Then what's –'

The sun went out, and the table was swept into darkness.

Above the Wheel floated a huge sphere, a mottled brown globe. It stank, Ace realized with a wince. It smelt of slaughter-houses.

Screams burst from the Travellers. Ace suddenly found herself unable to move.

The air was turning to glass, and freezing in her lungs. The pressure on her arms was huge. The table began to creak and groan. The wood split in lightning patterns across the pentagram, and the thing began to tilt alarmingly in its spin.

Jan was trying to stand, almost resisting the vast gravity around them.

And then Christopher roared.

The roar blasted from his mouth like a thunderclap. It sustained, sweeping aside the pressure that had forced them all down. Travellers began to vanish as they cut their links with the Puterspace Deck. Christopher stared up at the sphere from his seat, still roaring, throwing out a blanket of sound.

The note was getting higher. He couldn't hold it long.

Jan was climbing towards him, over the table, the cord between him and Ace stretching. They were the only three people left there now. His arms were wide. He wanted to rescue Christopher. Oh God, he needed to do it.

But Ace could see that he wasn't going to make it.

The note would fail before his outstretched grasp reached Christopher's hand. And then the sky would fall. Then they'd all die.

Ace made the decision. She grabbed the linking cord with both hands, and heaved.

'Christopher!' Jan was screaming. 'Don't –'

A hand pulled the wire crown from Ace's head, taking some hair with it.

The hand belonged to Máire.

'What happened?' she cried, anguished.

Ace looked up. The Travellers were all standing up shakily, weeping. Jan was staring at the Puterspace deck.

Christopher lay across it, still connected. A faint wisp of smoke drifted from the back of his neck. His eyes were gazing emptily upwards at the sky.

Jan's face creased in a silent scream.

'War,' whispered Ace.

4:

Twenties Kicks

The picture of the Doctor was fuzzy and distant. It was decaying as it replayed for the hundredth time. It shimmered across a fibre screen, suspended in darkness.

Fetid gasses drifted across the picture, and rasping breath could be heard. The gasping increased, until a hiss burst from the silence.

'Time . . . lord!'

'Not . . . possible,' a second rasping voice countered. 'They have not . . . interfered for . . . centuries . . . '

'No,' a third voice agreed with the first. 'He smells like a Time Lord!'

'Nerve fibres have been stabilized . . . ' the first voice hissed. 'I wish the fourth of us were here . . . the knowledge in that area is more . . . specialized. However . . . I have . . . sound.'

'Let me through,' the Doctor said, advancing on the screen yet again. 'I'm the Doctor.'

'Doc . . . tor?' hissed the second voice. 'He . . . is the Doctor!'

A low hiss of surprise and fear echoed round the chamber.

Finally, the third voice spoke. 'A worthy . . . adversary. He must be . . . dealt with . . . '

Bernice Summerfield wiped the sweat from her brow with a cloth. It was warm underground, the chemical lamps generating heat as well as light.

She'd told the crew to knock off about an hour ago. They were sagging on their feet, and, besides, she could think better when she was alone. The official survey of Heaven had somewhat speculatively labelled the arch as the 'Temple Of The Sun', hypothesizing that the silver construction was aligned with the rising of heaven's sun on the solstices. Well, computer simulations had shown that to be rubbish. Typical of old archaelogists to call anything they couldn't understand a church.

Benny was dusting around the outlines of the door now, feeling guilty for not having been there when the thing had been found in the earthen wall. Three days before the money ran out. She already had a pass on a Draconian freighter heading out across their empire. She'd look around a bit in Draconian space, see what they had on the fringes, maybe excavate something, maybe see if he'd come out that way . . .

But she was damned if she wasn't going to open this door first.

'Fine brush,' she muttered, reaching down into the kit bag she'd placed on the floor.

'Fine brush,' a voice replied, handling her the tool.

Bernice turned around slowly. Standing behind her, peering intensely at the carvings around the door, was a strange little man in a paisley scarf.

'Who are you?' said Benny, amused by the childlike look of concentration on the stranger's face.

He seemed to snap out of his trance, and flashed her a lovely grin, doffing his hat and offering her his hand. 'I'm the Doctor,' he said.

'I'm the Professor.' Benny shook his hand firmly. 'And I'm very busy, so –'

'Yes, so am I. Perigosto Stick . . . ' The Doctor began to search through his pockets until he found what he was looking for: a thin silver probe with a tiny sphere on top. 'Now, we need a small object . . . '

Bernice looked around the chamber. It was as if suddenly she was in the wrong movie. 'Excuse me, but is this important? I've got a door to open.'

'Doors. Tricky. Ah!' The Doctor produced a small cube from his pocket, and Bernice was suddenly very interested. The thing was almost invisible, like a ghost cube. Or . . . no, it was solid as steel. Or maybe it was shining brightly.

'I see.' Benny leaned on the wall and nodded. 'All right, this is a dream isn't it?' She pinched herself. 'Come on, I haven't got all night. Wake up, Benny, time to work!'

'No time for dreams.' The Doctor smiled secretly. 'You're awake. This is a tesseract, the shadow of a four-dimensional hypercube. It can do all sorts of things, and I prepared it for a special task. But it can also be used to prove that what goes up –' he threw the cube into the air and his hand flashed over the sphere on the Perigosto Stick in a complex pattern.

The cube vanished. Benny blinked.

The Doctor relaxed, and tapped his chin with the Stick. 'It's a game played between Time Lords. Manoeuvring an object across the dimensions. The loser is the one who lets it drop back into normal space. The Prydonians play it with spheres of pure platinum. I preferred rotten fruit. As we used to say, time flies like an arrow, but fruit flies like a banana.'

Benny paused, raising a finger. 'Wait. Tesseracts, Perigosto thingies, Time Lords . . . do you know a young woman called Ace?'

'Yes,' the Doctor said darkly. 'I travel with her.'

'Through time?'

'And space. In a police box that's bigger on the inside than the outside. Any more questions?'

Benny reflected for a moment, then decided. 'What's the best Isley Brothers song?'

' "This Old Heart of Mine".'

Benny nodded solemnly. 'Correct.'

'Surprising question,' grinned the Doctor.

'Ah, well, surprise is my middle name. Bernice Surprise Summerfield. My poor Mum wanted to hammer that point home, I think. Now, listen, I'm stacking up all these fascinating conversations to have later, but I really do need to open this door. What's the time?'

'The relative measurement of states of decay,' muttered the Doctor. 'But that's not important now. Are you ever going to get it open?'

'Well, yes, I hope so –'

The Doctor made another quick pass over his Perigosto Stick. There was a solid-sounding click from the other side of the door.

'Yes,' smiled the Doctor. 'It took you a while, but you did it.'

Benny looked between the Doctor and the door. 'This,' she sighed, 'is going to take all the fun out of archaeology.'

The met in Jan's tent. Cathlan, Ace, Máire, Roisa and Jan.

It looked for a while like nobody was going to say anything. They sat in a circle, both Ace and Roisa at Jan's side. Cathlan just shook his head and sighed.

It was Máire who broke the silence. 'We'll have the funeral tonight, if nobody has any objections. It'll bring us together, like the Great Wheel was supposed to. Besides, we don't want the authorities asking any questions about this.'

Jan leaned down close to Ace and whispered. 'I'm sorry. I'm just all . . . I don't know. Christopher used his powers against that thing. He gave his life for . . . for . . . '

Roisa and Ace glanced at each other. After a moment's eye contact, Ace put an arm around the man.

'It's okay,' she told him.

'I don't understand . . . ' Jan sighed. 'Don't understand anything anymore.'

Máire ran a hand along the tent material. 'There's a threat here, to all of us. We need to band together to fight it. We don't need any more problems.'

'Can anybody tell me what happened in there?' Ace asked. 'I mean, we all saw the same thing, but what was it?'

'We should have been safe . . . ' Cathlan muttered. 'We are prey in the woods, but safe when we reach the Wheel. Everybody knows that. Something must have brought that intruder upon us . . . Somebody's inner flaw, it followed us to the Wheel!'

'Hush, Cathlan.' Roisa had been looking despondently at her boots. 'It doesn't matter now, does it? We've lost Christopher. We just lost him. Everybody dies sometime, you know? I loved him very much, so did we all.'

Máire had been staring intensely at Roisa. 'You're not obliged to answer, now that we're not on the Wheel, but why do you want to stay on Heaven? And why do you want the rest of us to go?'

Roisa shook her head. 'I . . . I don't want to talk about it. Christopher would have understood, love. Let me go, will you?'

She stood and walked quickly from the tent.

Ace had seen the tears that were welling in the woman's eyes, and felt horribly guilty. But Jan was staring into the distance again.

It might be months before he could come to terms with the grief, years before he could really dispose of it. The horror was going to carry on in front of his eyes for a long time.

Ace gave Jan's arm a gentle squeeze, and knew that she had to be with him tonight.

Benny pushed the door open carefully.

There was a rustle as new air rushed in to move the old dust. It was a round room, with a strange rodlike mechanism mounted on a turntable in the centre. The roof was a slatted half-globe. The walls were covered with a strange, rough lettering, done in a tiny hand. The whole place was coloured dark blue, and the mechanism was bright gold.

'That's the only thing we know about the Heavenites,' Benny muttered. 'Great colour sense.'

The Doctor had walked around the central podium, and had stopped. 'We know something else now . . .' he said.

Benny walked round to look.

It was a skeleton, a tall, rather top-heavy creature with an angular skull. It was hanging from three manacles, chained to the wall. The remaining manacle hung free behind the thing's ribcage, the arm swinging lightly in the air that had entered the chamber.

'Ritual sacrifice?' suggested Bernice, then corrected herself. 'No, that's just the sort of assumption I hate.'

'Indeed.' The Doctor reached out his umbrella and gently tapped the shackles. 'This is a scientific building. Have a look at the device over there.'

Benny gently stepped up on to the podium and, without touching it, examined the long rod that was balanced amid a mesh of gears and levers. 'Aha! A telescope. A refractor, not amazingly powerful. Didn't have to be, since this observatory's underground.' She put her eye to the telescope, and sighed. 'I see absolutely no ships.'

'The shackles don't belong here. They've been roughly welded to the wall. You can see the heat marks. He wasn't wounded . . . ' the Doctor was musing. 'At least, his bones weren't broken.'

'She.' Benny hopped off the podium and joined him. 'Or a

male who just happened to have a huge pelvic girdle. Mammalian, probably something like a bear with an opposable thumb. Oh yes . . . I see!'

'What?' The Doctor frowned as Benny stood in front of the skeletal creature.

She mimicked doing up the shackles on both her legs, then the one on the right arm. 'She was left-handed, unlike me. She couldn't fasten her own left cuff with only one free hand.'

'Yes!' The Doctor dropped to his knees and began to scuffle about the floor.

'No need to grovel,' said Benny. 'I'm fairly secure in my brilliance.'

'You managed to find . . . ' The Doctor suddenly spotted something and grabbed it, holding it up to the light. A tiny sliver of metal. 'The key!'

'So why should Ms Astronomer Bear shackle herself to the wall?' Benny asked, looking at the key. 'Should we enquire too deeply?'

'Oh yes.' The Doctor nodded, jumping up. He wandered towards the skeleton and sniffed the bones. 'Not much bone marrow, no smell of putrefication.' He squatted again, and examined the floor. Traces of fine grey dust stuck to his fingers. 'Smell that.'

'Very olfactory, aren't you?' Benny took a sniff. 'Mushroom omelette?'

'Close.' The Doctor looked around the observatory, his face darkening as his eyes looked into the distance of space and time. 'After all these years,' he whispered. He turned to Bernice. 'I must get back to Joycetown.'

Bernice pretended to consider. 'Well, I think I can spare a moment . . . '

'Good. Something terrible is happening here. We may already be too late.' The Doctor jumped to his feet. 'Do you have any transport? Miller had business at his base . . . '

'I have a horse.' Bernice took the key from the Doctor. 'But there's something I have to do first.' She unlocked the manacles on the skeleton and it fell. As it did so, a tiny scroll dropped from its hand. Benny picked it up. 'Hmm. Do you want to examine this?'

The Doctor was already at the door. 'On the way,' he muttered urgently.

Ace and Jan walked slowly around the dying embers of the fire. They were holding hands, but Ace wasn't sure if Jan knew about that or not. He was quite lost, curled up inside, not looking at her.

And she'd come to this place to grieve herself. Not a lot of time for that. Well, Jules wouldn't have minded. He'd have said to go for it. He'd driven up to those gates like a madman, the big arclights shining down on the battered old car. That was all such a long time ago. Ace wasn't sure why that particular scene kept coming back to her.

The Travellers had wrapped Christopher's body in a black sheet, and given him a Puterspace crown to clutch. Then every one of them, even the children, had walked up and touched the corpse – corpse, what a crap word for a dead person – and said goodbye. Ace had said thanks to Christopher for saving her life, but had asked him in a whisper not to torment Jan with it. She told him that he was still exactly what he wanted to be.

They had danced for an hour, a very controlled dance. The Travellers knew it by heart. Ace had joined in, holding warm and solid hands with Máire and Jan. She'd tripped and stumbled at the steps, but she wouldn't have missed it. They formed a circle around the fire, and nobody was excluded. William the Cook called the patterns in a Palare rhyme, and the circle flexed back and forth.

As they danced, Jan had started to wail, a big low cry that spread across the Travellers until they were all doing it.

Roisa had taken a huge breath and bellowed at the sky, longer and louder than anyone else. Ace watched her, wishing that she could get rid of it all like that.

But as the scream faded, Ace felt the weight settle back on to the woman's shoulders. Whatever had died with the scream, pain still lived inside her.

That had made Ace cold with the slow horror of it.

After it was over, they took Christopher to a shallow hole a mile from the camp, covered him over and left him.

Máire said that he was in the arms of the Goddess, and was

a man again now, lucky in the love of the earth.

Then they had trudged back to camp, singing an old song in Palare that was full of hope and dreams.

Jan and Ace had sat by the fire and watched it burn out, the cinders drifting upwards in a spiral. They were silent until Ace had stood up and made Jan walk with her. She was cold, and Jan must have been freezing.

'Take me up into the woods,' she said.

'Yeah.' Jan nodded, dully. 'If you want. I was just remembering . . . '

'Bring your guitar, or whatever you call it.'

So Jan did.

Bernice had urged the horse on, and now they were galloping across the plains, towards the light of Joycetown in the distance.

The Doctor was sitting straight in the saddle behind Benny, not holding on with his hands but supporting his umbrella across his lap. He'd already stared at the scrap of parchment, shaken his head, and replaced it in his pocket. He seemed deep in thought. 'Where do you come from?' he asked Bernice.

'Originally?' Benny shouted over the sound of the hooves. 'Beta Caprisis. Earth colony. My Dad was a bigwig with Spacefleet. Mum stayed at home with me, until I was seven.'

'What happened then?'

'Oh, the Daleks did. When the war broke out, we were suddenly tactically important. Dad was at the front, of course, but they broke through. Mum grabbed me and my doll Rebecca, and ran for one of the shelters. She, ah, well, she dropped Rebecca, and shoved me through the door. It shut after me, but Mum could have opened it again. Only she'd run back down the street for Rebecca. Silly thing. The Daleks started bombarding the city with plasma beams. Mum was caught in the first blast.'

The Doctor closed his eyes. 'I'm very sorry.'

'No, no. Long time ago now. Not very important. Loads of people lost family. Dad never came back. He vanished after a scrap with the Daleks. Bunch of idiots said he'd run away, but that's totally impossible, you see, Dad wasn't like that at all.'

'No.'

'So I was sent to military academy as an orphan. I wasn't very good at it, though, because –'

A plasma bolt shot between Benny and the Doctor.

The horse bucked, sending the Doctor flying.

Benny pulled hard on the reins and grabbed a handgun from the saddle. Blasts of blue light skittered across the ground, and the Doctor rolled, clods of earth flying up around him.

As the horse bucked beneath her, Benny aimed carefully out into the darkness, watching for the source of the blasts.

'There,' she whispered, squeezing the trigger.

A little copse of trees was illuminated by the blast, and a figure flew backwards.

Benny calmed the horse and jumped down. The Doctor had stood up, shielding his eyes against the glare.

'Because I was such a bad shot,' Benny said. 'I've got better since then.'

Ace and Jan sat, their backs to a tree, looking down the valley in the moonlight. A light mist had risen, and owls were hooting mournfully in the dark forest behind them.

Jan had began to pluck randomly at the strings of his guitar, and at first Ace had been dispirited by the noise. Just single, isolated notes, floating out across the valley and dying.

But gradually, the notes began to form sequences, and the sequences turned into a worked-out series of chords. A melody began to drift through the forest. It was a sad tune, simple and gentle, and it caressed around its central motifs. Ace could hear patterns rise and fall, sometimes like great empires fighting, sometimes like a single person speaking up and then vanishing into the melody again.

Despite herself, her thoughts drifted back to Julian again.She was surprised to find herself sobbing. Not hard sobs, letting something awful out, like they'd usually been in the past. This was soft, the only thing you could do when you heard the music.

Julian would have been crying too.

Finally, the music died away, a last gentle note echoing across the valley. Jan looked up, and Ace saw he was sadly smiling.

'Jan . . . ' she murmured. 'I . . . oh God . . . no, wait . . . ' She wiped her face roughly and took a deep breath.

'It's fine now,' Jan sighed, putting his guitar down. 'At least for the moment it's fine. Shall we talk about something good? About space or something?'

So Ace leaned back into his arms, pulling them around her like a pullover. She told him about her life, about faraway Perivale. Jan believed every word, because he believed in magic.

'I want to come too,' he chuckled. 'Take me away in your TARDIS and we'll go duff up some clowns!'

'Yeah.' Ace nodded firmly. 'I wouldn't mind. I'll ask the Doctor.' That didn't sound good as she said it, but then Jan kissed her for the first time in the real world.

The kiss was solid and warm, and it got so passionate and angry that Ace knew she didn't want to be out there in the cold anymore.

'All night,' she whispered, 'I've been thinking about something I want you to do. Why don't we go back to your tent?'

Jan looked at her, surprised. 'Gods,' he muttered. 'That sounded gorgeous. You're on.' He stood up, pulling her up into his arms.

'Bad mistake,' Ace grinned, running her hand down his spine. 'You don't know what I want you to do yet, do you?'

Jan shook his head, and looked into Ace's eyes. His pupils were huge with the night. 'Whatever you wish,' he breathed. 'I don't care.'

They ran down the hill, into the camp, and past Máire's tent. From inside came the sounds of low female conversation. Roisa and Máire were together tonight.

Ace was glad at that, and smiled as she opened Jan's tent flap and pulled him inside.

They fell on a mess of rugs, kissing.

After a while, Ace gently disengaged herself from Jan's mouth. 'You're eager,' she whispered. 'We haven't done what I've been thinking about yet.'

'Well, no –' Jan gasped, his voice gruff.

'So now it's time. Sit up.'

Jan did so, but from his expression it was clear that he was in no mood for games.

'Right.' Ace slapped the man's knees. 'I've been into this idea since I met you. You see all this hair, all this stuff that's bound up on to my head?'

'Yes.'

'Take it down. Get rid of the clips and all that. But gently, right? Pull it and I'll go off back to Joycetown.'

Jan was smiling now. 'Turn your back, then.'

Ace did so, and shivered deliciously as Jan began to undo the clips that kept her hair in place. 'We're both alive, right?' she whispered.

'Yes.'

'And we've both had enough of death. You're very good at that you know. How are you with bras?'

'Oh . . . ' Jan muttered, stretching a hand forward so that Ace could see it. He made a little undoing motion. 'Easy as –'

And his fingers burst into flame.

Ace jerked back.

'Ah, no . . . ' Jan let go of her hair and moved the burning digits away from her. 'Don't be afraid. I'm sorry. Maybe you ought to just go back to town.'

'What is it?' Ace asked, staring. He wasn't being burnt, she was sure.

Jan moved around to face her. 'My power. What I got from the military. That's what I meant when I said that there was one thing thing I could do well. I'm a pyrokinetic. I can make tiny fires. I do it when my blood's up about something. Useful, eh?'

'Yeah! 'Course it is.'

Jan concentrated on his hand, and the flame vanished. Ace touched the flesh. It wasn't particularly warm.

'Well,' Jan sighed, 'that's the end of that, so –'

So Ace kissed him again, and shoved him back on to the rugs, pulling open the knots at his collar, kissing his snake. 'So if I get burnt,' she whispered, 'I get burnt. Don't I?'

The arm lay in the bracken, still twitching. Smoke curled from its shoulder end. There was no sign of its owner.

'Now that's what I call self-control,' said Bernice.

The Doctor looked back towards the lights of the town, and frowned. 'Exactly the opposite,' he whispered.

5:

Ace Dreaming

In the early hours of the morning, Ace rolled over and looked down at Jan's sleeping body.

He was very beautiful. There had, indeed, been a lot of hair in that pony tail. The snake tattoo ran all the way down his chest, and it wasn't nasty and macho, like most tattoos, but, well, meaningful. Like he meant it. She gently ran her fingers around the jackhole at the base of his neck, circled it and popped her little finger inside. He stirred slightly. The area was slightly inflamed. Ace wondered if it hurt and stopped.

She pulled the rugs closer around her. At this point, generally, she liked to be away, 'cos hearing all the things men came out with in the morning was an awful experience.

But this time she wanted to stay. Jan would say good things. Jan. That was a good name.

Ace sighed and shook her head, curling up again beside him.

Snuggled in the crook of her lover's arm, breathing in his scent, Ace allowed herself to fall down into dreams.

This was the good stuff, she thought. The time of being together when nothing could hurt you, and you could fool yourself into thinking that nothing would ever hurt again. He'd protect you, you could protect him. You could suckle him, offer yourself up as sacrifice to him . . . not that he'd want that if he thought about it . . . but you win. In the downfall afterglow, when he was sleepy and small, wrapped about you, you were where you wanted to be, on the way to dreams.

Yeah.

Gentle rain began to beat against the fabric of the tent.

A dream arrived.

The Doctor walked across the surface of the dream. Ace briefly wondered if he was dreaming himself, in some room at an inn.

Ace's hair wrapped across her head as it turned in the first jerk of deepest sleep.

Now, it was at this time, child, when the stars had turned about the nail of heaven, that the great mage known as the Doctor returned to the cave – what cave? Where? Hush, Ace – Dark it was, like the hidden face of the moon. Or like the womb that the Doctor had twice left. Sweet was the path there. The Doctor cast salt to his left and right as he walked.

At the cave entrance, the Doctor stopped.

'Death?' he called. 'Your sister Time said I could visit. Will you receive me?'

'I shall let you in, wily raven, but it will be a long while before I receive you!' a female voice cried, echoing from the cave.

The Doctor entered, doffing his hat.

Inside the cave sat Death, in a robe of black silk. Ace tried to see her face, and couldn't. The Doctor sat beside the figure, and offered her a gift, a tiny, burning candle, which Death silently took.

'Last time we met, we danced,' he began.

'Did you enjoy that dance?'

'Not very much, I'm afraid. I've come to bargain with you.'

'Again? The way I bargain with you, I should entertain every life of every cat! You only have thirteen to give me, Time Lord!'

'I gave you my sixth life for wisdom –'

Death laughed, and raised a soft finger between the Doctor's eyes. 'Don't lie to me! You sacrificed the colourful jester because you needed to be born! Time would have her champion, and he was just the compost for your blooming. You ran your TARDIS into the Rani's beam joyfully. Hah! Your sixth self hates you for that, he will become Valeyard for that –'

'Yes. I know. Now I offer myself.'

Death considered, grinning. 'Why?' she asked finally.

'My life for that of my companion.'

'Which one?'

Ace was suddenly afraid, jealous. Was there another?

'Ace!' the Doctor growled. 'My life for hers. I know what will happen on this world. I know how many you intend to take. Take me with you. Replace me with someone who doesn't know his legacy, who would never trouble the Eternals. I would be good company.'

But Death was already shaking her head. 'I cannot take your life, Doctor. Have you another one to offer me, instead? Do you have a plan?'

Ace didn't care. She was already sobbing in her sleep, bawling out the love she had seen the Doctor give. In the dream, the Doctor suddenly looked around, aware of the sudden noise, aghast. He had so much more to say.

The dream broke, and the bits flew off to become fiction.

Ace woke up crying, full of relief. As dreams sometimes do, this one had given her great fondness for a friend again, a glance at what your heart really thinks of them.

The air in the tent was cool, and Ace knew she was twice in love, in different ways, and had to have her two loves meet and like each other.

She could do it. She could pull the future together with her hands. She could make it work, whatever time wanted.

She reached out to Jan, and began to stroke him awake.

6:

I Could Never Take The Place Of Your Man

The next morning, Ace wandered into Joycetown's market square, having hitched a lift with Cathlan. The big man had ridden into town to barter, and Ace had enjoyed his company on the ride as he told riddles and sang obscene songs.

The air was clear and tasty, and Ace began to whistle to herself as she walked, despite what had happened to Christopher. It was hard, she thought, to feel bad in these circumstances. That was bad, really. Maybe Christopher would have liked it like that, but maybe he wouldn't.

She'd kissed Jan goodbye this morning, saying that she'd see him later in the day. His smile was so big – and so it should be – that Ace hoped he wouldn't fall back into sorrow today. At least maybe he'd avoid this big complex about sacrifice and just basically miss his old friend.

Jan had said good things, and told her that she was the most wonderful lover he'd ever had.

Yeah. She could believe that. For once.

It'd be cool to see the Doctor again now, to hug him, and show him that she could wander off, be herself, and then come back and be his mate too.

In a corner of the market square, three children were poking at something with a stick. They were jumping back and squealing at it. Ace wandered over, full of the joys of autumn. It wasn't so long since she'd been playing games like that.

The two boys and a girl looked up at her, scared, but she squatted down and peered at the muddy corner, grinning.

'What you got?'

'It's a monster!' the girl whispered, and used a twig to hitch aside a leaf. Under the leaf twitched one of the tiny white fibres like Benny had caught in that jar. It jerked and tried to get under the leaf again, not liking the bright low sun. The children squealed.

Ace frowned. 'That looks great. Can I keep it?'

'No,' the little girl complained. 'It's ours.'

Ace reached into her backpack, finding an empty nitro-nine flask and . . . well, what would kids here like? Her hand chanced upon something she'd always meant to get rid of, but never had. 'Swap you it for this?' she asked, flicking the yo-yo along the ground and spinning it back into her hand. Good that she could still do that. It had taken two weeks, and tons of peer pressure, to learn it.

'Yeah!' gasped the girl, and the children began to fight over the toy. Ace bent down to scoop the creature into the flask with the twig. She crushed a vaguely irritated thought that the Doctor better appreciate the thing.

She could buy a yo-yo anywhere, couldn't she?

The Doctor was pacing his room in intense concentration. His fingers were describing a complex pattern, like a musician composing a symphony.

He'd booked into the inn late last night, Benny heading back to the dig. It had taken him an hour to convince her that he'd be perfectly safe, and it had taken an intimation that her own crew might be in danger to send her away.

There was a knock at the door. The Doctor stopped his pacing and pulled it quickly open without answering the knock.

Ace stood there, holding a nitro-nine flask. 'Present!' she said, throwing it on to the bed.

The Doctor flinched.

Ace grinned. 'Got you!' she said, and wandered into the room.

'Where were you last night?' the Doctor asked.

Ace ran a hand over her hair as she plopped down in a chair, wondering why this felt so odd. Then she got it. The question sounded like something her Mum might have asked. She smiled up at the Doctor, but found that he was looking deadly serious.

'Wandered about a bit. Went and saw the Travellers.'

'Yes.' The Doctor closed the door. 'I thought so.'

'We went into Puterspace . . . and, listen, something really bad's going on.' She told the Doctor about Christopher's death.

The Time Lord's expression grew darker as he listened. He shook his head. 'You might have been killed. Travellers don't know the technology. Only ever just enough for anything. They fly their ships from the manual, they live off other people, they cause more misery and suffering than –'

'Wait a minute!' Ace stood up and put a hand on the Doctor's lapel. 'You knew there was something going on, right? You didn't tell me what it was. Well, okay, the Zargoids are here, how do I know what's safe and what isn't?'

'You could have stayed with me.'

'Yeah, right, that's usually the safest place to be, isn't it?'

'What do you mean?'

'I'm supposed to be on your side, not blundering into stuff like this 'cos you don't want to tell me about it. I'm Ace, remember?'

'I remember.' The Doctor was looking at her with a distracted air. 'That boy . . . the one I saved. You haven't mentioned him. Was he there?'

'Yeah.' Ace glanced down at her boots. 'Crashed in his tent –'

'I don't think you should go back . . .' The Doctor had turned aside, and Ace couldn't see the expression on his face, but his tone was deceptively mild. It was the first time the Time Lord had ever sounded like a parent to Ace. Previously, his love had been like a real friend's was, without all the blackmail bullshit.

'You what?'

'It might be dangerous, you don't know the people. All sorts of reasons.' He was muttering, trying to stop what he'd started.

Ace paused. She'd sounded something really deep inside him. She put a hand on his, and a moment later, as if considering the action, he held it.

'Give us a better reason, eh?' she asked.

'No. I was wrong. Forget I said it.' After a moment he finally turned to look at her. The Doctor's face betrayed no emotion. 'Sorry,' he muttered. 'You're free. You can do what you want.'

'I want to stay with you.' It had come out more directly than she'd wanted. She didn't want to hear an answer. 'Just tell me what's going on.'

'I don't know myself. Not yet.'

'So why don't you look at the thing in the flask?'

As if sensing that Ace wanted to change the subject, the Doctor picked up the container and unscrewed it, throwing the contents on to the table. 'Where did you find it?' he asked, bending closer to the surface.

'The market square. Some kids had it.'

The Doctor took a probe from his pocket, and inspected the twitching filament. He flicked a control on the probe, and a tiny burst of laser light killed the thing.

'Hey!' murmured Ace.

'It's all right,' the Doctor said, lifting it with tweezers. 'It's part of a group organism. You can't kill the whole thing by switching off one of its parts. It's a fungal spore.'

'What, like a mushroom seed?'

'Yes. But alien. I've seen something like it before. Long ago. But the structure seems different. I must take this back to the TARDIS lab. You were going to talk to the Librarian, weren't you?'

'Yeah.' Ace had been watching the Doctor engrossed in his work. It was like he'd clicked back into being him. Whatever his problem with Jan was, the Doctor she was used to was back again.

'I need to find *The Papers of Felsecar*. Urgently. I found a piece of paper last night . . . I can't read it.'

'I though you could read anything?'

'No. I can only understand speech. Words on paper don't have minds that you can read. So I need another key. Perhaps you could have a word, ask Trench if he knows where the book went.'

'Sure.' Ace went to the door. The Doctor was still bending over the spore. 'I'll be off then.' Ace glanced at the Doctor worriedly.

'Yes.' The Doctor heard the door close behind him. Then he slowly lowered the spore to the table. He leaned on the chair, and his face creased into an expression of pain.

Operative Miller frowned at the man standing in front of his desk. 'What happened to you?'

Kale cradled his arm in its sling, glaring at his superior. 'Creatures, sir. Horrible things. I took a routine patrol out into the Forest of Arden. I wandered off, saw what I thought was a campfire . . .'

'I'm reading between the lines, Kale.'

'This huge thing came at me out of the dark. Smashed my arm. It was all dressed in black, had a helmet on. I dropped my weapon, I had to, and I ran. I made it back to the patrol and we came in straight away.'

Miller stood, angrily. 'Why did nobody wake me?'

'I was in the medical bay, sir. I'd ordered the patrol to stand down, I must have been in a daze . . . '

'So what's new, lad?' Miller punched a communicator control. 'Security state yellow. I want a general notice out to all ships in the equatorial docks to report anything strange.' Miller closed the link.

Kale raised his free arm. 'The orbital platform, sir –'

'Yes, I was just thinking about that. We'd better warn them.' Miller scratched his chin. Every colony had a small orbiting space station, a place where incoming ships could drop cargo without having to make planetfall. Heaven was no exception. The crew of the platform were particularly vulnerable to any form of spaceborne attack.

'What I was going to say, sir . . . Well, I've not been a very good soldier.'

'True.'

'That bastard could have killed me, sir. I want a piece of it. I'm in no condition to fight, but I specialized in scanner work when I was training with the mining corporation. I could take a shuttle up there, put the whole planet through a scanner sweep –'

'The data from which might be of huge commercial value . . .'

'Yes, sir.' Kale's glance flickered across his superior's face, sizing him up. 'But, on the other hand, it would show up anything unusual on the surface of Heaven. It would be useful to both of us.'

Miller inwardly winced. He'd never got used to this sort of compromise, but he was going to need the troopers' loyalty soon, and Kale had always had their ear. 'Very well. Keep me informed.'

'Yes sir!' Kale saluted and exited.

Miller nodded, slowly. He'd have to tell the Doctor about this. He punched another control. 'Judith,' he ordered, 'find me everything we've got on file about the Sontarans.'

Why did everything always have to get complicated? Ace stamped up the steps to the Library, angry.

She felt guilty, damn it. That was the first time the Doctor had come on like a parent, giving his love all sorts of conditions. Was he jealous? It wasn't as if Jan was any threat to him . . .

She stepped inside the Library building, and made her way quickly past the security system in the same way the Doctor had last time. It was just a code to punch into a keyboard. Not hard to break. Mind you, on this planet, who was there to break it?

As soon as she was inside the vaulted hall she heard singing. A sad old song, the words too low for her to hear. Ace recognized the voice as that of Trench, the old librarian. She made her way through the shelves until she found him.

The old man was taking documents from a shelf down on to a small cart, the kind that was used for loading spaceships. Thc cart was already piled high with manuscripts.

'Hi!' Ace stepped forward. Trench jumped and looked round quickly. He put a hand to his chest.

'Oh . . . hello. You scared me.'

'Sorry, didn't mean to. What you doing?'

'Oh . . . ah . . .' Trench glanced between the cart and the shelves. 'Just taking some of the stock into storage. I expected you to knock, you know. This is supposed to be a secure area.'

Ace squatted down by the cart and read some of the titles on the documents. 'Poetry,' she murmured. 'And novels. A manuscript of *The Bell Jar*. Yeah, I read this when I was fourteen.'

'But it has been banned for decades!'

'Can't see why.'

'No.' A smile spread across Trench's face. 'Neither can I. Would you like a cup of chocolate?'

Jan was clearing out Christopher's tent, folding and packing things into crates. Nothing could be wasted, but anything that was special to Christopher would be preserved in a small collection of memories that Máire kept. That was the trouble. Jan couldn't think of one thing that Christopher would have kept.

Roisa entered and stopped. 'I didn't expect to find you here . . .' she murmured.

'No.' Jan sat down and looked up at her. 'Forgive me, Roisa. I never meant to hurt you.'

Roisa sat beside him and quickly stroked his hair. 'I love you. It hurt to find you with Ace, it's always hurt with every one of them.'

'I'm sorry, if I could offer you my hand, you know I –'

'Things have changed now. I want you to be happy with Ace. You should take her and leave here, quickly. Ah, Jan, if you only knew what I know . . .'

'And what's that? Can't you even tell Máire?'

'No. Hold me for a while, can you?'

'Always.' The couple embraced with an old ease. 'I don't know if she wants me, you know,' Jan said. 'She might be on her way again, soon. And whatever happens with her, I can't lose sight of you, lass . . .'

Roisa closed her eyes tightly. 'You'll have to,' she whispered.

There was a cough from the door. The Doctor stood there, glaring down at Jan.

'Doctor!' Jan jumped up, pulling Roisa after him. 'Roisa, this man saved my life in the market square!' He turned to the Time Lord. 'You must meet the rest of the tribe, Doctor. Ace has told me all about you.'

'I'm sure . . .'

Roisa nodded to the Time Lord, staring at his face with intense interest. 'Thank you for saving Jan's life,' she said.

'I've come to talk to you.' The Doctor turned to Jan.

'Well, I'll leave you alone.' Roisa left the tent. As she opened the flap, Jan glimpsed the unusual shape of a police box near the ashes of the fire.

'So Doctor, please have some mead at my tent.'

'No.' The Doctor sat down, crossing his legs. 'We must talk. Tell me, what's your definition of love?'

'I . . .' Jan looked around the tent, perplexed. 'I don't know.

I know I feel it. It's caring, isn't it, making sure that the people you love don't come to harm. Now, if you had asked Christopher –'

'Should you make sacrifices for love? If staying would hurt the one you love –'

'Then I'd go,' Jan said firmly, staring into the Time Lord's eyes. 'Do you know something I don't?'

'Many things.' The Doctor paused, unsure. 'But nothing urgent.' He seemed to make a decision, and stood up. 'I'm glad we talked.'

Jan stood also, laughing and shaking his head. 'Well, I have no idea what we just talked about. There is something you should know, though ' He took a pace closer to the Doctor, his face serious. 'I care about what happens to Ace. By god, I care about her!'

'Yes.' The Doctor closed his eyes, and put a hand gently on Jan's shoulder. 'I believe you. So do I. You've just made my job so much more dangerous.'

'What is your job?'

'Waking this world from the nightmare of its history.' The Doctor glanced around the tent, businesslike again. 'You have a Puterspace deck. I need to use it.'

'Of course,' Jan laughed, leading the Doctor outside. 'But you'd best be careful, there are things in Puterspace these days –'

'I know,' muttered the Doctor, shading his eyes against the morning sun. 'I know all too well. I had hoped not to meet them there.' He looked at Jan again, and the Traveller saw desperate pity in his eyes. 'But now I have to try.'

'You were saving those volumes,' Ace blew the steam off her cup of chocolate, 'getting them ready for transport. Why?'

Trench shook his head, quickly. 'No, no! Why, what is there to save them from? They are just literature, as you said. No value in them.'

''Course there is. They're originals.'

'I forget that not everybody thinks like a soldier.'

The two of them had set up a makeshift table on a crate. Trench and Ace had talked for ages about poetry. Now Ace felt that it was time to get to the point.

'Do you know where *The Papers Of Felsecar* has got to?' she asked. 'It's important.'

'No, I have no idea.' Trench said quickly, glancing upwards. 'The volume simply went missing. I think it must have been stolen.'

Yeah. The place was bugged. 'Want to take a walk outside?'

'No, I must get on with my work, there's no time to waste.'

'Yes, there is! What's the hurry?'

'You misunderstand.' Trench reached out and held Ace's hand. The poor man was shaking. 'I am an old man. I have to finish my business, my vast job here, before I die.'

'That's not gonna be for years,' Ace smiled. 'But I'll let you get on with it.' She stood up. 'You know what I hate?'

'What?'

'Bullies. Me and the Doctor find them and bully them back. It sometimes takes a while, but eventually –' she snapped her fingers. 'No problem.'

Trench smiled again, a sad old smile. 'That,' he murmured, 'is a wonderful dream to have.'

'It's not a dream.' Ace squeezed his hand. 'It's true. It works.'

'Perhaps it does.' Trench took a deep breath. 'Of course, there are records of the book on our computer system. Perhaps they would indicate where you could find another copy. But I couldn't possibly look it up for you at the moment. I am much too busy.'

'I'm sure you are,' grinned Ace, wishing she could tell the librarian how brave she thought he was. 'I'm off. See you later, curator.'

As she left, Trench allowed himself a smile, and began to chuckle. Then he put a hand to his chest once more, afraid, and returned to his work.

'Your pawn is in place.' Phaedrus knelt before what had once been his friend.

'We ... know!' hissed the tentacled mass in the metal frame. 'We turned a ... misjudged attack ... into a ... subtle advance. We have ... other advances planned. Everything must be ... perfect ... before we strike!'

Phaedrus sighed. 'Must we create so much, invest so much

time in plans, before the destruction can begin?'

'Yes!' hissed the fungus. 'We . . . have been planning for one . . . million . . . years! We . . . are the masters of traps and . . . misdirections! And as yet we are . . . still . . . vulnerable!'

'What must I do?' asked Phaedrus obediently.

'Steal a Puterspace deck . . . and send three acolytes . . . into Puterspace. We shall . . . guide them to their . . . prey.'

'It shall be so.' Phaedrus stepped towards the cellar door. Then he halted. A tentacle was gripping lightly at the hem of his smock.

'And bring me some . . . blood!' hissed the creature. 'I have need of . . . sustenance!'

'Of course.' Phaedrus smiled. 'There's always some about the place.'

7:
Necropolis

The Doctor walked down the colourful corridors of Puterspace, quietly interfacing with puffs of data as they fluttered by.

His way was subtle, of course. He followed no ritual, and trod three paces ahead of any alien contact. In the real world, his body lay in Jan's tent, his head entwined in the mesh of a wire crown. Every now and then, this body mumbled worried words about one last try, about doing things the right way, the old way. Every now and then, that body forgot who it was in its dreams, and called those watching Dodo, or Susan, or Rassilon.

But the Doctor didn't know that in the Matrix.

Through a maze of tightly folded information, he approached his goal. Stretched before him in the transparent void of Puterspace were a thousand colourful blocks. Corporate and Imperial datafields.

'Heaven!' called the Doctor. 'Economic history!'

A grey block rushed up and engulfed him.

The Doctor watched as bureaucrats typed casualty lists. Whole screens full of them were routed into growing black bubbles of files that were Heaven's allocations. The image fast-forwarded. More wars, more lists, more corpses. The bubbles grew bigger, and then something strange happened. All the other bubbles, all those that indicated where the other corpses were going – ejected into space; cremated; even taken back to Earth – all of them merged with the black bubbles.

The Time Lord nodded grimly. For three decades, he watched every dead human in space being sent to Heaven. He saw the programs that did this, little dark buzzing things that pumped the data into the balloons.

Then the Doctor left. He returned to the datafields and found the Travellers' private space, the Land Under The Hills.

When he read the name, he laughed.

The green block folded into forest under his feet.

He was standing in the clearing where the Great Wheel lay, resting askew on its pivot. The air was full of smoke, and the static charge of a battle lost.

'Hello!' he called. No answer came, so he wandered up to where the sword protruded from the table.

Sadly, he put a foot to the wood and pulled the blade out.

That was when the three dark figures stepped from out of the trees. They were cloaked from head to toe in black silk, and their faces were hidden.

'Good afternoon,' the Doctor grinned, swinging the sword gently. 'Wonderful place for a picnic.'

They didn't stop to bargain. Each figure snapped out a tiny silver disc and threw it. Computer viruses, designed to strip the Doctor's image down and kill his body in the real world.

Leaping up on to the table, the Doctor swatted all three aside with one stroke of the sword. One of the discs leapt straight back at its owner, and he exploded into a mass of splattered data.

'We don't have to fight!' yelled the Doctor. 'I have battled in the Matrix of Gallifrey! Go back to your homes!'

Mere bluff. The two remaining figures advanced on the Doctor from different directions, knowing that he could not fight them both off hand to hand.

The Doctor looked between them, detesting the weight of the blade in his hand, even as he knew he would have to use it.

Then another figure stepped from hiding.

He was clad in a long purple robe, and his head was hidden in a hood. He pointed at the two assassins. They stumbled, as if they were on the deck of a ship, and fell straight through the forest floor, with only a little rustle of leaves. The ground closed behind them.

The Doctor felt their minds disengage from Puterspace. He looked up at his rescuer.

'Thank you,' he muttered. 'I though I was alone.'

'Since I died,' Christopher sighed, pulling back his hood, 'nobody in Puterspace has been alone.'

The two acolytes of the Vacuum Church stared down at their

companion. All three had been connected to the same deck, but they had returned to the Temple unharmed.

The man's hair was gently charring as he lay across the table in the basement of the Church. The other two cultists looked at each other. They envied his interesting death.

Phaedrus shook his head, knowing that the creature below in the cellar would be angered by this failure. Still, he could follow its philosophy of no wastage.

'I shall enter Puterspace myself,' he told the acolytes. 'Attach the Trap software to the deck.' He gestured to the corpse. 'Take that down to the cellar. In death, he can still serve the Brotherhood.'

'How did you survive?' The Doctor wandered with Christopher through the woodlands of the virtual reality. 'From what Ace said –'

'My body is dead.' Christopher shivered slightly. 'Forgive me, I've become used to a lot, but that thought, it still . . . it still terrifies me. The enemy sent a shock through me that killed my flesh, and then vanished. They did not think that my powers would allow me to drag my memory entirely into the Matrix. Here, I still live.'

'And your physical form?'

'There are still connections. I have yet to see what is possible.'

'I must find out where the enemy are. It's vital. If I can find out now, I can save so many lives. I could actually call Spacefleet, before any of this tragedy comes to be, I could stop it happening –'

'That road is closed.' Christopher seemed angry. 'I have become aware of so much since I became one with the Dreaming. I know the future.'

'Terrible, isn't it?'

'The future?'

'Knowing it.'

'I am starting to realize that, Doctor. But it is too late. There is no way to locate the enemy through the Matrix. They are too strong here. Now you can only do what you do best.'

The Doctor stopped, and shook his head, his face once more an expression of pain. 'Lose before I win,' he sighed. 'She won't forgive me.'

'She may.' The purple figure placed a hand on the Time Lord's shoulder. He was about to say something else, but suddenly, a surprised expression washed over his face. 'Oh,' he said. 'Something is –'

Alone. Wandering in the vortex. Dying.

The Doctor was lying in the corner of the TARDIS, the radiation from the Great One's cave ravaging his body. It had taken years . . . ten years of slow decomposition.

Years he'd forgotten. The memory of pain fades with time. So how was he here now? Did he have to go through all this again?

He reached a hand out towards the console from where he lay. The hand was his own . . . his seventh hand. It wavered in his failing vision, and for a moment it had the ruffled cuff of his third incarnation.

'You probably see yourself as you are now.' Phaedrus stepped into the Doctor's field of view. He was looking around the TARDIS with interest. 'My name is Phaedrus, I work for the Church of Vacuum. I am sorry to see you in such pain.'

'Are you?'

'We trapped you. We used some special software of ours on this area of Puterspace. It's a very complex program, a Rutan one, I believe. It makes use of our huge banks of memory data, accesses the worst memories of the person in Puterspace, and then turns the Matrix around them into a representation of that memory. I'd be done for too, if it wasn't for my rescue line.' Phaedrus gestured at the golden cord that lay by his feet.

'Why?' The question was a dry croak.

'My church doesn't want you on Heaven. I don't have to give my reasons for that, I'm sure you've made guesses of your own.'

'How?'

'A mindscan was covertly taken of you at your second trial. That scan found its way into the possession of a rather compromised Time Lord. He must have read it before dying at the hands of my masters, and his mind was absorbed into their consciousness. Any corpse, any living mind that falls to them . . . they know all it knows. I have an offer to make you.'

The Doctor raised an eyebrow slightly. It took all his strength to make the effort.

Phaedrus looked down at him with compassion. 'Die,' he said gently. 'Simply die. The alternative is to be stranded here for ten years of your time. You will slowly rot away, as you did before. This will be very bad. Please, accept our mercy.'

The Doctor shivered, gathering his strength. 'I will never surrender to you!' he spat. 'You are an abomination!'

'No.' Phaedrus shook his head quickly. 'We are realists. Only that. I will return, please don't worry. I'll be back in a few minutes of my time. That will, perhaps, be a year or so of yours. *Adieu*.'

Phaedrus stepped aside, pulled on his cord, and vanished.

'No,' the Doctor whispered. 'No.' He tried to rise, and fell back again. His body was weak as a baby's, his every cell ruptured by the killing radiation. 'Death,' he whispered. 'Again.'

Ace popped her head around the flap of Jan's tent suspiciously. She'd seen the TARDIS standing by the bonfire and run straight in. She'd thought that they'd been talking about her, behind her back. That was way scary.

What she saw when she entered was worse.

The Doctor lay against some pillows, his head propped up. Around his brow was fastened the wire crown of a Puterspace terminal. He was deathly white, and his breathing came in slow, fitful gasps.

Jan, Roisa and Máire stood over him, their faces desperate. Jan put an arm around Ace.

'What's he doing?' she asked, fearfully.

'He wanted to go in, I told him it was dangerous now –'

'He's in a bad way.' Roisa looked up, her glance registering Ace for a moment then darting away. 'We don't dare pull off the crown, it could result in severe brain damage.'

Ace threw off her jacket. 'Get me a terminal.'

'No!' Jan pulled her to face him. 'He's dying, I don't want you to –'

Ace carefully took his hands off her. 'If he's fighting something he can't handle, if he's surrounded by enemies, then I have to be there. Always. That's the deal.'

'What, so he won't die alone?'

'Yeah.' Ace nodded. 'If it comes to that. So get me a terminal.'

The Doctor had crawled across the TARDIS control room floor, leaving a trail of blood from a sore that had developed in his leg. The ship was in flight, the column slowly rising and falling.

All those years ago. It had taken a decade. The TARDIS had brought him home in the end, of course, but it had taken so many years.

Bad memories. Memories they'd got from some dead Time Lord. Memories stolen from Gallifrey. Bad memories given to him like a plague.

He was trying to reach the console. Trying to reach the big red lever that would open the doors.

If the doors opened in flight, the emergency system would cut in. If that happened, then, if he could somehow hold on as the air exploded out into the vortex, the ship would make an emergency landing. Somewhere. If the conditions outside were life-supporting, then maybe the Doctor could crawl to find help. If he found help, he could organize resistance, put together a fighting force. Win.

He didn't stop to think that this was all illusion, that his tormentors would just throw him back into his memories.

His hand shook an inch from the console. The muscles in his wrist were cramped. He stretched . . . and he felt his strength failing.

And then a hand took his and pulled him upright.

Ace stood inside the console room, supporting the Doctor in her arms. 'Johnny Piper's back!' she grinned.

'No!' the Doctor whispered, spitting blood. 'Should have left me.'

'No chance. We're out of here.'

'Should have left me because –'

It was a dark hallway. The wallpaper was purple. Distant television sounds came from downstairs. The two adventurers were standing, suddenly, in an ordinary surburban house.

'Oh my God,' Ace breathed.

'Because the system's set to take intruders back to –'

'Their worst time ever,' Ace groaned. 'Perivale in the eighties!'

They stepped carefully down the stairs, Ace helping the Doctor with each little drop. He was still weak, though his wounds had vanished. Ace guessed that the computer world was having trouble keeping up with all these little plot details. 'My house . . .' she told the Doctor. 'But it's strange. Like that picture up there.'

On the stairwell hung a painting, an abstract mass of colours.

'That's meant to be a little boy with a dog. Crap picture. Why is it so vague?'

The Doctor sat down on the steps, and Ace sat with him. 'Because this place is made from somebody else's memories. Somebody who hadn't ever stopped to really look at that picture. Our enemies have been active for millions of years, their feelers are everwhere. Somebody you knew . . . has been absorbed into their group mind.'

'Who?'

'I don't know.'

'Is there any way out of this?'

'I don't know . . .'

'Don't keep saying that, it makes me nervous.'

'The enemy control this place. But perhaps there are remnants of the Travellers' Dreaming, hidden in this world. Perhaps we can use them to get out. I can't say too much. Our foes might be listening.'

'What will they do back in Jan's tent? With our bodies?'

'This isn't taking much real time. We've only been only been here seconds.'

'Why do we always get into this stuff?' Ace shook her head. 'It'd make a change to have an adventure in my own body. Nah, on the other hand I'll rephrase that –'

'Come on, Dorry, it's on the table!'

The woman who had stepped from the kitchen was in her early forties. She was wearing make-up, and an evening dress that was just out of fashion.

Her name was Audrey. She was Ace's mother.

She looked her daughter up and down, and sighed. 'I don't know where you found that old teddy bear. You're too old, you know.'

And she went back inside the kitchen.

The Doctor coughed. 'You've grown a bit since she saw you last.'

'So's she,' Ace murmured.

They sat around the kitchen table, *Top of the Pops* on the telly. Totally ignored by Audrey, the Doctor was examining the details of the place.

Ace was gazing around in astonishment. The kitchen was an exact copy. Everything was perfect. She glanced up at her Mum, realizing that she'd been hunched over the table, almost hiding. 'So how have you been?'

'What do you mean how have I been?' Audrey slammed a plate of fish fingers down in front of Ace. 'You see me often enough, don't you?'

'No,' Ace replied, remembering. 'No, I don't. You were never here when I wanted you to be here, you were always out somewhere, always off with Frank or Joe or Ricky ...'

Audrey sat down opposite her, looking only at her own plate. 'I've a right. Jack's off on his travels so much. You can't begrudge me my friends.'

'It's cool to have men for mates, but that's not it, is it?'

'Eat your food. I'm off in a minute.'

Ace turned to watch Depeche Mode prancing about. She was trying not to let all these old feelings out. Trying to be an adult. It wasn't that hard anymore. This was good, really. She could say it now. 'Don't go,' she said. 'Stay here with me tonight. We can talk a bit. Have a laugh.'

'I can't, my love. Joe's booked us a table.'

'You grew up without a dad. You must know what it's like.'

'Oh, I do! And I didn't do so badly now, did I? I've got you.'

'Still aren't listening, eh? Just as well you're an illusion.'

'I don't know what you've been reading. Eat your tea.'

Ace found herself getting more into this by the second. All sorts of stuff was bubbling to the surface. It was like being hit across the head, meeting your Mum in such a strange place, so suddenly.

Easy questions. Ones that she'd never got to ask.

'Why did you give me that crap name, anyway?'

'Don't swear. Mum always loved that movie. *The Wizard of Oz*. She said it took her away from all her miseries.'

Ace leaned forward excitedly. 'I never knew that! That's all right. Grandma was really cool.'

'You never met her.'

'I did.'

'You're always imagining things, you are. Always full of fantasies. You've got to learn to live in the real world.'

Ace smiled sadly. 'Yeah. Right.'

'Well, I'll be off then.' Audrey stood up, putting her plate on to the sink. 'You'll be all right, won't you?'

'Aren't you going to ask how I did in school? I smashed a boy's head across a desk, 'cos I thought he'd made a face at me. I set fire to the curtains in the main hall. I put laxative in the head's tea. That's why they put a social worker on me, Audrey. Because you weren't there.'

'I wish you'd call me Mum.' Audrey took her coat from a peg and put it on. 'See you later.'

And she left.

Ace sighed, and buried her head in her hands on the table. 'Yeah,' she whispered. 'Probably.'

'There's always hope.' The Doctor had been sitting quietly, staring at his hands. He reached out and stroked the back of Ace's head.

'You don't have to go to school tomorrow.'

'Neither do you. You've been thrown into this world, but you don't have to take part in it.'

'But all the usual crap'll happen though. Police, my social worker, all that?'

'If it did the first time, it will here.'

'Not too different then, is it? I treated it like fantasy last time round. Only difference is my teddy bear.'

The Doctor shook his head violently. 'You mustn't start accepting it, Ace. We must get back. There's a war to be won. Alien monsters to fight.'

'Are they worse than the ones here, then?'

'No.' The Doctor pulled her close and held her in his weakened arms. 'No, they never are.'

They stayed at the kitchen table for a long time, listening to the old clock ticking.

Ace locked the door behind her, and looked along the surburban crescent. Houses stretched around a curve of tarmac road. Cars were parked at intervals. The sky shone the orange black of a London evening. The air was chilly, and the two adventurers' breath bloomed out in clouds. Somewhere, a dog was distantly barking.

'Perfect.' The Doctor turned slowly on his heel. 'I can't see any flaws, any holes in the pattern.'

'Well, if we're here for a bit, then I might as well go and see some friends, eh?' Ace swung open the gate and the Doctor followed her down the road.

'I can see why you so dislike this place. No architecture. No soul. No music.'

'No money for any of that. Well, no, this place is really a bit rich. It's not cardboard city, is it? But people just live . . . oh, I dunno, like they think they have to. Not a lot of anarchy about in the eighties.'

'So who are we going to see?'

'Somebody who I've been thinking about a lot lately.'

When they got to Goldfinch Avenue, Ace leaned on the bell. Julian opened the door and grinned at her. He was clad in a typically extravagant shirt, and his hair . . . Ace sighed. Perfect.

'Hiya, Jules.' She swallowed the ache that welled up in her, seeing him again. 'Coming down the park?'

Julian walked ahead of Ace and the Doctor, whom he hadn't noticed. He spun around every now and then, walking backwards and laughing gossip. 'So I think Tim was erm, involved there, eh? I tried to mime it to him, sort of . . . *she's with Anthony* . . . but it didn't work. He just said "book or film?" and I cracked up.'

Ace was smiling, looking at him. Until she remembered the thump of soil on his coffin. And Jan, whom she wanted to see more than anybody else right now. Maybe walking and walking could get you out of this dream. Maybe you could walk to Heaven from Perivale.

They had reached the park, down by the railway station, a large would-be cricket pitch where people walked their dogs. A low mist hung in the air, and a few kids were kicking a ball about down by a skip. Ace's lot used to hang around by the swings, or run around down the narrow walkways between the factories. Jules wasn't really into all that. Ace had first met him in a pub, one day when she thought that Midge was being too childish. He'd started talking to her without the slightest hesitation, and they'd got on ever since.

'Who're you with now?' she asked.

Julian looked at her steadily for a minute. 'Last time I told you, you got all stupid and sulked. So, love, the answer's nobody special. Haven't seen you for a week, let's not spoil it. There's still lots to tell you.'

'Do you remember that day out we had, taking the old Allegro up to Lincolnshire?'

''Course I do. I still remember the lights of that place. All those men running about.'

Ace had a suspicion forming in her mind. 'I saw Mum tonight.'

'*Quelle surprise*.'

'She told me that she named me after –'

'Dorothy in *The Wizard of Oz*! Yes, she told me that once, too. One of those nights when you brought me back for a coffee and she came in late. We sat around the kitchen table, and when you went to the loo, she asked me if I was going to marry you.'

The Doctor was frowning, looking at Julian closely. 'Ask him about the picture,' he muttered.

'You what? Why?'

'Ask him!'

'What kind of picture hangs on our stairs?'

Julian raised an eyebrow. 'It's a green . . . something. Are you all right? Who're you talking to?'

Ace put a hand to her head. 'God, Julian. They got you, didn't they, whoever they are. They took your memories.'

The Doctor stepped forward and walked straight at Julian.

Straight at him, and then through him.

Julian gasped. 'Ace! Oh God, what's happened? Where am I?'

Ace ran forward and held him. 'Where do you think you are?'

'I don't know. It's all so strange. I'm part of something else, some great . . . there's so many other people in here. So many voices.' He looked around him, as if trying to match the world he saw and felt everywhere with the ideas that had rushed into his head. 'I'm dead, aren't I? I'm dead!'

Ace held on tightly, hoping he'd feel her warmth. 'I'm here, Jules, I'm real, don't be scared.'

'Can you hear me?' the Doctor asked.

'Yes, yes!' Julian looked around again. 'But I can't see you. Ace, where are we?'

'We're in Perivale,' Ace whispered to him, enjoying his familiar smell. 'We're at home.'

'I want you to imagine someone,' the Doctor cut in. 'Will you do that for me, Julian?'

'Why? What's going on? I was just sitting at home and . . . and this is only dreams, isn't it? I remember lying in hospital, and somebody saying something I couldn't hear, and then . . . oh Ace, why weren't you there?'

'If I'd known, I would have been. You know that.'

'I want you to imagine a tall person, a sexless being, once a man. He's tall, and dressed in purple robes . . .'

'Shut up for a minute, for Christ's sake!' Ace yelled.

The Doctor looked at her. It was a dangerous look.

After a second, Ace patted Julian on the arm. 'Listen to him. He knows what he's talking about. I just get a bit wound up by him sometimes. I won't leave you alone, Jules. I won't.'

'Don't. I don't know what's going on, Ace.'

'Purple robes –' the Doctor began again.

'Yeah, right.' Julian blinked, and concentrated.

Ace watched as a figure formed on the grass of Perivale park. 'You're changing the world, Jules,' she told him. 'With your imagination. You always did.'

The creature in the cellar of the temple thrashed in anger. Filaments sprayed out of its head. 'Phaedrus!' it hissed.

The priest hurried down the steps. He'd been on his way to

report his success inside the Matrix. 'Yes, my lords?'

'There is . . . activity . . . inside the Matrix! We have been . . . maintaining . . . the trap! But it is . . . changing! How?'

'I can't imagine.'

'Old data is being . . . recalled to memory. We cannot . . . erase it! You must . . . go back inside . . . and . . . stop it!'

Phaedrus bowed quickly and ran back up the steps.

Christopher looked straight ahead. His body was fully formed, and the Doctor had been advising Julian on details of face and colour.

The strange figure stood motionless in front of the cricket screens.

The Doctor frowned. 'That's perfect. He hasn't been erased from the program. Our enemies didn't have time to get rid of anything. All they did was write new data over the old. Julian managed to find him again.'

'Wait a minute, Professor. I thought that Christopher was dead!' Ace had one arm wrapped round Julian's shoulder still. 'What's he doing here?'

'He transferred his consciousness completely into Puterspace.' The Doctor was pacing, his hands wrapped behind his back. 'His mind will live on here, for a while at least. So why can't we retrieve it?'

Julian was looking between Ace and the Doctor, blinking as the Time Lord swam in and out of vision. 'Listen! There are other things that I can see! Underneath Perivale there's a whole forest, and in the forest there are wonderful things. Old things. People from old stories.'

'Those stories are under everything,' the Doctor nodded. 'They are retold and replayed many times. And the people in them are real. Nothing is ever forgotten.'

'Just what I was thinking!' The figure stepped forward from the bushes, brushing twigs off his silver suit. He seemed to become more solid with every step. He smiled brightly at the Doctor. 'I don't know about you,' the Trickster said, glancing up at the sky. 'But it's about this time in the evening that I like to put a sparkler into a corpse!'

A fizzing sparkler appeared in his hand, and he reached quickly across to Christopher, bouncing the fiery wand off his head.

Christopher opened his eyes and laughed. 'Oh,' he said. 'What a strange place the universe is!'

'My thoughts exactly,' muttered Ace.

'How are you then, Merlin?' the Trickster asked the Doctor.

'I've had better days.'

Christopher looked quickly around. 'What is this place?' he asked.

'Perivale,' Julian told him. 'I'm Jules, this is Ace, that's Vic and he's called the Doctor! I think I'm dead, but we're very sorry about Perivale itself, it's – ah!' He gave a little cry, and his eyes rolled upwards.

'Julian!' Ace exclaimed. But he was gone from her arms. Vanished.

Behind Ace stood Phaedrus, holding the bloody sword he'd pushed into Julian's back. 'Back into the group mind he goes,' the priest said, glancing around the group. 'I'm astonished at what you've done here, but this is the end of it. This sword is a very powerful attack program. I'd advise you to surrender and accept a quick death. Julian can't imagine anything else to help you now.'

'You're gonna die.' Ace turned, but Phaedrus gestured at her to stay at arm's length. Angry, she took a step back.

'I hope so,' the priest replied evenly.

The surroundings were blurring back into a vague white void. The Doctor looked down. 'Still got your cord?'

'Indeed. I wouldn't want to be trapped in this myself.'

The Trickster wandered up to Phaedrus and put his hands on his hips. 'That's fine workmanship, that sword is.'

'I will have none of your words, Trickster,' Phaedrus muttered. 'You're just an illusion, the product of the superstitious minds of the Travellers.'

'Oh, I am, am I?' The god figure turned to face the others. 'Well, I've got a better sword than that one, anyhow.' With a flourish, he produced the sword that had been embedded in the centre of the Great Wheel.

'Where could you get a sword like that, then?' the Doctor

asked, playfully.

'This is a Diana and Trickster sword, and it's ooooh, miles better than that one!' The Trickster suddenly tossed it to Ace, and vanished with a grin just as Phaedrus swung a blow at his head.

Ace weighed the blade carefully as the priest spun, ready to attack her. She could still half see Perivale, remember the smell of Julian. Aftershave and love. 'You're so wrong,' she told Phaedrus. 'D'you really think we're gonna line up and get killed?'

'I would prefer it!' Phaedrus leapt at her, smashing down at her with his sword. Ace parried easily, swinging his blade aside.

The Doctor and Christopher were apparently ignoring the fight, muttering together. Ace glanced over at them, and gritted her teeth. Just her then. Her and a fight for whatever Julian stood for.

She took three blows straight on the sword, parrying down, up, down, forcing Phaedrus to step back. There was no art to his swordsmanship. He was simply trying to impale her, as quickly as possible. 'Where's Julian gone?' she yelled at him.

'He's part of the group mind again, as I said. One of us.'

'He's not one of you!' Ace smashed aside the priest's blows. 'He doesn't belong with you, he's alive! He'll always be alive! And I'm gonna set him free!'

'That's impossible!' Phaedrus shouted.

'You stupid bastard!' Ace slashed hard and sent Phaedrus's sword flying. 'Anything's possible! Don't you know that from Julian?'

With a flick of the blade, the cord that held Phaedrus to the real world was snapped in two.

Suddenly, they were in a low dark room. The wooden panelling smelled of death. Phaedrus looked around himself, panicking.

'No!' he bellowed. 'Not here!'

'We're all in the same boat,' the Doctor said, putting a hand on the priest's shoulder. 'What's your nightmare? Where have your fears brought us?'

In the corner of the fetid room was a bed, and someone lay in it, dying. Phaedrus ran over to it, and knelt. In the bed lay an old woman, gasping for air. 'Mother!' the priest cried. 'Don't go! Don't go!'

'I must,' a hissing voice replied. 'Please, Phaedrus . . . don't let it end like this. Give me my medicine.'

The other inhabitants of the room could only watch. It was, Ace thought, like they were suddenly in a theatre, watching a play.

Phaedrus stood, his eyes full of fear. 'Yes,' he whispered. He glanced at his audience as he ran to a side cabinet. 'She asked me,' he assured them. 'She asked me.'

Ace stared, horrified.

Phaedrus was feeding his mother something with a spoon. She smiled at him, and then coughed, belching up blood. Her head fell to the pillow quite suddenly.

Phaedrus looked up, expecting something. His eyes were full of sadness. The door opened, and in walked a terrifying giant, his hands and head huge in proportion to his body.

'What have you done?' bellowed Phaedrus' father, rushing to the bed.

Christopher silently pointed. Through the door, golden sunlight was beaming. The forested dales of the Land Under The Hills lay outside. Cool air that smelt of summer gently wafted in.

The huge father was screaming into the dead woman's face. Phaedrus was standing to one side, watching.

As Christopher hurried out of the door, Ace turned back for a moment. Her eyes met those of Phaedrus. 'You don't have to stay –' she began.

The Doctor put a hand on her shoulder. 'No,' he said. 'Come away.'

The doorway vanished as they stepped out into the sunlight.

'Trapped in a loop,' the Doctor snarled. 'Very neat. The Trap program trapped the person who brought it in here, and that looped it back to his terminal. Very lucky.'

Ace stretched, and spat on the ground. The whole thing had made her feel dirty. 'Damn it,' she whispered. 'Julian.' God, she wanted to get back to Jan.

'We'd better go,' the Doctor told Christopher.

'Indeed. I will see you soon. Now you must go out into the

real world and win.' The being in purple waved his hand.

And the forest vanished.

'I can't win!' the Doctor shouted, tossing his head. 'Whatever I do I'll lose something!'

A gentle hand squeezed his, and a voice reassured him. 'Gently . . . you're back in the real world . . .' Roisa was bending over him. Beside her crouched Jan, gently massaging Ace's wrists.

Roisa took the wire crown off the Doctor, and wiped his brow with a damp cloth. He blinked, and his eyes slowly focussed.

'We nearly lost you,' Roisa told him. 'Here, drink this.'

She placed a goblet to the Doctor's lips. Gasping, the Doctor drank.

Ace woke a few seconds after the Doctor. She grasped Jan's hand and held on, smiling at him.

'I was so afraid,' Jan whispered. 'You're a real warrior, you are.'

Unseen by either of them, Roisa shivered, watching the Doctor drink.

'Too right,' Ace pulled Jan close and hugged him, sitting up.

'That's the best use for the Vacuum Church's goblet,' Jan nodded to Roisa. 'Perhaps that's what the Trickster meant, that it would be used to help save a life.'

'I should have asked him,' Ace grinned. 'Hey, Professor, is Phaedrus trapped in the Matrix?'

'No . . .' The Doctor made an effort and sat up. 'He'll leave when he wants to.' He looked between them all, and smiled a giddy smile. 'I think it's time we all worked together. Perhaps there are alternatives, things I haven't thought of. Time I told you some of what's going on.'

Ace reached over and smoothed a hair back from his sweat-soaked brow. 'Smartest thing you've said since we got here,' she grinned.

Phaedrus jumped upright from the table, and pulled the wire crown from his head violently.

He stared down at it for a minute, shivering. Gradually, he became aware of his converts around him. 'The book!' he gasped, after a moment. 'I didn't stop him, he's like a fox! We must stop him finding the book. Kill them all if necessary –'

A pain burst into his head, and he grabbed his brow. Through clenched teeth Phaedrus corrected himself. 'No. No. The Doctor is not to be harmed.' He calmed once more. 'He's useful to us now.'

Phaedrus didn't look up as his acolytes rushed to obey his orders. He continued to stare at the wire crown on the table. After a few minutes, certain he was alone, his lips formed a silent word.

The word was 'mother'.

8:

Burning Bridges

The circle of Travellers watched as the Doctor paced in front of them. Dusk was falling once more, and Jan was lighting the bonfire, applying his burning hands to strategic pieces of wood.

Ace had told the Doctor of her conversation with Trench, and how she'd returned with Cathlan only to find the Time Lord at the camp.

Now he was pacing, considering. It was as if he was reluctant to tell them anything, but found he had to. He was just working out what was okay to say. Ace frowned. What detail was he trying to hide?

'I need your help . . .' The Doctor waited until the crowd had hushed and addressed the assembled group, clad in their leathers and bright bandoliers. 'I need your help with a robbery!'

There was a cheer from the Travellers. Ace circled round beside Jan and embraced him.

'He knows how to appeal to them,' whispered the man.

'He's a Traveller himself,' Ace replied, quickly kissing him.

The Doctor had continued. 'There are huge things happening on this planet, and much of it I don't understand yet. I do know that we're in a race against time, even though the enemy haven't revealed their hand.'

'Who are the enemy?' asked Máire. 'Is it the Daleks?'

A whisper went round the campfire at the mention of the name. Little children buried their heads in their mothers' shoulders.

The expression on the Doctor's face was deadly serious. The name meant all that and more to him. 'No. Not this time. But it could be worse.'

'Ah, what's worse?' called out a Traveller.

'What's worse?' The Doctor walked over to where the man was sitting. 'There are things in this universe that even the

Daleks fear. Terrible things that use what we are, make it into something evil.' His gaze flicked over the crowd, and Ace got the impression that he was looking for something, and missing it. 'Things that play the most devious games. You can fight a Dalek, exterminate it. There are few ways to fight what's inside your neighbour, or inside you . . .' He paused, as if thinking twice about what he was going to say. 'What you all met in Puterspace was just a hint of their power. But there's still time to bring the enemy out into the open. Time to fight them in a normal way.'

'What are we going to do?' asked Jan. 'Raid the Vacuum Church?'

There was a general murmur of assent.

'No. We're going to raid somewhere else. I need a computer operator and five bodyguards.'

'Four!' shouted Ace.

The Doctor turned and grinned. 'As well as you,' he murmured shyly.

'It's still four!' called Jan. 'She's worth two women!'

It was just as well, Ace thought. She was replacing at least one. She looked up to see that Roisa's eyes were upon her again.

Night over Joycetown. A few farmers wandered out of inns, and late traders were folding down their stalls. A light shone in the tower of the Vacuum Church, as it always did. Cold breezes swept in from over the fields, making the last drinkers shiver as they headed for their horses.

A party of armed Travellers crouched behind the wall of the market square. They had tethered their mounts outside the town and climbed the walls, rather than sneak past the guards at the gate.

'It's late enough,' the Doctor whispered.

'Are you sure there's no alternative?' Roisa asked, checking her blaster. 'We've a bad enough public image in this town.'

'Talent borrows, genius steals,' Jan told her. Roisa had been sticking by the Doctor's side since they'd left camp, asking the Time Lord about his life and adventures. If she was trying to make Jan jealous, she wasn't succeeding.

'But what's the point of robbery if nothing is worth taking?'

Ace grinned. She had a Traveller bandolier containing a variety of weapons slung over one shoulder.

The Doctor pondered the quote. 'Shakespeare?'

'Adam Ant.'

'Ah.'

The rest of the party comprised Cathlan, Máire, and a young boy called Alec, who was, so Jan said, the best computer hacker in the camp now that Christopher was gone.

'Shall we go?' The Doctor motioned them out of their hiding place, and the group scampered through the darkened township, towards the tall tower of the Library.

The Doctor and Ace got there first, the Time Lord quickly tapping in the entry codes at the door. The Travellers followed them up the steps, glancing around for signs of pursuit.

Shepherding everyone in, Ace took the opportunity to whisper to the Doctor. 'If this turns into a firefight, make sure Jan's at the back.'

'Why?'

'Because I don't want him getting hurt.'

'He'd say the same about you.'

'Yeah. But I'm better at this than he is.'

The Doctor frowned. 'People get hurt. All the time. It's not up to me.'

Ace gave him an edgy glance before she ducked inside the building. 'Sometimes it is,' she whispered.

The vast shelves of books towered over the Doctor's party as they crept along the aisles of the Library.

Ace was looking around. The place seemed so much more foreign at night. They must have been cool aliens. Not the sort of bunch that went about invading other people's planets. Or maybe they were, and they just didn't talk about it in their architecture. Like, what does a grave say about the guy in it? Here lies Ace, had a life, hope you heard about it. Nah, she'd want a statue. A bazooka on her shoulder, a grin on her face, and Teenage Fanclub trying to look up her skirt.

She stopped herself and glanced at Jan, who was looking around the hall in tense interest. She never used to think about death.

'Which way?' Máire asked the Doctor, never taking her eyes off the narrow avenues between the racks. She was carrying her Dalek gun, attached to a powerpack.

'Follow me,' the Doctor pointed his umbrella. 'Two of you stay back here as lookouts.'

Máire picked out Roisa and Jan, much to Ace's relief. The remaining five stealthily made their way to an office at the back of the Library, through the windows of which Ace could see a small computer terminal on a desk.

Cathlan tried the door, and made to kick it in, but the Doctor stopped him. 'Ace ... hairpin.'

'What would you do without me?' Ace whispered, removing one. 'Ever had a companion with short hair?'

'No. It's part of the job description.' The Doctor quickly opened the mechanical lock, and the team hurried inside. Máire and Cathlan took up positions by the door.

Alec flexed his fingers against each other and turned the terminal on. He pulled on a pair of white silk gloves. 'So, what delights can I offer you?' he asked.

'Documents removed,' the Doctor muttered. '*The Papers of Felsecar*. Who's got the book?'

Alec's fingers blurred over the keyboard. 'Normally, I'd plug myself in,' he said. 'But that's getting dangerous lately. Don't worry, this sort of stuff is just as easy with ... aha, security! Damn, it needs a fingerprint. This is going to take time.'

Ace grinned. She remembered kids like this from her school-days. 'D'you think that Trench left the data on here?' she asked the Doctor.

'Yes. That's why he told you about it. It was the best he could do, if he felt he was being observed. He's probably been doing his best to sneak things past ...' he checked himself, 'past the enemy.'

A light flashed through the office window. The team fell to the floor, covering the chemical lamps they carried.

Ace crawled to the window and peeped over the sill.

In one of the aisles, a group of three black-robed figures were having an urgent conversation with Trench, who carried an oil lamp. One of them was prodding the old man's chest with his finger. The Librarian stumbled, sobbing in pain.

Ace scrambled to her feet.

'Ace!' hissed the Doctor. But it was too late.

She flung the door open, and shone her lamp at the group of intruders. 'Evening lads, what's the problem here?' She was worried about Jan. Had these three come past him or through him?

Máire and Cathlan dashed out behind her, bringing their weapons to bear.

One of the robed figures stepped forward, laughing. 'We were just asking our friend Fyan a few questions,' he yelled. 'Isn't that true, Trench?'

'Yes,' the Librarian muttered, weakly. 'There's no trouble here, Ace, really ...'

'Well, maybe there wasn't.' Ace grinned. 'But there is now!' She grabbed for a blaster from the bandolier.

The man smiled and ran straight at her. He didn't even bother to draw his gun.

So Ace shot him in the shoulder.

He spun, fell, and got to his feet again, pulling his gun from his belt. The Travellers gasped. He wasn't even injured, though his robe sizzled and sparked where the blast had hit him. The other two figures watched, nodding, as if they were pleasantly surprised by this demonstration of invulnerability.

Shots from the man began to blaze into the office space, slicing through the glass. The Travellers dived into cover. After a second, the other robed figures joined in.

'By the Goddess, I'm sorry to use this.' Máire drew her Dalek gun. 'Only four shots left in the power pack.'

'That's the way it goes,' Ace murmured.

The noise from the gun made everybody wince, familiar as it was. The figure was blown aside into the racks and lay still. Ace fired a salvo of shots into the floor near the others, and they backed away, as if confused by a weapon that could hurt them.

Trench dived for the office, terrified. The sound of blaster fire was echoing all around the huge building.

Ace grabbed the Librarian's hand and pushed him and his lamp into the office. She was about to tell the Doctor that they'd better hurry.

But then the man Máire had shot got to his feet again.

Theatrically, he dusted down his robe. Ace realized that the figures who had retreated were working their way round. She could see shadows creeping through the aisles.

The office had become an island of light in the dark Library.

The dead man walked slowly forward. 'You should have surrendered peacefully,' he called. 'We are peaceful folk. But now you will meet the void before us!'

Máire raised an eyebrow and fired again. The blast sent the man tumbling backwards, his internal organs illuminated.

This time, he had screamed. He raised his head, finally, smiled . . . and then fell back, dead.

'Dalek gun'll kill anything . . .' Máire whispered. 'Eventually.'

The Doctor rolled to the door space and tapped Máire on the shoulder. 'Don't use it again unless you have to. You must fire twice if . . . if they still look human. If they don't, there's no point at all.'

Ace reached into her backpack. 'I'm gonna regret this,' she muttered. 'But let's close the door.'

The Doctor was peering over the window sill, watching the forms creeping about the Library. 'Vacuum Church assassins,' he said. 'Ideal. Obvious. Here as well as in Puterspace.'

'Get down, Professor!' Ace whispered, pulling the Time Lord under the window sill. 'Close your eyes and count to five!'

The assassins had gathered outside the door, and were slowly stalking towards it. 'There is no other exit!' hissed one. 'We have them!'

'Why five?' said the Doctor.

'Short fuse.' Ace popped open the door, and gently rolled a can of nitro-nine through it.

Then she closed the door and threw herself back to the floor. 'Why are monsters always so –'

The window blasted inwards in an explosion of glass. Ace pulled Trench under her, sheltering the old man as shards smashed into the office.

The alien metal of the walls shielded the Travellers, though the human-made windowframe bounced off the far wall.

And then all was silence.

The Doctor raised his head over the parapet and nodded grimly. Pieces of black robe were scattered everywhere. 'Slow,' he muttered. 'Yes, I know. Useful, isn't it?'

Trench was fighting his way upright, crying out. Ace tried to calm him, but he shrugged her aside, diving on the computer. 'I only have seconds!' he shouted, jamming his fingerprint on to a sensor pad. 'They thought I'd destroyed the book! But they were wrong!'

A file sprang on to the screen at the touch of Trench's frantic fingers.

THE PAPERS OF FELSECAR: MSS. LENT BY GOV. REMIT TO PROF. BERNICE SUMMERFIELD.

'I've met her,' Ace gasped.

'So have I. I should have mentioned it to her,' the Doctor mumbled, bashfully.

Trench was gasping, holding his chest. 'Now you know. Get away from here!'

'Why?' asked the Doctor. 'What are you afraid of?'

'Get away!' Trench was reeling, clutching his chest. He began to pull at his loose nightshirt, ripping it open as if he couldn't breathe.

The Travellers stepped back, looking at each other nervously.

Ace stared, horrified. On the centre of the man's chest there was a grey patch of fungus.

And then, suddenly, it spread.

One second, Trench had a human face, limbs, hair –

And then something inside the old man exploded.

Tentacles burst from his fingertips, his head blasted open into a mass of thrashing fungal filaments.

The thing roared, an ear-splitting shriek of bloodlust.

It sprang straight for the Doctor's eyes.

9:

The Armies Of The Night

The Doctor sprang back into a corner, clutching the oil lamp.

Cathlan fired a burst of shells into the monster's thrashing form. It spun round, screeching but unharmed.

'Get back!' shouted the Doctor. He was quickly unscrewing the base of the lamp.

'Hoi!' Ace dodged in front of the creature, waving her arms. 'Fyan Trench! You still in there?!'

The monster paused, as if listening. Then, as Ace drew closer, a tentacle flashed out.

Ace rolled aside. A barrage of plasma fire engulfed the creature, and small pieces of it flew in all directions, but still it advanced, backing the Travellers into the other side of the office.

'Excuse me!' the Doctor shouted.

The tentacled thing turned.

A burst of flame wooshed across the office, catching the creature full on. The Doctor was spraying fire from his mouth, holding the naked oil lamp near his lips.

The creature ignited, and reeled for a moment, screaming.

'Now!' shouted the Doctor. 'Everybody out!' He threw aside the lamp and leapt the barrier where the window had been. Ace and the Travellers followed.

They sprinted along an aisle. The creature, still ablaze, followed, its tentacles hissing ahead of it, one lashing a book from the wall by Ace's cheek.

Ahead, Jan and Roisa were standing either side of the aisle, their weapons drawn. 'Get out!' shouted Ace. She was amazed to see that Jan was shaking his head. He slapped her shoulder as she ran up to him.

'Go on! We'll cover you!'

'But –'

'Go on!' He levered a foot to her bottom and pushed, sending her dashing ahead.

As the creature galloped up the aisle, Jan and Roisa looked at each other. It was nearing them. In a second, it would be on them.

'Now!' shouted Jan.

They both kicked out the wedges from the shelves they had spent five minutes manoeuvring into position. The twin metal constructions collapsed in front of the approaching beast, blocking its path.

They turned and ran after the others.

The doors of the Library burst open, and the Doctor dashed down the stairs.

He ran straight into James Miller's chest.

The Travellers found themselves surrounded by a party of guards, who instantly went into firing postures.

There was an explosion from inside the Library. 'Messy!' shouted the Doctor.

Miller nodded. 'We'd better get a fire crew in there . . .'

'No. Let it burn. There's something in there that doesn't die easily.'

Ace looked around the soldiers, exasperated. 'Hey!' she called. 'Leave off, we're on your side!'

Miller waved a hand, and the guards stepped back. The Travellers lowered their weapons also. 'Sontarans,' smiled Miller. 'Always leave chaos in their wake.'

The Doctor frowned, puzzled. Then suddenly his face broke into an amazed smile. 'The person that told you there were Sontarans involved –'

'Yes?'

'What was wrong with their arm?'

Miller stared at the Doctor.

Kale took a key from his pocket, and switched off the communications deck of the orbital platform.

His shuttle had arrived only minutes before. The platform was a small post, crewed by three troopers. It maintained a geostationary orbit above Joycetown, and was mainly used as an early warning station, its sensors trained in the direction of the Draconian Empire. The tiny control room was crammed with sophisticated detection equipment.

'It's only for an hour or so,' Kale reassured the Duty Officer. 'I've got to realign the sensors to sweep the planet's surface. You read the letter of authorization.'

The man nodded. He and Kale were employed by the same mining company. He gestured to Kale's plaster cast. 'What happened to your arm?' he asked.

'Broken,' Kale sighed, pulling open the sensor panel with his free hand. 'Mechanical accident.'

'He knows where the book is!' hissed a voice in the steaming darkness.

'But . . . so do we,' said a second voice.

'It is . . . of no matter,' added the third voice. 'We have . . . misled the military . . . and now blinded their . . . detectors! The Doctor cannot . . . help. Soon he will not be able to . . . help himself!'

Miller had been trying to contact the orbital platform for an hour now. He threw down the communicator in disgust, then quickly picked it up again.

'Judith, tell Howarth to take a copter down to the equatorial dock. He can requisition a shuttle and get up there . . . what? Damn it!'

'What is it?' Ace asked. The Travellers and soldiers were gathered in Miller's HQ, the former looking around at the corporate logos suspiciously.

'Kale took the last bloody one today!' Miller sighed. 'The rest are all in for repair.'

'Yes.' The Doctor was sitting crosslegged on Miller's desk, his eyes closed. 'Of course, They would be.'

'You could call for reinforcements,' suggested Máire.

'Aye, I have done. I've used the Priority Link. Instantaneous communication, you see, absolutely new –'

'Really?' the Doctor sighed.

'And very expensive too, lad. But the sixth fleet won't get here for a week. Until then we're virtually blind.'

'Since our eyes are closed,' the Doctor murmured, opening his, 'now would be a good time to get some sleep. And I need to go visiting. Can you take us back to the Travellers' camp?'

Miller looked around the raggamuffins in his office, and sighed. 'Yes, Doctor. I'll get a bulk flyer together. Anything else?'

The Doctor considered. 'A bottle of metal cleaner,' he decided.

The night air was sweet, cool breezes shuffling the grasslands under the moon. Ace and Jan lead their horses down the ramp of the bulk flyer, a huge VTOL aircraft, towards the applauding Travellers, who were waving from around the bonfire.

'I want a word with you,' Ace said.

'I want to get you into my bed,' Jan grinned back.

Ace would have answered in similar fashion, but the Doctor appeared out of the crowd and took her arm. 'Sorry,' he mumbled. 'I know it's late. But now I know where my book is, it's vital that I go and find it. Do you want to come with me?'

''Course I do,' Ace told him. 'Who else is gonna ride shotgun for you?'

'Who indeed?' muttered the Doctor, leading her off.

'I could come along –' began Jan, but the two adventurers were already selecting horses.

Ace turned back to him and blew a kiss. 'Wait up for me!' she called.

'Need some company?' asked Roisa, leaning on Jan's shoulder.

'Yes,' said the Traveller, wryly. 'I think I do.'

'What did you get from the thingy in the flask?' Ace asked as they trotted out of the Valley.

'I've been examining the filament in the TARDIS labs. It's very complex, highly specialized . . . the structure almost transcends biology. The cells contain something like the symbiotic nuclei that enable Time Lords to regenerate, they can control vast amounts of energy. The fibres can burn through matter, interface with living cells. They're all part of the intelligence of the enemy.'

'And is this Vacuum Church place in on it, too?'

'Yes.'

'So why not raid the place?'

'Because it wouldn't really achieve anything.'

'Wipe the smile off that creep Phaedrus's face.'

'It would. But what's more important, winning or feeling good about yourself?'

'Doesn't one lead to the other, Professor?'

'Not always.'

Ace could see that the subject was closed. 'Any word about that guy, Kale?'

'No. Miller was trying to requisition a ship. He hasn't succeeded, of course.'

'Couldn't we just hop up there in the TARDIS?'

'We could. But that could be exactly what the enemy wants us to do.'

'Who are the enemy, anyway?'

'Hush. Later. Walls have ears. Even tent walls . . .' The Doctor urged his horse into a gallop, and Ace followed.

They thundered across the moonlit plains, swapping the lead, until the two companions saw the brilliant silver arch picked out in the ghostly light.

The Doctor slowed his horse to a stop and dismounted. Ace did likewise. They led their animals towards the distant tents of the archaeologists. The Doctor began to talk about his friendship with Christopher Marlowe, and, although Ace could see that his thoughts were mostly elsewhere, she asked questions, and they laughed together.

After a while she felt confident enough to ask the question. 'Professor, do you always pick the people who are gonna travel with you?'

'Sometimes. Often they pick me. Why?'

'I'm . . . I want to stay with you, but I – well, me and Jan, we're –'

The Doctor stopped walking. 'I see,' he said. 'You'd better decide. Pathways. You can never take both.'

'You mean I have to decide between you?'

'Yes.' The Doctor wasn't looking at her. 'My granddaughter did, a long time ago. She'd fallen in love. With an Earthman.

Like marrying a mayfly . . .'

Ace heard such bitterness in the Doctor's voice then that she winced. 'But me and Jan –'

'You think you've fallen in love. One day you'll wake up and he'll be gone.'

That touched a nerve. 'Shut up! What the hell do you know about love? You don't do it, do you?'

'Not lately.'

Ace let go of her horse, and pulled the Doctor round to face her. 'What are you getting so worked up about? I didn't have it off with a bloody Dalek!'

'Would it have made a difference?'

She slapped him. Hard.

The Doctor turned away.

Ace stood there, shuddering. She wanted to hold him, to ask him why he was like this, suddenly. Why had he changed so much? What could she do to make it all better? Oh God, why had she hit him?

The Doctor spoke first, quietly, his back to her. 'I was shown the worst time of my life in Puterspace,' he said. 'I was alone. Wandering in the vortex. Dying. It was terrible. I don't want to be . . . I don't want to be alone.'

It sounded like the hardest thing the Doctor had ever said.

Ace rubbed a hand across her eyes. 'You're not alone, who says you have to be alone? Where am I gonna go?'

'With him.' The Doctor whispered.

Ace was astonished. 'You're jealous!' she cried. 'You're actually jealous!'

'No.' The Doctor turned around, his face creased with tension. 'I don't want to see you hurt. There's evil on this world, infinite evil –'

'Well it's got nothing to do with Jan. He's a good person . . . you've got a lot in common.'

'Have we? Perhaps. But if you stay with him, you'll be hurt. Badly.'

Sighing, Ace took the Doctor's scarf in her hands. 'I am never, ever, going to leave you. You needn't worry, you sad old man. Come here.'

They hugged. Ace felt the Doctor relax, but only slightly.

This was way disturbing, the whole bit. Usually he was up on the whole game, way beyond anything dull and stupid like jealousy. She was used to him being in control. The idea that he wasn't was scary.

It wasn't cool to be jealous. She remembered how she'd met the first guy that Julian had gone out with, and had tried so hard not to show her jealousy that Jules had said she was trying to chat the guy up. If only he'd known. Or maybe he had.

'Will you think about giving Jan a lift?' she asked. 'Please. I can't choose between you.'

The Doctor put a hand up to her cheek, and touched it gently. 'You won't have to choose,' he whispered.

Ace saw the infinite sadness in his eyes.

'Hello!' a cheery voice boomed from behind them.

Bernice stood there, waving a trowel.

'You really should have said . . .' Benny muttered, rummaging through a pile of books by the side of her bunk. 'Ah!'

She blew the dust off a slim, leather bound volume. Gold leaf on the cover declared it to be *The Papers Of Felsecar*.

The Doctor grabbed the book and leafed quickly through it. Ace and Benny peered over his shoulders. 'The monks of Felsecar have taken it as their mission to preserve some of the most dangerous objects and information in the universe,' he said. 'They've been doing that for a quarter of a million years.'

'Ah, now, wait.' Benny raised a finger. 'That's before human beings started standing upright.'

'Too right!' Ace grinned at her. 'Broadens your mind, doesn't it?' She'd been looking at the Doctor for some recognition of their conversation outside the dig, but he was acting like it had never happened. Maybe that was for the best.

'This is a collection of some random manuscripts from their collection. They somehow found their way off-planet, and, as such curios do, hung around for centuries. Somebody brought them to human space, and they were bound in accordance with this note attached to the inner cover.' He glanced at a dirty post-it note that was firmly stuck in the book. 'Oh dear, one of mine.'

Benny laughed out loud. 'You mean you –'

'Had to tell them what the book was called. Probably so I

could find it now. I must remember to get around to doing that. Now –' the Doctor began to flip quickly through the pages. 'Recipes from Rigel, a palimpest of poems, notes on Dalek design down the decades . . .'

Benny shared a smile with Ace. The various manuscripts bound into the book were in a dozen different languages.

'Here we are. Written in Draconian on the top of the page. In felt-tip. I'd never do that, this must have been done by a very crude future incarnation.'

Benny was about to ask. Ace put a finger to her lips.

The Doctor was reading. 'This is a volume of Heavenite poetry. Written in Heavenite. With Gallifreyan translation by . . . my goodness! Castellan Lode! She was the greatest literary historian the Time Lords ever had. Before the laws of time were enforced, some of them must have visited here . . .'

'Poetry.' Ace sighed. 'Not very useful, is it?'

'About as useful as the Rosetta Stone,' gasped Benny. 'You know, that wasn't too important a document: Wednesday, did the washing, et cetera, but it was written in both hieroglyphics and Greek. The archaeologists back then knew Greek. This can be used –'

'To read anything else in Heavenite! I get it! But if you're going to write this, Professor, why didn't you add anything more useful?'

'Because I remembered that this was what I found. Tricky thing, temporal paradox. You can't do deals with time.'

'Only with Death,' Ace muttered.

The Doctor frowned, and fumbled for a pencil. 'How's the dig going?' he asked Benny.

'Not long left.' She poured cups of coffee from a flask for herself and Ace, and motioned the Doctor to use her folding desk. 'We haven't found anything new, but did you realize how thoroughly the observatory's covered in Heavenite writing? It's been written everywhere in a tiny hand, burnt into the walls, the telescope –'

'I know.' The Doctor placed his can of metal cleaner on the desk.

Ace slurped her coffee and grinned at Benny's surprised expression. 'Fancy a walk?' she asked.

'Indeed I do,' the archaeologist said, getting to her feet. 'I think. Should I ask him if I do?'

'You do,' said the Doctor, absorbed in the scroll.

Ace hoped that he was joking.

The two women wandered towards the arch, its slim shadow falling over them as they passed between it and the moon. They exchanged information about the events of the past few days Bernice asked if Ace ever knew what the Doctor was doing.

'He's playing,' Ace told her. 'Playing chess against some alien thingy. Usually, it's a bit one-sided, but this time . . .' she hugged herself against the cold. 'This time I think the other lot are as fast as he is. And he's losing his touch. He didn't half lay into me just now.'

'What about?' Benny stuffed her hands into her pockets.

'Jan. The Doctor's getting very sad about that.'

'Are you two –?'

'Yeah. Very.'

'Can't help you there. Total failure, boywise.' Benny leaned back and stared at the arch. 'Why can't you ever meet a man like that thing? Beautiful, elegant . . .'

'Doesn't talk much. Yeah, I could get used to that.'

Benny laughed. 'When I was at the Academy, I went a bit wild. Didn't like the way they wanted to make us all into troopers. I certainly can shoot, but I prefer not to have to. Can't stand soldiers, guns, all that business.'

'I dunno. Guns are okay if I'm using them. So are soldiers. Prefer grenades, though.'

Benny raised an eyebrow. 'I think we'll agree to differ there. I went AWOL and hid in the woods by the Academy. They couldn't find me. Word got out, though, and after a while girls at the Academy started to visit me for advice. Boys, periods, anti-aircraft weapons. I was sort of a gymslip guru. Anyway, a boy started to visit with the girls. I taught him everything I knew. Simon, his name was. We rolled about in the bracken a bit, I fell in love, he betrayed me to the authorities . . .'

'Typical,' Ace nodded. 'But me and Jan are gonna be okay. We're different.'

'That's what they all say.'

Ace shook her head. She didn't want to hear that. 'This Simon. Was he your first?'

'Oh yes. And, apart from a couple of times when my heart has overruled my head, the last. The Academy decided that I was obviously qualified for frontline service, made me the youngest private in the corps, and put me on a troopship bound for Capella.'

'You fought the Daleks?' Ace was impressed.

'Ah, no. I jumped ship in an escape pod. Found myself on some strange colony halfway to nowhere –'

'You and me both. Pain, isn't it?'

'It is. I started to work with an archaeological unit. Now, this is the point in the story where I do something very bad. I, ah, I faked my qualifications . . .'

'You mean, you're not a real professor?'

'That's right. Do you know, I've never told anybody about that before?'

Ace felt suitably honoured. Benny was looking at her a little nervously, as if she might rush down the diggings and yell the news to everyone. 'It's okay,' she smiled. 'Neither's the Professor.'

'How did you meet him?'

'Well.' Ace took a deep breath. 'I was working as a waitress in a cocktail bar . . .'

Kale slid into the ventilation duct and dragged the access port closed behind him.

From the ready room of the platform, he could hear the three troopers discussing how long it would be before the communications net was back on line. They were merry and lacksadaisical, waiting out the week before their replacements arrived.

In the darkness, Kale snapped open the catches of his false arm, and took it off, removing the bulky plaster. From his shoulder socket, grey filaments relaxed and swayed, no longer having to support the weight of the limb.

Kale opened the shoulder end of the metal arm, and reached into the cool internal chamber with his fingers. One by one, he removed three thin white filaments. They twisted in his grasp and sang to him.

Ace and Benny climed down the ladder into the excavations, Benny nodding to Clive and several others of the team who were still carefully sifting material from various areas of the floor. They were visibly tired, at this early hour of the morning, working by the light of chemical lamps.

'Trouble is,' Benny confided, 'there's nothing disused or destroyed to find. All the tiny objects we find are discarded. And we generally can't make head or tail of them. The Heavenites must have had one hell of a recycling plan. Come on through to the observatory.'

They stepped carefully through the doorway into the chamber beyond. Ace went over to the pile of bones in the corner.

'My fault,' Benny told Ace. 'Not good archaeology. She was a skeleton, she'd eaten that parchment the Doctor's got. I had to let her out. I've got a thing about people being locked up.'

'Haven't we all?' Ace sighed.

The Doctor was carefully looking between the slip of parchment-like material and *The Papers of Felsecar*, making notes.

A head poked into the tent. It was Paul Magrs, the archaeology student who had given his name to the observatory door. 'Oh, hiya. Sorry, I just wanted to get a probe.'

'Come in,' the Doctor finished his note with a flourish. 'I'd just finished.'

Paul reached into an open pocket of Benny's toolkit, and pulled out a thin rod. 'Who're you? he asked. 'I haven't seen you about.'

'I'm the Doctor, and this is my friend . . . oh, no she's not here.' The Doctor looked around, puzzled. He seemed to make a decision. 'I was just deciphering this note. Have a look.'

The student glanced at the page of the Doctor's notebook. 'It's not *Pride and Prejudice*, is it? But then, what is?'

'Very few people would criticise the literary style.'

'Well, everybody's different, aren't they?' Paul shrugged. 'I was born to deconstruct.'

'How are you on ethics? Would you say that it was worth sacrificing one person to save a whole galaxy?'

'Depends on the person, I suppose.'

'A very human answer.' The Doctor nodded. 'Thank you.'

Paul grinned, gave the Doctor back his piece of paper, and left. On his way back to the dig, he thought about what the strange little man had said, and started to feel uneasy.

A few minutes after he'd resumed the examination of the tunnel floor, the Doctor wandered past, on his way to the Observatory.

'No, listen, I've thought some more about it, and –'

The Time Lord looked at him as if they hadn't met before. He doffed his hat. 'Hello, I'm the Doctor and this is –' He checked himself. 'Ah, no, she's in there. I'd better go and find her.'

And he walked on.

Paul shook his head and got back to work.

Ace was looking at the masses of Heavenite symbols visible on the observatory walls. They were exactly like those she'd seen on the Library and other buildings. 'I thought those were just decorations . . .'

'No.' The Doctor bustled in, glancing around the walls. 'They're a highly complex alphabet, derived from a representational, rather than a phonetic, source.'

'Have you deciphered our skeleton's dinner?' asked Bernice.

'Yes. She ate something that disagreed with her.' The Doctor walked up to the telescope and sprayed it with the metal cleaner solution. 'I'll have to translate the contents of this room.'

'So what does the note say?' Ace asked, exasperated.

'It says . . .' the Doctor pulled it from his pocket once more and held it up to scrutiny, ' "Forgive me. I cannot (or will not) take part in the Resurrection Dance, for I know what it is and what it is about. You who read this, beware At'Ky'Tch – which is what they called this world – for we have been abused by our gods. The walls will tell you of the Resurrection Dance, and will show you how to predict when the Time has come again. Once more, forgive me. I must imprison myself now, lest all this work be for nothing." She doesn't sign her name.'

'Brave woman,' Ace sighed. 'She must have written all this stuff on the walls.'

'She burnt it in with the same device she used to seal the manacles to the wall,' Benny added. 'We've found some tiny shards of metal which might be it. Is that important?'

'No.' The Doctor was polishing the telescope with his handkerchief. 'This will take a few hours.'

'Okay, we'll leave you alone. I'd better get back to camp anyway.' Ace paused at the door. 'She got turned into one of those fungus things, didn't she?'

'Yes.' The Doctor nodded. 'That's why she chained herself up and wrote the note on something that wouldn't be dissolved in her stomach. So she wouldn't destroy all this work.'

'That's horrible,' Benny sighed, looking at the bones in the corner.

'Respect is due,' Ace agreed.

Roisa and Jan lay, propped up by cushions, against each other. They were holding hands and listening to the massive radio receiver that Jan had assembled in one corner of his tent. The aerial stretched around the whole canopy.

'Yeatsland, dry and cold,' the voice on the radio announced. 'Wind force four, increasing. Lake Wobegon, some rain, becoming dry later. Shepherdshay, storms towards morning . . .'

'When we first came here, we always used to listen to this,' Jan whispered. 'It makes me feel safe, like somebody's watching over the whole world.'

Roisa shivered, and clutched his hand. 'It's just a weather station, somewhere. A few people in a hut, drinking coffee in the middle of the night. They're alone too.' She closed her eyes, and began to cry. 'Oh Goddess . . . why did this have to happen to us?'

'What?' Jan cradled her head on his shoulder. 'What's wrong? Please tell me. Whatever it is, we can all fight it together . . .'

'No, we can't!' Roisa wailed. 'It's too late! Oh Jan, take Ace with you and go, get away from here tonight!'

'Why?'

'Because –'

Ace stepped into the tent. She took one look at Jan and Roisa and tried to step out again.

Jan leapt up and caught her. 'No, come back, it's not –'

'I know what it is.' Ace smiled gently. 'I'll be back in a few minutes, okay?'

But Roisa had stood up herself, touching Ace gently on the sleeve. 'It's all right,' she whispered, wiping her tears with a hand. 'I'll go.' She stepped outside, but turned back after a moment. 'Take good care of him,' she whispered. 'Don't let anything . . . keep him safe.'

'I will!' Ace insisted, moved. 'I wouldn't ever let . . .'

But Roisa was gone into the night.

An hour later, Jan and Ace lay curled in their makeshift bed. Jan was massaging Ace's back, expertly relaxing her muscles.

'Don't you ever do that to me again,' she said distractedly.

'What?'

'Push me out of the way in a fight.'

'Oh, this is what you wanted to say, is it?'

'If it had been anybody else I'd have smashed their face in.'

'So why not me?'

'Because I love you.'

'Oh.' Jan stopped massaging.

Ace turned over and looked up at him. 'Close your mouth,' she said. 'I was just thinking about that poor old librarian. He was brave, and he wanted to help us, and somehow the bad guys did that to him. We're not here on holiday. We're gonna be in fights again, and I thought I'd tell you tonight. Get it over with. Okay?'

'Okay.' Jan lay down beside her, watching her face. 'I love you too.'

'No, you don't have to say that –'

'I didn't bloody well think I had to! I just do. And we're going to be together, right? Here or in space with your mate . . .'

'If he lets you.'

'Let's see him stop me.' Jan kissed her gently.

'He could.' Ace whispered. 'Let's hope he doesn't want to try.'

'I have something to tell you.'

'What, you're pregnant?'

'Hush, this is serious. You've already told me all your names.'

'No.' Ace closed her eyes. 'Um . . . Dotty sometimes, and my Mum used to call me Dorry. That's it.'

'Well, it's time you heard my secret names, if we're going

to be together. If you know these, you can steal my heart and soul away, but you've already done that, so where's the harm?'

Ace hugged him for that.

'When I was young,' Jan told her, 'I was Ramany-Pashy, which is a reference to a wild bull in Romany tradition. It means that I used to throw myself at lots of women who didn't want me, and succeeded a few times through keeping on trying . . .'

'That doesn't suit you now,' Ace murmured, not wanting to show Jan how moved she was by all this.

'No. That's why I changed it in the last year. I'm now Aradrath, the one big fire. I wanted to have something about my power, and rather than be trivial, I thought I'd look forward to the time when I'd make a good big fire, one really useful one. I think that's the one I've lit with you.'

'That's beautiful,' Ace held him tightly. 'You're beautiful, and I love you.'

They made love once more, Ace wondering how it was that she drew strength from this man, how it was that she trusted him, just as much – more – than she trusted the Doctor?

Trust was new for her.

Poor Roisa. Ace wondered briefly if she could tolerate a time-share on Jan's company. Roisa really cared about him, and she was unselfish enough to give him up. Damn it, why did ex-girlfriends never turn out to be complete villains? You'd get more sleep that way.

They talked for a while about children's stories after they'd finished, caressing. Jan fell asleep, and Ace rolled over, pulling a book from his pile of reading matter beside the rugs. Byron. Yeah, it would be. She found a page at random.

'The Assyrian came down like the wolf on the fold . . .' Ace read to the sleeping Jan, whispering.

Colm Wylie stood at the edge of the Travellers' camp, shifting the weight of his plasma rifle from one shoulder to another.

He blew into his hands. The Travellers took turns on guard duty, as with everything else, and tonight was Colm's turn. He was an ex-marine, and still sometimes had trouble sleeping, with all the dreams of vapourized blood. He'd given it up for anarchy, and didn't mind wandering the camp at three in the morning.

There was a shuffling noise from out on the perimeter. Colm looked up. Past the light of the stake-mounted lamps, something was moving in the darkness. It might be a herd animal, of course, a grazer wandering up to see what the lights were.

But these days, it might not be. Colm found the alarm beacon in his pocket, but he didn't press the button.

He could see vague shapes now, moving outside of the stone circle. Human shapes, swaying listlessly, their steps taking them in a ritualistic circle around the camp. They were moving so quietly . . . Colm shook his head. He wasn't dreaming. He couldn't make out any features, but there was a whole army of people out there.

He tightened his grip on his gun. 'Hoi!' he shouted. 'Who are you?'

The only response was a strange keening sound. Right on the edge of audibility, it sliced through the night air like static.

With the noise came something else. Colm saw it arriving, a cloud of white fibres, floating in on the breeze. A snowstorm of thin, hairy, flecks. It wafted towards the camp, scattering amongst the tents, wrapping around the stones and poles.

One of the fibres landed on Colm's glove, and twitched.

He yelled, throwing off the glove, and hit the alarm button. A blaring siren shrilled out from a speaker attached to a central pole, and Travellers began to tumble from their tents, snatching up weapons. They ran towards the sentry point.

Ace ran out into the night in a robe, carrying a belt of grenades. She got to Colm before anyone else did. The man was shivering, clutching his hand.

'They're going!' he gasped.

Ace peered out into the murk. In the middle distance, she could make out a parade of retreating figures.

'Should we go after them?' asked Alec, running up barefoot.

'No . . .' Ace shook her head. 'That's a good way to get killed, running after a retreating enemy.'

Máire and Roisa arrived, in identical black robes. Roisa had been shining a torch ahead of her, gesturning to Máire to be careful.

'These things!' she cried to Colm. 'They're all over the place!'

'Are they dangerous?' asked the sentry. He showed Roisa

his hand. The tiny fibre had somehow gone straight through the glove, and was embedded in the flesh of his wrist.

'I don't know,' the woman whispered, her face filling with fear. 'We'll take a look back at my tent, I'll bathe it.' She turned to Ace. 'Make sure nobody else gets near the fibres, whatever they are.'

Ace and Máire looked at the number of semi-naked Travellers that had gathered around the sentry post. 'Bloody fibres again,' Ace muttered.

'We'll clear a path back to the centre,' Máire decided. 'Everybody follow me, and then take a good look around your own tents.' She pointed to three burly Travellers with weapons. 'I think it'd be an idea if you kept a watch until dawn.'

'They won't be back,' Ace muttered. 'I think they've done what they came for. Oh my God!'

Jan was drowsily wandering towards them, his feet bare. 'What's wrong?' he muttered. 'I think the sky fell in just now . . .'

Ace ran to him, hopping over fibres, and quickly inspected the soles of his feet. After a moment, she sighed in relief. 'You're the luckiest bloody man alive, you are.'

'Aye, I'm with you, aren't I?'

Ace made him walk very carefully back to their tent.

Benny had gone back to her tent for a cup of coffee, and was sitting alone, looking at photos.

Dad. Where was he? Dead on some frontier world? A wisp of gas in space? Or was he off on some secret mission that nobody knew about?

No. That was absolute rubbish. That was just fantasy.

Sometimes she'd thought she'd found leads, descriptions of a man a bit like him. Once she'd walked into a bar and thought she'd seen him across the room. It had turned out to be some old space pirate, but for five minutes, how her heart had beaten.

Dad.

A shadow moved across the surface of the tent. Benny pulled her gun. She slipped quickly outside, and relaxed in the moonlight.

The Doctor was gazing up at the moon, his face full of childish delight. He hadn't noticed her, but was staring up into the sky, his boy's eyes full of moon.

And he must have seen so many moons.

Benny found herself wishing that she could have fallen in love with somebody like him. As she wished, she knew that she wouldn't.

But, God, she wanted to be his friend.

A burst of shooting stars exploded silently overhead. The Doctor gazed at it, and his face fell into an expression of grim determination.

'Bernice,' he said. 'Take me to the place those stars have fallen.'

Ace woke suddenly, and shook her head, trying to figure out what was a dream and what wasn't.

The fibres were real. Yeah, and Jan was safely sleeping at her side.

Something had woken her up. Christ, if she wasn't so knackered, she wouldn't have been able to sleep in the first place.

The sound that had woken her came again. A light tap against the fabric of the tent. Like somebody was flicking their finger against it. Ace listened, until the tension drained out of her, and she was almost about to fall back to sleep. Then the sound came again.

She reached for Jan's gun, afraid. Was this going to be it? Grabbed by fungus monsters in the middle of the night?

Hell, let them try. Ace crept up to the tent flap, still wondering if she was dreaming. She undid the whole thing with one tug of the ties, and threw the flap open.

Before the tent stood a tall figure in a black shroud.

'My God,' Ace whispered. 'Are you real?'

'Indeed.' The being held out a whitened hand. 'For a while. Come with me.'

Glancing back at Jan, Ace took Christopher's hand.

10:

No More Mister Nice Guy

The dark-robed figure stalked across the hillside, its garments rustling in the night breezes.

Ace followed at a distance, the gun tucked into the belt of her robe. She wasn't feeling cold, which was probably something to do with Christopher. They had walked through the camp like it wasn't there, the nervous sentries looking straight past them. It was like a dream, like sleepwalking.

Christopher had been silent as he lead the way up the hillside. When he reached the white horse, he stopped, and turned to look down at the lights of the camp.

Ace joined him, watching as two owls swooped above the downlands, hunting.

'So,' she began, when it became clear that Christopher wasn't going to talk first. 'How you doing?'

'I am dead,' the robed figure rumbled. 'I control this body from Puterspace, where I live on, having transferred my soul there.' He pulled the cowl from his head. Ace was shocked to see the pallor of his skin, and the lifeless tilt of his eyes. His lips barely moved, and they were already caked and cracked. 'Already that life is fading. Soon I shall be gone, and this body will obey the demands of our enemy.'

'What? Why?'

Christopher showed her his palm. Under the skin, a number of the white fibres were moving. 'I have walked the camp, taken in as many as I could. They still identify me as a target. Tell me, do you believe in destiny?'

Ace sat down on the grass, pulling her robe over her knees. 'No. You get the breaks, you make what you can of them.' She looked up at Christopher. 'Look, the Doctor knows a lot about computers, maybe he could . . .'

'My heart has stopped.' Christopher's dead eyes swept over

the landscape. 'And the only electrical activity in my brain is that which I create there. There are no options left for me. Sometimes the paths to be taken are obvious. If you stay here, stay with Ramany-Pashy –'

'Aradrath,' Ace corrected him, and then gasped. 'Hey, look, did you know that too?'

'Yes.' Christopher looked away quickly. 'But I have known him too long to be used to it. If you stay with him, then you will have to make a sacrifice.'

'Why is everybody telling me that? What's wrong with living happily ever after, anyway?' Ace rubbed her brow, wondering why she had come out with Jan's name like that. It was precious to her, something wonderful. Although she trusted Christopher, it was as if the magic of this encounter had eased the word out of her brain.

Christopher's cracked lips smiled as he looked down at her confusion. 'It is a dream. A good dream, but death will end it, sooner or later. You are the best beloved of Time, the steward to the Doctor, who calls himself Time's Champion. But Time is the lover of change. Soon, nothing will be the same.'

'How do you know all this?'

'I am part of everything now. I wonder if dying in the matrix will be like dying at all . . . But then, I don't know what dying is like.' He put a hand to Ace's head. 'Do not trust those with the spores on them.'

Then he turned, and began to walk down the hill. Ace watched him go, distractedly hitting the earth with her hand.

'I don't care about destiny!' she whispered. 'Don't care about anything but him.'

Benny lead the Doctor to a line of low pylons that stretched across a hillside. A wire hummed between the pylons, and small lights blinked on top of them.

They'd left the horses tethered to a tree, and walked the quarter mile to the fence.

'This is the edge of the current landing zone.' Benny pointed. 'These barriers are designed to keep herd animals out.'

'What about people?'

'There's precious little chance of anybody getting hit by one of the pods, and there's too big an area to guard. Besides, if you knew that several tons of dead people were about to descend pretty rapidly overhead, would you go wandering around sightseeing? I think not.'

'No.' The Doctor ducked under the fence. 'Coming?'

Benny nodded. 'We've got six hours until the next drop time. Will that do?'

'Oh yes.' The Doctor raised the wire with his umbrella. 'I'm only sightseeing.'

They trudged down into the valley. Bernice looked at the Doctor occasionally as they went. 'So,' she asked. 'Do you have a girlfriend?'

'No.'

'Boyfriend?'

'No.'

'Model railway set?'

'Somewhere.' The Doctor was staring down into the valley, observing the fiery shapes that lay there. 'The TARDIS is full of surprises.'

'But you're not the sort of person that keeps a big table, with tiny trees and signalboxes and things?'

'No.'

'Ah, then you must be interested in law and order.'

The Doctor stopped, and turned to face Bernice. 'No,' he said, a slow grin spreading over his features. 'I like chaos, big explosions, rebellions, that sort of thing. Why do you ask?'

'Because I want to know why you go around in a police box!'

'You know what one is?'

'It's from my favourite era.'

'I could have changed it ages ago,' the Doctor confided. 'But I like the shape. And the motto. Call here for help. That's what I do. I let little children sleep safely at night, because I've searched through all the shadows and chased the baddies away. I'm what monsters have nightmares about!'

He sounded quite satisfied with that for a moment, and Bernice smiled. But as they approached the fires that guttered and flared in the valley, she could see from his face that he wasn't content with his definition of himself.

'But everybody's a monster sometimes.' The Doctor picked

his way through the great impact craters that had been blasted into the grasslands. He bent down to watch a mole trying to rebuild its home. 'We all do things we regret. And sometimes we have to lose things very precious to us.' He stood again suddenly, and looked around. 'Are these craters formed where the pods have landed?'

'Yes.' Benny led the way down into a crater, slipping on the smooth earthern walls. At the bottom of the hole, ploughed into the earth, lay a sizzling black pod, about the size of a coffin. Deposits on its surface were still burning. 'Remains of a sash,' Benny explained. 'This one would have been a corporate soldier. Can't tell which company now. In the morning, robot gardeners buzz the area and plough everything under. The caskets are made of hard cellulose, so they're biodegradable.'

'Do all the dead arrive on Heaven like this?'

'No. The majority are shipped in and given a traditional burial. The bones are miles thick in some areas. There are a great many corpses in Draconian and Human space, and lots of them end up here. Several alien species are convinced the place is sacred as well . . .'

'They would be. Their computer records have been interfered with for centuries. Everybody's been conned into sending their dead here.'

'Why?'

'Open the casket.'

Benny shrugged. 'If I was a religious person, I'd find the idea very distasteful. But I'm a tomb robber, so here we go.' She removed a device from her belt and ran it along the seam of the casket.

The Doctor lifted the lid and peered inside. He knelt and pulled a skull out, turning it over in his hand. 'Do you think we should take arms against a sea of troubles?' he asked the skull.

'Mixed metaphor,' sighed Benny.

'Deliberately.' The Doctor upturned the skull. A host of white filaments dropped on to the soil, and swiftly began to bury their way in. 'You can't fight the sea, no matter what you do.'

Ace watched the owls circling above the forest as she trudged back to camp. Dawn was breaking over the hills. It felt like the last dawn ever, cold and a bit half-hearted.

The Travellers were packing their tents away, folding them up into wooden boxes, which were then slung over the backs of the horses. They left white circles on the ground where they'd restricted the growth of grass. Máire was walking from stone to stone around the circle, touching each one as if to say goodbye.

Jan shouted and ran forward, lifting Ace up in a whirling hug. 'Where were you?' he laughed. 'I thought you'd left me!'

'Never.' Ace kissed him soundly, wondering whether she should tell him about Christopher. 'I went up to the hill, to think a bit.'

'After last night? Gods, you're a warrior aren't you?'

'Yeah. What's going on? Why's everybody leaving?'

'We're moving on. The decision was made around the fire this morning. We'd searched the camp for any fibres, and didn't find many, but the site's not really safe anymore. Roisa's been trying to remove the threads from the people who got touched. We think there's three of them. She argued that we should move right off-planet, but Máire brought it down to just getting a little nearer civilization. We're going towards Joycetown.'

'That'll take us near Benny's dig.'

'Aye, that's where we're stopping. Safety in numbers. Hey, you said "us"!'

'So I did.' Ace kissed him again.

They wandered back to Jan's tent, or what remained of it. The central pole had been removed, and piles of cutlery, fabrics and tools were stacked outside of it. Ace piled in, placing things carefully in the wooden trunks.

She pulled the goblet from a silk scarf, and examined the carving on the golden stem. 'This is the one you're worried about, right? The one you got from the Vacuum Church?'

'That's the one.'

Ace finger found the hollow of the base. 'This must be really valuable.'

'It might be, but that's where Roisa's wrong, you see. I wouldn't do anything for money.' His tone was irritated, and Ace remembered how sensitive he was about the cup.

'It's good that you've got it,' she said. 'Even if it was filled with blood in the Dreaming. They don't deserve –'

The goblet had suddenly got deeper. A false bottom in the cup had vanished when she'd pushed her finger into the base. 'Here, have you seen this?'

Jan looked over her shoulder. 'No,' he whispered. 'That's going to be for poison or something, isn't it?'

'Well, it's empty now.' Ace dropped the goblet into the case. 'Maybe that's the secret of the goblet,' she told Jan. 'Maybe Vic will stop bothering you about it now.'

'I doubt it,' Jan smiled, returning to his packing.

On a distant hillside many hours later, as Christopher's body walked to wherever it was going, it passed the Doctor.

The Doctor was staring down at the camp also, his eyes fixed on Jan's tent. He seemed to be fighting something inside himself, his eyes dark.

Christopher paused, and looked at him coldly. 'Aradrath,' he spat.

The Doctor glowered back. 'Yes,' was all he said.

Then both resumed the paths they had been walking.

Phaedrus looked around his congregation, nodding eagerly. 'We are pawns,' he told them. 'We are only soldiers, dying for futility. We are used by our masters, as others are. Our only boon is that we know, we are allowed to see. Are the new acolytes ready?'

Two young men and an old woman stepped forward. They were dressed in grey robes. The woman was dying, as converts often were. She'd read one of the Church's books on making more of your passing, and had spent three weeks being counselled by Phaedrus himself. One of the boys was a runaway, an apprentice farmhand. He probably thought that this was a good gang to belong to, the ultimate way to display your individuality. The last boy had not offered any reasons. He'd only insisted.

Normally, they'd have had some more time. Ah well, things were hard for everybody.

'Bring the worms!' Phaedrus commanded. An acolyte stepped

forward, carrying three white fibres on the end of a baton. He showed the initiates the creatures. 'If you wish, you may go in peace,' Phaedrus told them. 'But it you wish to die alive, and be whole in the knowledge of your death, then seize the worm.'

The old woman already had, watching it squirm on the surface of her palm, working its way under her skin. The runaway closed his eyes, and touched the fibre with the back of his hand, wincing.

The other boy stared at the baton. He reached his hand out, shaking.

Phaedrus watched, interested. He lived for these moments.

The boy smacked the baton aside and ran, shoving guards out of the way.

Phaedrus inclined his head to the two new acolytes. 'Welcome,' he said. 'Your comrade may have run away, but he will be with us soon enough. Now we all have a task to perform.'

The Doctor was lying on the floor, a notepad in hand, glancing between *The Papers Of Felsecar* and the base of the telescope. He made a final note, read back what he had written, and then jumped up.

Benny was leaning in the doorway, her arms folded. She'd caught three hours sleep, and was feeling a strong urge to resort to make up to hide the bags under her eyes. 'Eureka?' she asked.

'Yes.' The Doctor stuffed his hat back on his head and pointed to the ceiling. 'The observatory used to be at ground level. In the last few decades, the earth subsided.'

'Yes, yes –' Benny stopped him. 'I know. The arch is much bigger than what we see on the surface.'

'So we must dig it out.' The Doctor was flustered, pacing back and forth.

'No problem, the crew still owe me a day's work.' Benny put a hand on the Doctor's shoulder. 'Look, digging it straight out will ruin anything we might find in the infill. It's against my code of ethics.' She paused. 'When you said last night that the mixed metaphor in *Hamlet* was deliberate, was that a critical opinion, or first-hand knowledge?'

'I was there when Will composed it,' the Doctor snapped.

'I was a friend of his, and, when I'm not dealing with threats to life and liberty, I spend most of my time correcting idiots who misquote him!'

Benny narrowed her eyes, staring keenly at the Doctor's expression. He was completely sincere. 'This is my career we're talking about. My whole life. Tell me it's vital.'

'Do it in an hour, and I might not have to . . . not have to do something I'll regret. Please. It's important.'

'One hour.' Benny nodded, sighed, and ran to tell her crew. She slapped Ace on the shoulder as they passed in the earthen corridor. 'I've just decided,' she shouted.

'What?' Ace called after her.

'I'm not an archaeologist!'

Benny vanished around the corner.

Operative Miller hit the button angrily. 'Damn it, Judith!' he muttered. 'Why can't we communicate with them?'

Judith, the communications officer at Miller's base, shook her head. 'The main antenna of the orbital platform has been rerouted, as we knew it would be, in order to monitor ground-based sources . . .'

'Any evidence that Kale's actually doing that?'

'The emission spectrum from the platform would suggest not. We can work out the angle of the antenna . . .' Fiona touched a control. 'It's pointed straight at Joycetown. Hasn't moved in three hours. And the secondary antenna's out.'

'So what's going on up there?' Miller looked up at the ceiling in frustration.

Suddenly, a red light appeared on the desk. 'Platform engines just fired, sir!' Fiona shouted. 'Sustained burst!'

'What?' Miller jumped into a chair and checked the instruments. 'My God,' he whispered. 'They're on a re-entry curve!'

Ace popped her head around the door of the observatory, and whistled to the Doctor. 'How's it going?'

'Terrible,' the Doctor growled. Ace stepped back a little, and he softened, reaching out to smooth her hair. 'How are the Travellers?'

'Come and see for yourself.' Ace led him out into the sunlight.

The Travellers were setting up camp all around the dig site. On the back of a cart stood the TARDIS. 'Thought we'd better bring it with us,' Ace smiled, taking the Doctor's arm.

'Good.' The Doctor had grinned at the sight, and Ace was full of things she wanted to say to him. I'm in love, she wanted to say, come to the wedding.

'Ah, you've found another man already!' Jan slapped the Doctor on the back.

Ace sighed. The Doctor was looking tense again. It was as if Jan made him nervous.

Benny had taken up a pick, and was hacking at the soft soil under the arch. Her students were clustered around her, helping out with spades and starting up power tools.

'Hoi!' she shouted, catching sight of Jan. 'Get your people over here and help us finish off a promising career, you lazy git!'

The three creatures stepped forward and bowed to Kale, the tendrils of their heads quivering. The remnants of corporate uniforms still clung to their fungoid bodies.

Kale smiled. The tentacles that had unfurled from his arm socket were holding down three of the rocket thrust controls. He turned his head to the viewing port, and saw the globe of Heaven growing gradually larger. The first flickers of outer atmosphere were already burning blue and red as they caught the external struts of the platform.

Kale licked his lips, suppressing a spasm of fear. He concentrated on the music, the music that was soaring up from the planet, roaring into the antenna, directing every subtle movement of his tentacles on the thrust controls.

The music was gradually increasing in volume.

Roisa heard the sound first. From the tents of the archaeologists was coming a steady beeping noise. She glanced at the large team of Travellers and students digging away under the arch. Cathlan was singing a rhythmic song as he shovelled aside great clods of mud, and Máire had picked up on it too. Dear Máire. Roisa hoped that, somewhere in the future, she'd forgive her for what she'd done.

She opened the flap of the tent, and picked up the receiver

of Benny's radio unit, reciting the callsign off the top of the pack.

'This is Miller!' a voice cut in, sounding desperate. 'You must all get away from there as soon as possible. The orbital platform is in a declining orbit. We've worked out that it will crash in your area. You must get away! Hello? Are you there?'

Roisa lowered the receiver, shaking. A burning pain was coming from her foot. 'What should I do?' she whispered. 'Who will save us now?'

A hand reached out and took the receiver.

The Doctor glared at the Traveller, his eyes full of steel. 'I will,' he growled.

Phaedrus and his congregation were singing, an incredibly complex melody, the vocal patterns interlacing in delicate strands. They had their eyes closed, and their thoughts were all the same, computations of falling spacecraft, visions of paths and vectors. They had been rehearsing this for months, the new intake trained in it as part of their instruction.

The song resounded through the architecture, echoing and spiralling off of the walls of the temple.

It concealed another sound from an anteroom. A wheezing, groaning sound.

Ace and Benny hopped up on to the lectern at one end of the temple, in front of the choir. Guards snatched for their guns, but Ace pulled two submachine guns and waved them randomly at the crowd, grinning. Benny aimed down her pistol, straight at Phaedrus's head.

Phaedrus kept singing, his eyes fixed on the weapon. With an effort of will, he closed his eyes.

The guards lowered their weapons.

Benny cleared her throat. 'Ladies and gentlemen!' she called, shouting over the choir. 'I'd like to introduce you to possibly the most important thing on this side of the universe! Let's have a big hand for . . . the Doctor!'

The congregation still had their eyes clenched tightly closed, still holding on to the song. They couldn't afford to lose concentration for a second. Phaedrus's brow was sweating as he held the singers together, coordinating the signals they were psychically beaming into space.

It was working. The platform was following the right arc, making tiny course corrections as it fell.

But then another voice joined in the chorus.

And it was singing a different tune.

The song told the congregation that she might have been weary, that they knew how girls got weary, wearing that same old dress . . . The Doctor was crooning into a stand-up microphone, speakers in the TARDIS throwing his voice into the massed choir. 'But when she gets weary, try a little tenderness . . .'

Benny leaned over the mike, hollering the lyrics of the chorus in a voice with more soul than training.

Ace shrugged at the guards. 'Not my style,' she mouthed.

The choir's melody began to break up as the other song entwined with it. Acolytes opened their eyes and looked round, trying to find their place in the tune again.

Phaedrus clenched his hands in rage, his nails biting into his palms.

He could still see it, it was still there – it was gone!

'What are you doing?' he bellowed.

The choir stopped, suddenly, and so did the Doctor. The Time Lord leapt off the stage, and grabbed Phaedrus by the collar. 'Winning!' he snarled. 'Now let me talk to your masters!'

A limb cracked from the platform, and spun away as the spacecraft tumbled into the atmosphere, clouds rushing up to meet it.

The exterior was already becoming molten, gobbets of metal spraying off into the void as the blast of friction fried the surface.

Kale had lost the song, and was screaming now, his teeth clenched. The three monsters behind him were becoming feathery, their skins erupting in masses of white fibre.

He was nearly there. He had been on the right course, he could feel it. If he could hold on for just a few more seconds . . .

Máire stared up at the glow that was blooming over the western horizon. The Travellers had gathered in a crowd, and were sheltering each other. Winds were beginning to whip across the planet's surface, faster and faster. The archaeology students had grabbed horses, and had been going to gallop away as fast as they could.

Máire had told them that it wouldn't be fast enough. The platform would hit the planet like an atomic bomb.

Some had gone anyway. Those that remained grasped the hands of the Travellers, and looked up into the sky. Máire had told them that Travellers didn't die with their eyes closed.

Jan gritted his teeth. He and Máire and Roisa had formed a line at the front of the group, holding hands.

'Ace got away at least,' Roisa smiled to him. 'I love you.'

'I love you,' Jan whispered back, without hesitation.

'We're all going to the Goddess together,' Máire told Roisa. 'I'll love you better next time.'

'I hope you get the chance . . .' Roisa's voice broke and she began to sob. 'But any way . . . any way you like is fine! You just find me! Whatever I am, a dog, a bloody snail, I'll take care of you in the next life!'

'Come on then!' Jan shouted up to the sky. 'Brigida!'

The Travellers took up the cry, a scream to the goddess of poetry and war.

The glow filled half the sky.

'I don't need you.' The Doctor slapped Phaedrus across the face. 'You're a puppet. Give me your masters!'

Phaedrus flushed with anger. Then he gasped as his head jerked back. A different voice gurgled from his throat. His eyes stared upwards lifelessly.

'So, Time Lord. What do you want of us?'

'Destroy the platform!'

'Why?'

'You need a pawn here, I know that. You need a powerful host mind to be able to broadcast your signal. For the moment, you need Phaedrus. Are you sure my song was random? Are you sure I haven't set the platform into a new trajectory? Perhaps to land here?'

The voice broke into a hissing laugh. 'We . . . know you . . . Time's Champion! You will not . . . take life!'

'I will!' Ace ran forward and shoved one of her SMGs into Phaedrus's throat. 'If it's Jan or you, you're dead! So back off or I'll blow his brains out! You know I will!'

Benny winced at what she heard in Ace's voice. It was just on the edge of hysteria.

The Doctor folded his hands behind his back. 'I'll leave her to it, then,' he murmured.

A low hiss escaped Phaedrus's throat.

Kale was laughing now as Heaven swept up towards him. He was going to achieve his great mission for the cause of death! He could see mountains and hills, and rivers and –

One of his tentacles jerked against a red switch.

The platform exploded into a ball of flaming gas.

The explosion lit up the sky above the dig, colouring the clouds. A moment later, a thunderclap echoed off the hills and dells.

A thousand daylit meteors burst across the blue, trailing fire and smoke.

And the Travellers fell to their knees in relief.

'Doctor,' whispered Máire. 'Thank you . . .'

'But don't cut it so bloody fine next time,' muttered Jan.

Phaedrus awoke to Ace grinning at him.

'Love does strange things to you,' she said.

'And nearly to you.' The Doctor let go of the priest. 'Tell your masters that if they leave now, I may choose not to harm them. Now, do we get out of here unmolested, or do the pawns have ideas above their station?'

Phaedrus didn't speak. He just raised an open palm. He was looking at Ace with a kind of longing.

It took a moment before Ace realized that he was actually looking at her gun.

The three companions dashed back to the TARDIS. At the last moment, Benny peeped back around the corner to the anteroom.

'But apart from all that,' she asked, 'what did you think of the song?'

A red umbrella handle pulled her off into the TARDIS.

11:
Continuity

Ace had run off into the interior of the TARDIS to get some more clothes.

Benny was still staring. Her first journey had only taken twenty seconds, during which time she'd just said: 'Oh.'

'Bigger on the inside than the outside,' the Doctor murmured, glancing at a control.

'I've heard that before.' Benny put a hand on the console to steady herself. 'It looks like a police box, and you travel through time and space in it.'

'Yes.'

'I hope it has an *en suite* bathroom.'

The Doctor pointed with his umbrella. 'First left after the zoo.'

'I see.' Benny raised an eyebrow.

'It's about time the TARDIS had a cleanout. Dodo keeps getting lost.'

'Who's Dodo?'

'My young companion.' The Doctor walked slowly around the console, flicking switches randomly. 'She talks using hip phrases, she comes from London, she's fashionable. She reminds me of my grandaughter.'

Benny didn't like the sound of the Doctor's voice. 'You're not well, are you? Is there something you want to talk to me about?'

'Oh.' The Doctor had his back to her now, and the hunched shoulders reminded Benny of some ancient horror movie. She straightened up, preparing. Oh God, was he going to become a monster, leap at her?

'So much.' The voice was a whisper. 'Tell me that we'll have time, one day. That I'll be able to explain all I've done . . .'

'Of course you will,' Benny blurted, extremely nervous now.

'Why, what have you done?'

Ace burst back in, heaving two haversacks full of provisions.

The Doctor looked up from the TARDIS console and grinned his funny grin at her. 'At the temple . . . you weren't really going to shoot?' he asked her, the old Doctor again.

'Nah . . .' Ace laughed. 'Well, not at the crowd. I could have topped Phaedrus, but, you know, if Jan had already died . . . Life's too short, eh, Professor?'

Benny slowly looked between the two of them.

Something deep in the Doctor's eyes still scared her.

The Doctor looked out at his audience, staring up at him as he stood against the light of the bonfire. It was early afternoon, and a token party were working away at uncovering the observatory. Everyone had returned, wondering that they hadn't been killed by the impacting platform. The TARDIS had landed amongst them to applause.

Students, their hair cut into spectacular fringes. Travellers in their rugged boots and coats. Ace, a bundle full of messages from previous centuries. Fathers held babies on their laps, and toddlers ran between adults' legs.

'Children,' the Doctor whispered to himself. He picked up a burning stick from the bonfire, and waved it in the air. 'It's time,' he told them. 'Time to tell you what you're facing.' He started to pace before the fire, twirling the stick to illustrate his story.

'Millions of years ago, while the Earth was still forming, the world of Gallifrey was doing business with another species. The Hoothi. The master strategists of the galaxy. Nobody knows where they evolved, or if they were artificially created. They're fungoid creatures, they live off decayed matter. They farmed whole worlds, kept sentient populations as herd animals. Now, these were the days when the Time Lords had interests of their own, planets where their influence was felt. The Hoothi began to take sides in a war on Tranmetgura, introduced their dead soldiers into the battle . . .'

'Dead?' asked Ace from somewhere inside Jan's bulky furs. 'What d'you mean?'

'They infest the bodies of their slain foes,' the Doctor paced along the fringes of the fire, 'and use them as pawns in their obscene plottings. The Time Lords had been negotiating with the Tranmetgurans, trying to organize a planetary government that they could deal with. The Hoothi damaged that plan. Full-scale war broke out, and biological agents reduced the planet's population by two-thirds.' The Doctor's face showed disgust. 'The slaughter was huge. The Hoothi took all the dead into their silent gas dirigibles, and used them as they do all dead matter.'

'Silent gas dirigibles?' Benny was sitting by the fire, glancing over her shoulder at Cathlan, who was staring at her in a way she didn't like. She had decided to keep a close watch on the Doctor, but he was so obviously himself at the moment that his outburst in the TARDIS seemed like a dream.

'Silent, steathly, invisible to tracking systems thanks to the Hoothi's vast psychic powers. That's why Operative Miller hasn't been able to find them. That's why I have to, and quickly. The Hoothi ingest a range of noxious atmospheric gases, all deadly to human life. Their vessels are inflated by them. Hence: dirigibles. They sail between the stars in their great spheres, hiding in hyperspace. Now, let me return to my story. The Time Lords sent an ambassador to the Hoothi worlds, intending to stop the creatures from interfering further in Time Lord affairs. The Hoothi used him as a host.' The Doctor looked into the light of the fire, unwilling to face the crowd, not wishing to pick out certain people with his eyes. 'Their attack on Gallifrey didn't last long. Time Lord biochemistry was more advanced than theirs – then, at least. And, when you can find them, the dirigibles are vulnerable. Full of explosive gases. Gallifrey opted to launch a devastating counterattack, they were going to time-loop the Hoothi worlds. The Hoothi vanished, fled the Milky Way. It was thought that they had decided to search for easier prizes elsewhere. But they haven't. They're back. And they're here.'

Jan raised a hand laconically. 'You said they were master strategists . . .'

'Yes. They plan their games well in advance. They prefer to let others do the work, and appear to act only at the last minute.'

'Look who's talking,' Ace whispered to Jan.

'They have a group mind, the whole species thinks as a single being. Very cunning, very dangerous.'

'If they were going to attack,' asked Máire from the crowd. 'Why haven't they done it already?'

'They will atttack,' the Doctor told her. 'They already have, by trying to destroy this site, by making sure of their ground in Puterspace, by trying to prevent me from finding *The Papers Of Felsecar*. They're waiting for something, they're still vulnerable, and their interest here means that I want to uncover the observatory even faster. Miller's sent a message to Spacefleet, and they could be here within a week. That will be too late. Now, I'd better tell you what the inscriptions in the observatory said.'

A cry came from the diggers. Clive, the archaeology student, was waving his spade in the air. 'Metal!' he shouted. 'We're nearly there!'

The Doctor watched from a distance as the massed forces of the Travellers and students dug away the final covering of the observatory dome.

'They look like children playing, don't they?' Roisa had wandered up to stand beside him.

'My thoughts,' the Doctor smiled. 'Exactly.'

Roisa took a deep breath. 'I'm not a fool, Doctor. You were talking about fungal infestation. Those spores that landed in the camp ...'

'Those with them on their skin have been touched by the Hoothi,' the Doctor turned and stared into Roisa's eyes. 'The Hoothi can use their senses to gather information, and can cause their bodies to erupt into full infestation within seconds. That's what happened to the librarian. Sometimes the process is slowed down, a gradual takeover.'

'Is there a cure?'

'No. The only hope is that the psychic command will never be given. If we can find the Hoothi and destroy them, then nobody else will have to die.'

'So what should I tell those of us with spores?'

'Tell them – no, tell them nothing. There's no point in spreading pain, no point in prolonging the process ...'

'No.' Roisa nodded firmly. 'No, you're right about that.'
And she walked away quickly.

Máire had spent an hour working on the dig, and then returned to her tent. She'd taken a reading on the surface of the metal, and it seemed to her that a fair-sized grenade wouldn't crack the dome if it was used to blow away the earth. Save a lot of digging time.

Passing Roisa's tent, she heard a sound she recognized. It sent her sprawling to the ground.

The safety catch of a blaster had just come off.

Máire crawled on her elbows towards the tent, getting her jacket covered in dew. She gently pulled the flap aside and peered in.

Roisa had a gun in her mouth.

Máire cried out and leapt forward.

They tumbled together, Máire aware of how the thing could go off, kill either of them, or both. She pulled it roughly from Roisa's face, and fought her for it, smashing her arm against the ground until, sobbing, the woman dropped the gun.

They held each other for a long time, Roisa screaming into Máire's shoulder.

'What is it? What is it? Why couldn't you tell me?' Máire cried.

Between gasps of breath, Roisa looked up at her. 'I tried to do it,' she sobbed. 'And I couldn't! I couldn't squeeze the trigger!'

'That's good.' Máire hugged her tighter.

'No,' Roisa whispered. 'No it isn't.' She gazed down at her fingers.

They were twitching now.

And she wasn't able to stop them.

The dome of the observatory was completely uncovered now. It was a hemisphere, directly under the great arch, much higher now that all the earth had been cleared away. It lay in a large depression, mounds of soil all around. The Doctor walked once around it as it glittered in the sun. Then he ran into the dig, climbing swiftly down a ladder.

Ace followed. She'd been wanting to ask the Doctor about Jan, and he seemed, well, on the case again. Fighting monsters, like he was supposed to.

She wandered into the telescope room, and watched as the Doctor took a last look at the inscriptions on the instrument. He inspected the levers that stuck out from the frame where it was mounted.

'Professor.'

'Yes?'

'Can Jan come with us then? When this is all over?'

The Doctor looked up for a moment, but he didn't turn around. There was a pause. 'Are you sure?' he asked. 'He's not very like you. Not very adventurous.'

'He is! He's just been stranded here too long. He's a lot like both of us.'

'I know you better than he does.'

Ace gritted her teeth. She'd been about to answer that one a bit too directly. 'I dunno. Maybe.'

'This lever will open the canopy. I think I'd better pull it.'

And he did. The canopy of the dome began to grind open, on ancient bearings. The Doctor rushed around the room, squirting oil on the rim from a small can he pulled from his pocket.

Low sunlight slowly filled the observatory as the slats moved aside. Ace looked up to see Travellers standing on the banked soil. Above them grew the darkening sky.

The slats stopped on a level with the arch, which then –

'Wicked!' Ace gasped.

The silver arch had vanished. Without a sound.

The Travellers whooped and applauded.

The Doctor began to read from his notebook, checking the right ascension and declination of the telescope, and turning dials to correct them. 'The Heavenites knew a thing or two about hyperspace technology . . .' he muttered. 'They must have learnt it from the Hoothi. Which is how our astronomer came to make this.' He beckoned for Ace to look through the telescope.

She lowered her head. It was like Julian's telescope, the one he had in his back garden. They couldn't see much, because of the light pollution from London. But once, on a freezing winter evening, Ace had peered down the viewfinder, and saw the disc of Saturn, surrounded by its rings.

It was a great moment. A world in space. A different planet that was part of real life, that you could see from Perivale.

Julian had danced her round the garden, telling her that they'd both go into space one day.

She'd made it, at least. And Julian was almost with her, in that terrrible afterlife . . . She pulled her head back from the telescope. 'Doctor, what about Julian? Is he part of –'

'Part of the Hoothi group mind. Absorbed by one of their spores. Individual filaments get everywhere, all through space and time. It's how the Hoothi collect intelligence. Even from dead brains. He can only be free, Ace, if I can destroy them. Or . . . No, before I tell you that, look down the telescope.'

Frowning, Ace did so. If Saturn had been everything good, everything transcendent about earthly life, what Ace saw now was everything that had ever hurt her.

In the deep blue was death, a tiny shining point of death. One star shone above it, and one below and to the left. The thing showed a disc. Even from here, Ace could feel the ache of it, the final conclusion it spoke of.

You lived, and then you died.

And if you were really unlucky, then you belonged to the Hoothi.

The Doctor opened a page of *The Papers Of Felsecar*. On it was a drawing, of exactly the view Ace saw through the telescope.

'Is that it?' the Doctor asked.

Ace nodded.

'That's the view that our astronomer associated with the ceremony called the Resurrection Dance . . .' The Doctor tapped the telescope. 'This uses lenses that are part of superstrings that lead into hyperspace. She designed it to see through all their stealth procedures. Do you feel bad looking at the sphere?'

'Yes.'

'That's the power of the Hoothi. All their psychic defences. If you were infected with their spores, you'd be a mass of fungus now.'

Ace shivered. 'So what were you going to tell me, about

freeing Julian?'

'Spacefleet will be here in three days, not a week. I'm hoping they'll wait that long. Traditionally, the Hoothi run away from bigger forces.'

'So, you think –'

'There are infected people in the Traveller camp, yes. They are the eyes and ears of the Hoothi. I didn't want to say that, because the ones everybody knows about won't be the only ones, and I don't want to see them become victims of the other Travellers.'

'They wouldn't do that.'

'Wouldn't they? They're human, aren't they?'

'But why don't the Hoothi just change them into fungus things now, and attack you?'

'Not enough of them. The Travellers reacted well to the spore scattering, and Christopher, yes, I do know about him, Christopher absorbed many himself.' The Doctor took out his notebook and frowned at it.

Ace raised a finger. 'Hey, did you know I wasn't infected?'

'I do now.' He glanced up at Ace's astonished face. 'Joke,' he said.

'Three . . . days.' The fungoid mass in the cellar was twitching again, flicking its tendrils past Phaedrus's face. 'We have a . . . shorter time than we . . . expected.'

'Is that important, Piers?'

There was a moment of silence from the fungus. 'We are not Piers. We are . . . the Hoothi.'

'Yes, yes of course, Haven't the spores infested enough people?'

'Amongst the . . . living. But we have . . . other interests. There may be . . . not enough time. It is important that . . . this form . . . remains intact. Bring me . . . more blood.'

'Your will be done.' Phaedrus nodded quickly and retreated.

Roisa gently ran a finger along Máire's lips. 'Don't ask me about it,' she said. 'It's one of those things.'

'One of those death things!' Máire exclaimed, grabbing the finger. 'Blessed be, Roisa, I love you! You can't expect me to stand there and let you die!'

Roisa lay down and closed her eyes. She'd been playing off-handedly with an open jar of salve while Máire had shouted at her for five minutes. 'Do you remember the moment I first saw you? You were backpacking from Ratty's ship, lugging a tent on your own through the Forest of Arden.'

'Yes.' Máire lay down beside her. 'I'd heard that you'd established a camp on Heaven. That was before they cut the white horse.'

'Right. And you'd got stuck in some farmer's trap, blood all over the place.'

'Without you I'd have died. Isn't that one reason why you –'

'No, listen. There isn't much time. I was so in love with Jan when I met you, so sure that we were always going to be together, that my first love would be my last. The moment I saw you, Máire Mab Finn, I knew that wasn't true. You were curled up, and you had your foot half off, but you weren't looking to die. You were watching a pair of owls on a branch.'

'I thought they were bloody going to eat me, you romantic idiot!' Máire laughed, and pulled one of Roisa's short locks.

'But you were smiling! And right here I knew, you see, that love isn't made of Jan or of anybody else. It'd be there if people weren't. If you died there in the forest, and I'd found your corpse, then those owls would have loved you. Loved you and eaten you, but then your love would support everything in the green. You'd become food, and a home, and a warm place to hide. The Goddess would welcome you right back inside her, and sometime in the future you'd be back, your soul in someone else.'

'I want to love you as you are, not when we're other people. I don't want to lose you.'

'Ah, lass.' Roisa pulled the laces from her boot and slipped off her sock. 'You already have.'

In the centre of Roisa's sole was a thin white mark. Beneath the skin, Máire bit her lip to see a spore, pulsing in a thin stream of blood.

'You've got to tell the Doctor.' Máire steadied herself on her lover's shoulders. 'He can help –'

'I asked him. There's no cure. And besides, Máire, I'm...

I'm losing control of my limbs. I might kill you. I've already done something . . . something terrible.'

'What?' Máire ran a hand down her face, fighting the desperation that was screaming inside her. 'Oh my love, what have you done?'

Roisa swallowed, and put a hand to her foot. 'I can't tell you. I was weak. I can hear them in my head, Máire. Don't you think sucking your own gun's a good way to go?'

'No. A Traveller doesn't give in to the system by killing herself. A Traveller dies with her eyes open.' Máire's voice dwindled to a whisper. 'What am I going to do?'

'You're going to do three things, my old love.' Roisa pulled her boot back on and laced it up. 'You're going to look after Jan, and marry him to Ace when you've retaken the Great Wheel. You're going to never forget me, or the love we had in the summer before this terrible autumn . . .'

'How could I? If you're going to go off and die somewhere, let me be with you when you go . . .'

'No. I can't do that, because of the third thing that you're going to do.'

'What's th – ' Máire shivered, and put a hand to her lips. Then she fell to one elbow, struggling to stay upright. Finally, she rolled on to her back with a terrible whimper. Her breathing became deep and steady.

Roisa kissed Máire's forehead tenderly, wiping her own finger with a cloth. 'Sleep,' she said.

Roisa gathered together a number of provisions, and wrapped them in a saddlebag. All the while she was singing an old Traveller saga, one of the Seven Tales. It took all her thoughts to remember it, all her mind to consider it.

As she left the tent, she took one look back, and watched Roisa smile as she fell into some blissful dream.

Roisa hoped the song would last her until Joycetown.

Benny and Ace were walking through the camp. The Doctor had showed all of the Travellers the image in *The Papers Of Felsecar*, and Jan had asked some informed question about orbital positioning and adjustment. Then he had told Ace that it was his turn to gather firewood, and that there would surely be a ceremony of thanks tonight, so he'd better get a lot of it.

The Doctor had dashed off to call Operative Miller on the radio.

'What's he like to travel with?' Benny asked. 'The Doctor, I mean.'

'Oh, it varies a bit.' Ace sighed. 'Sometimes he's way cool, really sweet. And sometimes he's angry and ... big. Like he's really important on the cosmic scene.'

'Have you ever heard of somebody called Dodo?'

'Only as in "dead as a". What's up?'

'The Doctor mentioned her. He seemed a bit confused.'

'Yeah, well, sometimes he is a few pages short of a full script.'

'Are you staying here, then? Setting up a pub with Jan?'

Ace took a deep breath. 'No. No, I want him to come with us in the TARDIS. We'll have to get a double room sorted out. Don't tell anybody, I dunno if Jan's made up his mind yet.'

'Well, I won't, but what about Roisa? You said that you were just staying for the weekend.'

'Well ...' Ace grinned. 'Nothing ever goes the way you plan, does it?'

Jan had assembled a pile of thick logs in a wooded glade, and was swinging an axe at them angrily.

He'd go with her. Leave all of them behind. Of course he would, desert everybody when death was about to descend, when horrible things walked the fields of Heaven.

He glanced up at the thought, suddenly uneasy with his isolation.

A figure in black was watching him from the edge of the forest.

'Christopher?' Jan asked.

But the figure was gone.

Jan dived into the trees after it, swinging the axe before him to clear the way of undergrowth. Animals and birds scattered out of his way. A glimpse of black sped before him, visible through a tangle of twigs and low branches.

He didn't think where the trail was leading him, only that mystery was running away from him, right on the edge of vision.

The shiny cloak flickered through the trees, and Jan crashed after it, saw it standing still on the other side of a bracken hedge, dived at it, calling . . .

And fell.

The scrap of black cloth ripped aside as Jan hurtled down the chalky slope, small pebbles skittering down the low incline with him.

He rolled, shoulder over shoulder, down into a low valley, and thumped to a halt on the grass at the bottom.

Groaning, he looked up. Lynn's Croft. Where Traveller Lynn, sister of Ursus, had fought her own father with a long staff and won, a decade back. The low red sun shone along its high banks, reflecting off the scattered chalk.

'Why have you brought me here, Trickster?' Jan growled, glancing back up at the wooded bank. The narrow track was a little-used causeway across the downlands, an awkward road to Joycetown.

The sound of oncoming hoofbeats was echoing through the valley. Jan watched as the shape of a horse and rider appeared around the end of the track and headed towards him.

While the shape was still far away, he recognized Roisa's style of horsewomanship. He stood up, and let the axe drop to his side.

The rider drew closer, and Jan knew that this was to be a test.

The look on Roisa's face as she approached was ashen. Then it became horrified. Her hand snatched for a pistol from the saddle holster, and she found her lips were sealed tightly together.

She was aiming at the man she loved. And he was just standing there.

Jan watched Roisa bring the gun to bear. One shot off horseback. He'd seen her do it, bring down straw targets in flames.

He waited until she was a hundred yeards away. Until their eyes met.

In that glance, there was everything love could ever teach you. Love taught you to open your arms and fall like a baby, like a straw target, fall and see if anybody caught you.

Jan looked at his old love's expression, and he closed his eyes.

Roisa screamed against her teeth and, with a mighty effort,

jerked her aim aside.

The blast shot past Jan's shoulder, missing his head by an inch.

He raised his arm and swung the axe, its weight carrying it where it would go, his eyes still closed against the roar of hooves.

There was a concussion, the axe thudded into the ground, and the horse galloped on by.

When Jan opened his eyes, Roisa's arm lay in the grass before him.

Her hand still grasped the pistol tightly. The hand had rings on its fingers. The fabric of her coat, the coat that he'd gently put over her, was frayed at the shoulder.

From the white of the shoulder bone, a thousand tiny filaments caressed the air.

Jan turned away, and took two shaking steps after the horse, trailing the axe behind him. Roisa had already vanished into the misty distance.

A tiny sound rose in his throat, a little noise that spoke of summers past and gentle, ordinary, words exchanged.

The sound became a roar, and Jan ran back to the arm.

He hacked at it with the axe, scattered it into pieces, kicked the pieces about the chalky grass, howling at it to stop looking like what it was.

After a while, it did.

Jan fell to his knees, panting, and felt something inside himself about to break.

A hand applied a gentle pressure to his shoulder, and he looked up.

'This is not the last time you will see me,' Christopher said. 'But it is the last but one. Do you know what you must do?'

'Oh yes.' Jan reached out and took up the axe again. 'I know.'

The Doctor put down the radio receiver, and stared at the fabric of Benny's tent.

Ace poked her head through the flap, agitated. 'Doctor, you'd better come out here, Jan's just got back to the camp, and –'

'I know.' The Doctor looked up at her with insane eyes. 'Operative Miller says that the launch codes of every ground-based weapon he's got have been scrambled. Either by hand or through the Puterspace net. I gave him the coordinates of the Hoothi sphere. He said he'll pass them on to the fleet. Too late.'

'He could go and raid the Vacuum Church, or if he's not allowed to, we can.'

'The Hoothi would just activate all their spores. Thousands of people would die now, instead of later. Then the Hoothi would wait for ... whatever they're waiting for. The sacrifice of the Heavenites was all in vain. There's nothing left to do. No other move to make.' He reached out a hand to touch the fabric, a kind of surprise in his voice. 'I've lost.'

Ace stared at him, wanting to grab the Time Lord by the shoulders and shake him instead. 'Don't be stupid. Jan's talking about taking a ship from the Irvingport docks.'

'Is he? Useless. He shouldn't do it.'

'I know! I've been trying to tell him that, but he won't listen to me, so why don't you –'

'Because I choose not to.' The Doctor looked around, as if looking for a solution. Then, he seemed to make a decision. He unfolded a portable chess set from his pocket. The game was already in progress. The Doctor quickly made a move, and then reversed the board, playing against himself.

Ace clenched her fists, hating him. 'So what're you going to do when the Hoothi get here?'

The Doctor appeared to consider the question. 'Leave,' he said.

Jan was swiftly packing a bag, pulling his sword from the block of wood and sliding it into a scabbard.

Ace stood watching him, her hand raised in a gesture of pacification. Damn the Doctor.She didn't know what to say. It'd have to be one thing, right? A good thing. Jan was like her. If you went on and on, pushed it, then he'd just get fed up and go anyway. But if you had a good reason, a real good reason ...

She couldn't think of one. She lowered her hand. 'Don't go.'

'I have to. Who else is going to do it?'

'The Doctor –'

'The Doctor's sitting there doing nothing. I can do something with a little ship. The military trained me to fly them. We know where the bastards are, now. And besides –'

He went to the tent flap, closed it, and opened his bag, showing Ace what was inside.

The Heavenite telescope. 'You told me what this can do, right?'

Ace shook her head. This was making far too much sense. 'Look, if there was any point in doing it, the Doctor would have thought of it.'

'Would he, now? He called Miller, he played his game as far as it went, and then he was surprised. Listen . . .' Jan walked up to Ace and took her shoulders in his strong hands. 'I've had to see a woman I loved, my best friend too, taken by this stuff. I can't just watch. I have to do something. If you love me, you'll understand that.'

'I do love you. But everybody's dying, and I don't want you to die too, right? At least . . . ask the Doctor, see what he says.' She knew it was crap as she said it, but who else had ever saved everybody? Maybe he was playing another waiting game, like with Fenric, maybe he couldn't tell her –

Jan slapped his forehead. 'By God! You can't face the idea, can you? He's lost it, he's got nothing left to frigging contribute!'

Ace bit her lip. 'What are you going to do?'

'Can't tell you, all that lot in the camp might be listening for the Hoothi. But there's a plan, a good one. I've asked Cathlan to come with me, Fiona and Patrick. The four of us can fly an orbiter.'

'And me. I told you –'

'Hush.' Jan put a finger to Ace's lips.

She opened them again in an expression of rage.

But the rage became peace, and Ace fell, asleep, onto the rug.

Jan pulled their sleeping furs over her. 'Me and Roisa, my love, we know the same tricks. I'll be back before you're awake, and then none of us will have anything to fear.'

And he left the tent.

A few moments later, a figure entered. It squatted above the sleeping form of Ace and dropped a few drips from a bottle on to her lips.

'The same trick . . .' Máire muttered, feeling Ace's pulse.

'Now we'll have to save both of the idiots!'

A bell rang out from the tower of the Vacuum Church building. Dusk was falling over Joycetown, and the tower was dark against the setting sun.

Roisa hid in an alcove, holding the stump of her arm.

No pain. That was so strange. She could feel the phantom presence of her arm, the nerves still fired. She could see filaments sticking out from the stump, filaments that staunched and controlled blood loss, applied anaesthetic.

So they nearly had her. She was still free to think though, and she still repeated her old song. Maybe she'd given away her plan, maybe they'd heard about –

No. Jan, think about –

No. Certainly not that. Not him.

Roisa forced herself back to remembering a chorus. She touched the two packs of chemicals that she'd strapped to her chest, and felt the fuse that ran between them.

Well, at least it wasn't going to hurt.

She watched as a procession of black-robed acolytes trod, heads down, into the church.

Roisa pulled her black silk robe tight about her waist, and pulled one of her own black wool shawls over her head. The very nature of the cult meant that no huge expenditure was made on robes, so her look wasn't that out of place.

She joined the end of the procession, keeping her head down. They walked slowly through the gateway. A large acolyte, rifle slung over his shoulder, watched them enter.

In a courtyard, each acolyte took a sip of water from a fountain as they passed. Roisa did likewise.

They passed inside the building, the man in front of Roisa turning to bolt the woden door behind them. She quickened her step, as if she'd got mixed up at the fountain, and he allowed her time to pass.

The acolytes dispersed to their cells amongst the corridors and stairwells of the Temple. A door closed in her face, and Roisa was alone, standing at the heart of the building.

Perhaps she should pull the fuse now. It would bring the place down, do enough damage.

No. If she was strong enough to blank the plan from them, to move against their will despite the infestation . . . then she was able to make sure.

It took an hour of searching, peering behind different doors, hiding in corners. The Temple wasn't exactly a secure installation, it had never needed to be, with such industrial and political support.

Perhaps they'd been in league with the Hoothi for a long time.

Phaedrus's office was indicated by his name, burnt on to the door. Roisa took a deep breath and walked straight in.

Phaedrus was sitting at a desk, a quill in his hand. He looked up as Roisa stepped into the room.

'This is for Christopher and my own sins!' Roisa whispered.

She reached for the fuse.

And her hand stopped an inch from the cord.

Phaedrus stood up. 'We were expecting you, I'm afraid. It's good that you've come to us. Now, there's someone living downstairs that I'd like you to meet.'

He touched Roisa's shoulder as he walked past her and, without wanting to, she followed him out of the door.

Roisa could barely feel the tears on her cheeks.

12:
Three Manuscripts

The Doctor turned the board again and sighed. 'Probably stalemate.'

Benny popped her head into her tent and frowned at him. 'Make yourself at home. Don't hesitate to use my favourite chair. If the urge strikes you, riffle through my belongings and discover my innermost secrets and appliances.'

'Sorry. Nothing to be done. Needed to wait.'

Benny sat down on her bedding roll. 'I've heard awful things from the Travellers. How you've given up completely, and wouldn't help Jan when he left to take on the Hoothi. Is this true?'

'What do you think?'

'I think you're in serious trouble. Move your right arm.'

The Doctor did so.

Benny pulled a thick volume from the stuffed bookshelf behind the Doctor. Resting it on her lap, she found a place with her finger and began to read. 'August the fourth. This is my diary, by the way . . . '

'Is this relevant?'

'Oh yes, very. This is from a year when I had a tremendous crush on a young research assistant. "Dear Diary, I hate myself. And I'm afraid that means I hate you too. Those who read this will just have to get used to a deterioration in our relationship" '

The Doctor was smiling. 'Do you often stage readings?'

'Yes, and I annotate all over the place, and sometimes I go back and stick notes over the bits I don't like. I don't want to erase them, so you can peel off the note, but I want to offer a . . . a new version, I suppose. This is one of those pieces. Here's where we get on to the note. This is the new version.' Benny peeled off a scrap of pink paper and read it out. 'I took Ian out dancing, to the Elderstrasse Ballroom, and it was great.

He told me that I was like a sister to him, which was very flattering.' She sighed, and crumpled the note up. 'History is written by the winning side. That's why nobody in this century has ever heard of Exeter City.'

'Ah . . . ' The Doctor looked puzzled once more.

'This, however, is what really happened. I took Ian dancing, had a few too many glasses of wine, told him that I loved him and got really hurt when he told me he thought of me as a sister.I ran out down the steps and ruined a perfectly good dress in the fall. A Styhian begger helped me out of the gutter. I told him that we were both looking at the stars, and gave him most of my cash.' Benny thumped the book closed. 'So what do you think?'

'The real version's better.'

'True. The new version . . . the game . . . is just there for a while, until I can face the real version.'

The Doctor narrowed his eyes. 'I see.'

Bernice glanced at the chessboard. 'Are you winning?'

'No.'

'Do you play chess often?'

'I've had a few games. Against some good opponents.'

'But only you can beat yourself?'

'Yes.'

Benny concentrated on the board for a moment. 'Which side do you want me to be?'

The Doctor looked up at her, and their eyes met. Benny winked, quickly.

'White,' the Doctor told her.

They played in silence. The Doctor was hard pressed by Benny's chaotic style of play. Sometimes it was childish, taking pieces thoughtlessly. Sometimes it was very thoughtful indeed.

'You're very lonely, aren't you?' Benny said after a while.

'No. Well . . . sometimes. I've lived a long time. Twice. It's hard to explain. Sometimes I get too close to a human. Sometimes we both get hurt.'

Benny took a pawn. 'How do you feel about Ace?'

The Doctor frowned, as if confused. 'I left her on Earth, with her boyfriend. I only saw her once more. She's living out her incarnation, waiting for him to die. Then she'll call for me.

Yes . . . she'll call. And I'll find her again.'

'Who are you talking about?'

'Susan. My grand-daughter.'

'I was talking about Ace. Do you know who that is?'

'Yes. Yes, I do. Bernice . . . Benny . . . I've never lost a game. And I think you're going to beat me.'

'Better than you beating yourself. Have you got loads of options left here, are you waiting for something to come along?' She waved at the board vaguely.

'No. But I still might win. You never know.' A slow smile spread across his face. 'There's something I'd like to do, if you're willing . . . '

'Hmm, now where have I heard that before?'

'It's something I don't usually ask of my companions, because I like to respect their privacy, but you've shown me so much of your life already. If you don't like it, tell me to stop.'

He reached out slowly and touched Benny in the centre of her forehead, with one finger. Benny smiled, enchanted, as she felt a gentle gaze flicker over her memories. She felt the Doctor shy away from embarrassing topics, and comment gently on the pain of her life. Finally, he took the finger away, and the process ended.

'Did you mind?' he asked, shyly.

'Not at all, but then I'm an exhibitionist. Why did you want to do that?'

'Because I'm alone. Or soon will be. Because I wanted to know you.'

'There are other ways.'

'Not for me.'

'No.' Benny pursed her lips. 'And that wouldn't have anything to do with wanting to know if I'd been grabbed by the Hoothi, would it?'

'No.'

Benny slowly nodded. 'You know, there was something else I was wondering. You never told me about the translation you made of the Heavenite script on the walls. I'd like to hear what our astronomer had to say for herself.'

'It isn't important. Not part of the game.'

'But the game version isn't the important one, is it? Go on, we've got a while until the end of the world ...'

'Plenty of time for the game.'

'And the story. Fancy some tea?' Benny jumped up and pulled a teapot from a straw-lined box. 'Tea is too small a word for what I have in this box. A better one would be detergent. You can read while I brew up.'

The Doctor took his notebook from his pocket and peered at it myopically, manouevering it at different lengths from his nose. Finally, as Benny placed a kettle on top of a trivet, he began.

'*My name is ... Alish'k'gresnal.* That doesn't seem to mean anything, I think it's a matrionymic ... '

'Go on, go on, never mind the footnotes.'

'*I have been ... offending, sinning, badly against the gods. I built my Observatory, with several bunches,* ah ... bales of help? *Bales of help from the clans of my three husbands. All the older folk forbade me, saying that their forebears had no observatory, so why did we have need of one? I said that since we had been given telescopes and measuring equipment by the gods, we should use them to discover our world ...* '

'Respect is due, as Ace would say.' Benny poured the kettle out into the pot, and switched off her bunsen burner.

'*I began to discover that the stars are many ... valleys away. I could not find the gods, they were not visible.*'

'Rather like old Galileo, eh?' Benny poured the Doctor a cup, her flippant tone concealing a pained frown.

'*When they are visible, it will be time for the Resurrection Dance, as the old folk are saying it will be soon. And then the dead will rise from the ground, and half the living shall go with the gods, and we will be told again how to remake this world.*'

'Remake?'

The Doctor nodded, and continued to read. '*My third brother's grandmother remembered a mountain that we have done away with. It was taken away in baskets, over many years. Many old folk remember the hibernation times, but now there are no hibernation times, and the old folk are getting frightened of the scratchings some of us feel in our fur and the white worms that move upon the ground.*'

'My God.' Benny warmed her hands on her mug.

'I say . . . ah . . . the worms can mate in a cold place.'
'Hah!'
'I have read some . . . accounts of the Resurrection Dance, and I cannot believe what the priestesses tell us, that going with the gods is good. I will not go with them, and I leave this message for you, because tonight the gods are in the sky. The arch will mark this place, even if the ground is remade. The door is locked, and I will shackle myself, and swallow the note, so I will not destroy all the message, even if I escape. I have an itch in my fur. You must prepare, take arms and beware. Remember me . . . in love.' The Doctor closed his notebook.

'We do remember you,' Benny whispered, pouring a drop from a hip flask into her tea. 'We do. You were a great scientist, Alish'k'gresnal.'

'She was. But that's the story. The Hoothi kept the Heavenites as a slave race, culled them every few years, gave them technology to turn their planet into a garden, to make it seem ideal. Not to their own eyes, but for newcomers they would never see. The Resurrection Dance that year was the last one. Every one of the Heavenites was infested and taken away, even the dead.'

'Totally recycled. So even Heaven is just a place where you work for the company and die in debt.' Bernice sighed. 'God, what for?'

'For a strategy. A move in a . . . game.' The Doctor spat the words out. 'I shouldn't have read it. No point. No meaning.'

'No meaning?' Benny exploded. She would have commented further on the Doctor's insensitivity, except that into the tent walked Alec. He hadn't made any signal of his approach. 'Oh, liberty hall, be my guest!' Benny threw back the last drop of tea and, after a moment's thought, threw the cup into the corner. Instead of breaking, it wedged in the mud by the tent peg.

'Alec,' the Doctor began, urgently. 'Do you remember what I said to you about the telescope, and what to do when –'

'The telescope's not there any more. I had to deliver this . . . ' Alec handed the Doctor an envelope. 'Exactly two hours after she'd gone.'

'After who'd gone?' the Doctor asked urgently.

'Ace,' Alec told him. 'I hope that they win. Because you're

not doing anything to help us.'

And he left again.

The Doctor clutched at the envelope. 'No!' he whispered. 'He'd knock her out, prevent her going! I know he would! She can't go with him, he wouldn't let her!'

'Open the letter.' Benny gently helped the Doctor's trembling fingers rip open the envelope. Over his shoulder, she read:

Heaven
The Milky Way

Dear Professor

You're really not going to like this, but I did it anyway. Máire woke me up, because Jan put me to sleep. He's off to steal a spaceship, and he's got a plan, which he won't tell anybody. (Told you you were alike!) I want to go with him, because I love him, and because I'm a better fighter than him, and 'cos I thought that maybe this time you really can't do anything? (Really can't? I hope you know what I mean about not looking down telescopes, etc, right?) I thought maybe this was what you wanted me to do, only you couldn't tell me. We're gonna catch up with him.

Anyway, it's all rubbish in the end, right? Life's hard and then you regenerate. See you afterwards. Oh, burn this, eh?

Love you (take Benny with you if we get zapped!)

The note was signed with a stylized 'Ace', big and bold, and a single kiss.

The Doctor let it fall from his hand.

'Did you really think she wouldn't go?' Benny asked.

'I didn't think she'd be able to.' The Doctor stood up, and peered down at his chessboard with a kind of loathing.

Suddenly, with a snarl, he kicked the board over. Pieces flew in all directions.

Benny stared as the Doctor jammed his hat back on to his head and grabbed his umbrella.

'I'm tired of this game,' he yelled. 'Time for the real version. Time to start writing this book.'

And he strode out of the tent. Benny quickly looked around,

nervous. If she knew this man at all, if what she'd seen of him was true . . .

She wasn't going to run after him.

The Doctor popped his head back inside the tent.

'Well?' he asked, his eyes full of the impending storm. 'Aren't you coming with me?'

13:
Something Terrible

The two horses carrying Máire and Ace had intercepted those of Jan, Cathlan, and the two Travellers Patrick and Fiona. They'd scrambled down a hillside, having driven their mounts across the downlands rather than along the roads, and nearly collided with the four galloping riders. Both horses were tired, white at the mouth. They neighed and bucked around their four fellows in the twilight.

'What are you doing here?' Jan shouted, angily.

'Not being bloody left behind!' Ace brought her mount up beside his, and smacked him lightly across the shoulder. 'Now we're here, you're not going to find some other reason to stop us coming, are you?'

'You're both uninfected?' Jan glanced at Máire. 'We've all checked each other out here . . . '

Ace raised an eyebrow at Fiona, a tall Traveller woman with a huge mane of dark hair. 'That must have been fun.'

'Ah, leave off,' Jan grinned. 'She's with Cathlan.'

'So when's that ever stopped you, you man?'

Máire was looking serious. 'I think I'm uninfected. I don't know how we could be sure. Why did you leave me sleeping, Jan?'

'Because the tribe's already lost a priest.'

'So what? We're going to come back, aren't we?'

'Well now, that's the plan . . .' Jan scratched the back of his neck.

'Roisa drugged me, she's gone to the Vacuum Church.'

'I know. We had an encounter. We'll save her quickest this way. Kill the problem at its source.'

'So, what is the plan?' Ace asked. 'You can tell us now.'

'I could.' Jan grinned. 'But I like to illustrate my explanations.'

'You are like him, aren't you?' Ace spurred her horse onwards again, and they headed for Irvingport, racing.

Irvingport was quite a bit different to Joycetown. Ace gazed around the gothic buildings, dark and mournful overlooking the sea. The town was set in a natural harbour, a Heavenite monument set on each spar of the two shale beaches that led out to form the bay.

The six riders cantered down the long spiral path into the town, dazzled by the moonlight across the ocean. The brown brick of the buildings was washed in silver, and Ace felt a sudden pang.

She hoped she was right, that this was what the Doctor had wanted her to do. His options might have run out big time.

They slowed their horses to a trot, and headed through the town's streets, passing a steady parade of Draconians, carrying their belongings, part of the southward winter migration to the warmer Draconian areas at the equator. They were all headed to the same destination. Beside the imposing edifice of the town hall stood a Heavenite dome, and a queue of various humans and Draconians was steadily moving towards it. Ace noted that there was no similar train of people coming out.

'What is it?'

'Transmat.' Patrick directed his horse towards a larger entrance in the side of the dome, where a Draconian merchant was carefully watching as several cases full of rugs were moved inside the building. 'The quick way to the equator.' His middle-aged, cold-scarred face cracked into a smile.

'But it'll cost a fortune!' Máire exclaimed. 'How were you going to pay?'

'Sell the horses,' Jan shrugged.

'To a bunch of Draconians heading home, ones who've already exchanged all their own horses? Brilliant, that is, Jan.' She sighed and dismounted, handing the reins of her horse to Ace. 'Don't let him sell it,' she told her.

When Máire came back, she was carrying a small bag of decacredits.

'What did you sell, then?' asked Jan , embarrassed. 'We could have found a buyer for the horse you know, I've been asking, and –'

'I took in two of my Dalek eyestalks for the bounty,' Máire sighed. 'That's enough for us and the horses. So we'd better get this right, eh?'

Ace put a hand on her shoulder. 'That was great. Thanks.'

'Well, this is personal, isn't it?' Máire quickly looked away.

'For all of us,' Jan agreed. 'Let's get on with it, eh?'

They led the horses into the silver dome, an official exchanging cash for receipts or wiping credit chips. He looked up at the Travellers as if he expected to be robbed, and Ace suddenly realized that she looked a bit like them now, with the bright braids that Jan had plaited into her hair, and the black stars that had been sewn into her jacket.

The bulk transmat booth was a large white room, shining with a dull electricity. One moment they were standing there, soothing their animals.

And then they were in another white room, identical but for the Draconian flag on the wall.

Ace had expected to feel the transmission, like she'd felt the time-storm all those years ago. She wondered about being atomized, broadcast, reassembled. Was something lost along the way?

The heat was glorious, a warm breeze billowing soft linen curtains at the booth exit. Jan and Cathlan pulled them aside to reveal a brilliantly sunlight market town, Uptakash, as Fiona informed them, named after a Draconian poet. It was teeming with life. Reptilian steeds and riders made their way through sunbleached paved streets and traders singing high-pitched songs in advertisement of their wares. Amongst them were a number of humans, wearing white clothes and large hats.

The Travellers began to pull off their heavy coats and woollens. A Draconian official checked their receipt and courteously told them that they had freedom to trade and to barter. He also gave them a printed slip of paper.

It was a rough drawing of one of the spores, with a Draconian warning below in startling blue. Ace and Jan exchanged glances.

'Do you think we should tell them?' Ace asked.

'No, let's just solve their problem.' Jan remounted his horse, and, carefully parting the crowds, led the riders towards the spaceport.

'Why are all the spaceports on the equator?' Ace asked.

'Better launch conditions, larger windows of opportunity . . . ' Jan had been looking at her as they rode together down the dry mud road that led the four miles out of town to the spaceport. 'I love you. Why did you come?'

'Because I love you, and all. We do things together, right?'

'Right. I'll never try to ease you out again.'

'Or knock me out?'

'Don't know about that.' They kissed, leaning from their horses. Máire overtook them, her mount at a trot. 'Come on,' she insisted. 'We may not have much time.'

'When we get home,' Ace whispered, as they urged the animals on, 'we'll have time.'

The blunt shapes of launch tubes threw long shadows over the carefully mown grass of the spaceport. It wasn't a big place, just five launchers and support facilities. A high perimeter fence ran around the boundary, limiting access to the booking and departure hall, a low Heavenite building with a pyramidal roof. Heat haze wobbled over the grass, giving the whole lazy complex the look of a mirage.

'Not a lot happening,' Ace decided. 'How do we get in?'

'Like this.' Jan produced a wire and two clips from his saddle pouch. 'I made this out of two Puterspace terminals.'

They rode along the perimeter fence, looking for an opportunity. Eventually they found it. An ornamented garden had been built behind a cluster of flat-roofs, probably living quarters for spaceport staff. Tall trees provided shade.

The horses were tethered to a post by the road some way off, and the team jogged towards the garden. By a small stream, to the sound of trickling water, Jan connected the wire between two poles of the fence, bypassing the alarms. Then, flames puffing from his fingers, he ran his hands in a circle across the mesh. Finally, he kicked the body-sized circle of fence he'd made on to the grass.

The team hopped through, and sprinted along the perimeter. Ace guessed that security here was probably even more lax than in the cold autumn of the north, but they were taking no chances.

They reached the main launch buildings after ten minutes, and hid in a cargo storage area, watching as technicians wandered the tarmac. No hurry was obvious. From a maintainence schedule, Máire read that only one large vessel was prepared for launch, the Draconian freighter that Bernice had booked a passage on.

'Ah, but that's not what we're after,' Jan scanned the list of craft quickly. 'Here we are, an orbital shuttle, no hyperspace capability.'

'But that's not going to be armed,' Máire told him.

'No, but nothing here is, otherwise Miller would have used it. This is an old Spacefleet trick, it's in the rule book. Trust me.' Jan quickly compared the maintenance schedule to a map of the spaceport. 'Right. Hangar ten.'

The group ran through the walkways of the spaceport in the sunlight. Ace smelt the hot tarmac and was reminded of those days she'd spent hiding from the police between Perivale factories. Good summers, with Midge and Jules and Manisha. Two dead now, one injured. And Jules wasn't even free yet. Well, maybe they'd do something about that.

The hanger was much like the ones that would house aircraft, a low building containing three heat-stained craft. They were stubby, brown and wingless, used to ferry people and goods up to larger ships. Jan pointed to the first one, plucked a tool from the hanger wall, and used it to twist open the airlock controls. The outer door hissed open, and the six adventurers climbed up into the craft.

Jan quickly checked the instrument panel. 'These old birds need a crew of three, but six is no problem. It might even help with the navigation. And since we're not filing a flight plan, we're going to need to keep a bloody close eye on the sensors, see if we're running into anything.'

'Not likely in Heaven's space . . .' Máire murmured, pulling on an acceleration harness. The Travellers had clambered into a seat on the flight deck. Máire showed Ace how to fasten her harness. The door closed.

They taxied out onto the runway, tiny antigrav generators pushing them along. Almost immediately, alarms began to sound across the field. Running Draconian guards gestured at them through the windows, bringing their blasters to bear.

'Preflight checks complete,' Jan shouted. 'Ready?'

Ace was going to say something.

But then her stomach slammed into her boots.

Out of the window, the spaceport had blasted away into buildings, a coastline, a continent, a cloudscape, the blue curve of the planet Heaven.

All of the Travellers had shouted as they went up, an involuntary scream. Ace gulped back the urge to throw up at the top of the arc. For a moment, they were in freefall, and it felt as if they were going to fall . . . back . . .

'Internal antigravs cutting in,' Jan said. And suddenly they were just sitting there, above the planet, with normal gravity.

This, Ace realized, was a lot different to her usual form of space travel. Give her the TARDIS anytime, she thought.

'Right.' Jan flicked a switch on the console and turned around in his seat. The black of space shone through the viewport behind him 'Nobody's coming after us, which isn't surprising. Now, the whole planet's between us and the Hoothi for another hour. We're going to have to move quickly. We're going to jettison everything non-essential in the craft. Tools, fuel pods, and the whole bit. Then we suit up and switch off the life support, the gravity, all the power sources. We come over the horizon as a randomly shaped cluster of objects in a quickly decaying orbit. The Hoothi will think of us as asteroidal material or space junk. They think that right up until the moment when we bail out, the engines activate and the ship rams them at high speed!'

Ace blinked. 'What about all their stealth stuff? Even with the telescope, we're never gonna get the computers to lock on to them in a second, especially if they're gonna do it from just being booted up.'

'Ah, well, we're not going to leave it to the computers. I'm going to line her up visually, using the scope, before I jump into the escape pod.'

Ace looked at him for a moment. Then she nodded. 'Fair

enough.'

'I thought you'd argue.'

'It'll work.'

They spent the next hour preparing the escape pods, and filling the airlock with debris. Jan switched off all the emergency power systems, and the Travellers climbed into the ship's spacesuits.

Ace was watching the horizon, a bright blue curve against the neon dark of space. Then she turned to watch Jan's fingers jumping over the control boards, checking that no secondary power sources were left functioning. She didn't want to say it. This was going to be the worst mistake of her life. For once she didn't want to hang on to something so hard it hurt, but hurt it did. After all this time, she was still hanging on. She moved closer to Jan, while the others were making checks. Close so that they couldn't be overheard.

'Listen, no big deal, but when we get back, d'you want to get married or something?'

Jan didn't stop working. 'Yeah, that'd be right.'

'Oh. Right. Okay then.' Ace started to move away.

'Tell you what . . . ' Jan motioned to Máire to come over, and took the woman's hand. 'Máire, ask Ace whether she'll keep me safe and warm, and hide with me from all pursuit.'

Máire looked between the two of them with amazement. 'Will you keep Jan safe and warm, and hide with him from all pursuit?' she asked quickly.

'I guess so . . . yeah.' Ace frowned.

'And will you, Jan, do the same?'

'Aye, I will and all.'

'Well, you're now betrothed in the sight of the Goddess.' Máire sighed. 'You soft fools!' She went back to her task.

'Does this mean we're engaged?' Ace asked Jan. 'That was always something I said I'd never do.'

'We are. What else did you say you'd never do?'

'Done most of it,' Ace smiled, kissing him.

Having checked their suits, the Travellers depressurized the ship, and switched off the lights and heating sources. Jan powered down the reactor to a level where it might be mistaken for a natural radiation source. Within ten minutes, they were huddled in the individual escape pods, tubular bins that ran down the lower wall of the small flight deck. Máire and Ace lay along one wall, beside Jan's empty capsule; Cathlan, Fiona and Patrick were curled along the other.

In the silence, Ace concentrated on the figure of Jan outlined in the darkness. He was poised awkwardly, one hand over the manoeuvre controls, standing half out of his seat. The Heavenite telescope was wired into the controls, pointing straight at the vision screen. Jan kept taking quick glimpses down it.

'You got the button?' he asked Máire.

'I have.' Máire was clutching the launch toggles for all six capsules. 'Soon as you're ready.'

Ace found that she was holding her breath. She watched as Jan quickly calculated some final course corrections, based on the position that the Doctor had worked out for the sphere.

The globe of Heaven rolled away beneath them. 'One minute until we're in sight,' Jan called.

Ace felt it when it came over the horizon.

It was a vague smudge in the viewport, a dark object against the dark. The sphere was rolling gently in geostationary orbit.

'Computers got it lined up.' Jan whispered. 'Nearly there. Making visual correction . . . '

He reached across to the ignition switch.

Something roared.

Cathlan was a raging mass of tentacles, struggling to get out of the escape pod. Remains of his jacket clung to the creature as it shot out filaments, grabbing bits of the hold to pull itself up.

Fiona was shivering, staring at her hands in amazement. Before the shivers reached a critical pitch, she hit a control, and the window of the pod slammed shut, locking her inside.

A second later, the pod was full of grey matter.

Patrick leapt up, and his head exploded in a puff of fungus. The creature turned to Jan, who was staring at the chaos that was happening all around him.

His finger hovered over the button.

His other hand was scratching his neck.

With an effort, he seemed to steady himself, and looked through the telescope. The creature that had been Patrick stood, and watched him look.

A great gasp came from Jan's lips. 'So that's it!'

He laughed, biting his lip, and looked straight at Ace.

She had been watching the creatures making themselves out of human flesh, like it was a dream.

'Can't push the button,' he said.

'I love you,' she said.

'I love you,' he said.

Something terrible happened.

And then the door slammed shut in front of Ace.

The escape pod blasted out of the ship on explosive bolts, falling away in fire.

Ace fell, staring, down towards the planet Heaven.

14:
Inside The Sphere

The TARDIS ground into existence on top of a huge tower of bones. The skulls, femurs and scapulae of a hundred races were piled atop each other, and moisture was slowly dripping down the sides. The atmosphere was cloudy and fetid, gouts of brown vapour belching across the tower in slow gusts.

Almost as soon as the time-craft had appeared, a translucent balloon raced up the tower and engulfed it. Its reflective surface shrank for a moment, rainbowing as it filtered certain gases in and out of the areas it now contained.

The TARDIS door opened and out stepped the Doctor, opening his umbrella. After a moment, Bernice followed him, her hands jammed into the pockets of her chinos. She glanced up at the murk outside the bubble. 'I suspect that this is the last thing that a doughnut sees . . . ' she muttered.

'Close.' The Doctor was deadly serious. 'The interior of a Hoothi sphere. No living being's been in one of these for centuries.' He poked the bubble with a finger. 'Protoplasm, designed to let us breathe the atmosphere. Filters in the chemicals we need. Filters out of the poison.'

Benny had walked to the edge of the tower. 'Oh, look where we are. On a pile of bones a mile high.'

'Then, let's get off.' The Doctor strolled to the edge of the tower and walked into space. Benny had a moment to stare wide-eyed before the Doctor's weight whipped the bubble off the top of the tower, and her with it.

They floated down gently through the smoggy atmosphere. Benny glimpsed humanoid shapes moving along galleries. She hugged herself, thinking about her Mum's religious beliefs. Before being exterminated, she'd been a good Catholic. This was a bit like the Hell she'd warned her only daughter of. The things you just glimpsed, half saw through the murk . . . they were the worst. There were little gangs of things the size of pixies, and huge, lumbering things with mushroom heads.

'The sphere is the size of a small moon,'the Doctor told her. 'It contains four Hoothi and as many slaves as they've collected. Each sphere has a group consciousness of its own, which is also a part of the greater Hoothi Consciousness.'

Benny was staring down as the bubble approached the floor. Three figures were waiting for them. 'Intelligent fungus. How is that possible?'

'Everything's possible. And some things just happen because we don't want them to. It's said the Hoothi evolved on a world where the climatic changes wiped out all other life in cycles. They grew up with death, and now they're exporting it. Ground floor. Victims, aggressors and chinaware.'

They had stopped, facing three gruesome beings. A Tereleptil with a huge growth of Hoothi fungus for a head, looking like it might overbalance at any moment; a naked human with a recognizable face, a handsome young man; and a small ball of fluff that moved along on the tips of its filaments. Benny glimpsed an uncomfortably organic-looking structure at its centre, a mass of tubes and concealed shapes.

The human stepped forward, tendrils waving from the top of his head. His lips moved experimentally, and, after a moment, words came out of them. He was whispering, but the thick atmosphere carried the sound very clearly. 'Doctor. Welcome to the domain of the Hoothi.'

'Take me to them.'

'Follow us. Do not attempt to puncture the bubble.' The three creatures moved away across the soft floor. It was, Benny realized, a mesh of muscle and bone, like a ribcage. She tried to step softly, but stopped after a while, being glad of the bubble. The base of the tower was surrounded by a honeycomb of grey caverns, seemingly formed out of mineral deposits. The Doctor and Benny followed the Hoothi slaves towards them. The scale of the place was vast, Benny looking up to see only a slight curve in the walls that vanished upwards into the murk. Giant organic bulbs glowed gently with internal light.

'That's for our benefit,' the Doctor muttered. 'They'd normally be working in darkness.'

'Two questions,' Benny murmured. 'Firstly, what's this place made of?'

'Animal remains,' the Doctor spat. 'Hoothi spheres are made from bone, skin, specially engineered slave creatures. They have a chemical reactor at the centre which keeps the necrosystem in order. The whole thing, from the bonded skin of the exterior to the ribbings that support it, is held together by the huge psychic will of the Hoothi.'

'Ta. Secondly, what is that fluffy thing?'

'That used to be a baby.'

Benny stopped walking and closed her eyes. After a moment, the Time Lord came back and put an arm around her shoulder, but she shrugged it off, shaking her head.

The three creatures led the TARDIS crew through the caverns. They passed groups of marching slaves from a mixture of species, about half of which Benny recognized. The beings were repairing walkways, moulding soft plasma with their hands. They moved aside to let the bubble that contained the Doctor and Benny through. The air that filtered into the bubble was becoming fetid as they progressed, full of the warm sweetness of decay.

A soft light was shining at the end of the rocky corridor, a low green glow that reminded Benny somehow of dentistry. They turned a corner, entered a large chamber, and were in the presence of the Hoothi.

Three of them were rooted in a semicircle, grey puffballs the size of trees, their surfaces wrinkled like brains. At their base, amid a tangle of filamentary tentacles, vocal organs were stretched tightly across bone. The fungi sat in a low canal, along which a thick liquid was flowing. Benny bit her lip when she saw that it was blood. They lived in a cathedral of bone, ribs stretching skin high into the fetid air. The apex was invisible in the stinking clouds.

'Welcome, Doctor,' said the humanoid slave, who had taken up a central position between the giant puffballs. 'I am the voice of the Hoothi. We are honoured to entertain a Time Lord.'

'I'm not honoured to be here.' The Doctor glanced around the chamber. 'I've come to bargain.'

'What with? Do you offer us the life of your companion?'

Benny flinched, looking quickly at the Doctor.

He slowly shook his head. 'No.'

'What else have you to bargain with? Our game is already over. We have won.'

Fascinated as she was by the conversation, Benny had been watching the behaviour of the Tereleptil. It had approached the channel of blood, and knelt in front of it. Putting both hands up to its neck, it pierced its own flesh with its claws. Shuffling forward, it collapsed into the channel and lay still. Benny could make out older, vaguer shapes under the flow of liquid.

The humanoid had been watching her reactions. 'We feed continually,' it told her.

'You really are obscene . . . ' Benny whispered.

'You haven't won yet,' the Doctor snapped, getting back to the point. 'Where's the other one of you, anyway? You always travel in fours.'

'The other of us is . . . elsewhere.'

'In waiting somewhere, of course, just in case your plan fails.'

'We leave nothing to chance. You spoke of a bargain. What is your offer?'

'I have only one offer for you. Withdraw your sphere from this place. Run away. I won't pursue you.'

A guttural hiss broke from the orifices of the fungi, their form of laughter. The Doctor stared back, unflinching.

The humanoid made an attempt at a smile. It was a strange expression, an alien memory of what a human smile was like. 'We have been manipulating the life forms and the appearance of this world for centuries, Doctor. We have transformed the planet into a popular Draconian and human vision of paradise. We have changed the chemical balance of its soil so that it better preserves dead matter. Apart from that, we have manipulated the computer systems and traditions of both great powers, making them bring their dead here. The fields of Heaven are thick with meat, Time Lord. Meat we can use. Billions of unstoppable soldiers, enough to conquer Gallifrey by sheer force of numbers. Once we have done that, then all of time will become our warm place of growing. We have planned this for longer than many races have existed. Tell us, why should we be afraid of you?'

'Afraid of me?' The Doctor wandered forward, his hands clasped behind his back. 'No. But you should be afraid of life. Life will always fight you, wherever you find it.' He gestured at the organic hall. 'The material of these walls loathes you, and deep in their lost minds your servants loathe you too. You could have lived on your homeworld, existed on the natural decay around you. Or you could have used your intelligence to change your diet, using minerals or genetically engineered animals. But you wanted conquest, made death into an active force in the universe.' He trailed the tip of his umbrella across the soft surface of one of the puffballs, causing the surrounding bubble to bulge. 'Can you imagine all the varied beauties of life? Jimi Hendrix . . . the first kiss . . . paddling? You stand against all that, against everything that any being in the universe holds dear. You're an abomination, an obscene error.' He strode up to the humanoid and glared at it. 'And I will put an end to you.'

'Will . . . you?' The booming, ragged voice roared out from one of the puffballs. 'You . . . dare . . . to talk to the Hoothi in this . . . manner? Watch!'

One of the skin sections of the wall glowed into murky life. A grainy vision appeared: Jan on horseback, smiling. 'I like to illustrate my explanations,' the soundtrack crackled.

'Your . . . words!'

The screen showed the Doctor frowning at Roisa. 'My thoughts . . . exactly,' his image muttered.

'Your . . . thoughts! All known to the . . . group mind!'

The screen showed Roisa pressing Jan's goblet to the Doctor's lips. The image zoomed in on her finger, softly pressing the indentation in the base of the cup.

The image became an internal scan, a colourful presentation of the Time Lord's internal organs. The two hearts of the Doctor's body were pulsing with life.

A thin white fibre shot down his throat, in a billow of liquid, and spiralled into his stomach, where it attached itself.

Benny put a hand to her mouth in sudden fear.

'We are . . . inside you, Doctor!' the Hoothi roared. 'Whenever we wish it, Time Lord, you are . . . ours!'

15:

Ace Falling

The escape pod whipped around Heaven in descending orbit, little flares of atmosphere skidding off its casing.

It was skipping on the edges of the air, bouncing across the sky. But in the end, there was only one place it could go. It would fall into Heaven's stratosphere and plummet towards the planet.

If its retros fired, it might make a soft landing.

Inside the pod there was something strange.

It was Ace, lying curled, her knees up to her chin. She was quite unharmed.

Something terrible had happened. Her eyes were wide, the darkness of space reflecting in them. The tiny fires from outside flashed across them every now and then, but they didn't react.

Something terrible.

When she was a child, Ace had woken in the night to hear owls, hooting in the distance of Perivale Park. The little girl had listened, scared, for a moment. Then she ran into Audrey's bedroom, hurtling under the covers. That was a dangerous thing to do, because Audrey wasn't always alone. All those bitter excuses and barriers. But that night, the owls had woken Audrey too. She just turned over and cuddled her daughter, and the two of them fell back into sleep.

Audrey was dead now, in this far future. And who was out there who ever cared for Ace? Sabalom . . . no, he never did. The Doctor? Could he care for her? Was it something he was able to do? Or was she just a piece in his games? She didn't want to think about him.

Jan loved her. He really loved her. His lovemaking had been so complete, so concerned, so full of desperate needing. He was the only person who'd ever needed like she needed. Needed love, needed strength, needed someone to say everything was always gonna be okay. That was why he was a warrior too, because sometimes you had to keep kicking.

Something terrible. Ace didn't know what. There was a big piece of her brain that knew something that she didn't want to know.

She'd seen something that she shouldn't have seen, that she didn't want to see, and the sight was running away down deep inside her. This time, she wasn't going to run after it. This time, never mind fighting it, she'd let it go. There were some things that you shouldn't fight, some times when you just had to curl up and say yes to death.

She really believed that, as the fires grew darker around the capsule. Not a muscle in her body moved, except her heart, and she'd have stopped that if she could. Just death, quiet death, up here without any fungus, up here away from people. Stupid people, stupid little clowns, and he'd sucked at her breast like a little child, a little boy they could have had together and it would have been okay, a family in the TARDIS, a family, a family –

People came and talked to her in the capsule. The Trickster was in a clown costume, and he had a completely different face. He told her that Jan was one of his, and it had all been a joke, couldn't she see? Ace cramped and twitched until he went away. Christopher came to her and said that he'd been jealous of the living, that he'd sacrificed himself again, and didn't see why Jan couldn't return that. Ace had punched his face in, hitting it and hitting it and hitting it – a clench of the teeth, a shudder and a gasp that stopped her on the edge of insanity – there was just a skull in the black cloak. Just a silly monster. Just a clown.

In the capsule, as it fell, Mother Mary came to her. Or it was Diana, with her owls on her arm. The Huntress told Ace that she was loved, and that this wasn't the end. There was more life yet to come. A man, no matter how loved, couldn't drag down and end the life of a woman warrior. She'd always whispered in her ear, the goddess told Ace. She'd seen her in the Land Under The Hills. The Trickster was just a stupid little boy and she shouldn't listen to him.

Don't run away, Diana told Ace. You already grabbed the rose once, already took reality instead of fantasy. You're much too important to lose, the steward of Time's Champion.

But Ace didn't want to be somebody's something. She wanted to be Ace. And at the moment, that wasn't possible, 'cos Jan made her Ace now.

And Jan was dead.

So she wanted to be dead too.

And if death wasn't going to come and see her, madness would look after her for a while.

This is all flowery nonsense, an old English teacher told her. You're not talking to gods and things, and madness won't just pop up and take you. You'll bite your own tongue, and run spirals into yourself, and never talk normally with anybody else again. Madness isn't about gods, it's about shivering outside Centre Point with a cardboard box and a begging cup.

Well, Christ, then just death, just let me die. I keep on surfacing for a second, and thinking that I can go on, that everything can be fairly all right. And then I get dragged back under, and everything's such shit. I can see the next wave coming too, I can feel that I'm about to fall, and I'm never gonna reach land again. This is all there's ever gonna be, lots of pain, special pain, pain made for me. This is hell, isn't it, over Heaven?

He was right out on the margins, Jan was. This is an obituary. He didn't want to submit, to the government or to death. So death came out to the provinces and took him by force. He never even got to be a hero, never even got to run at something with his sword.

The flames were building around the capsule now. Smoke was roasting off the hull, and colours were blasting across Ace's eyes, still oblivious.

Another shooting star had bloomed over Heaven.

Ace knew that, way down there below, somebody was watching it go. Maybe they were happy to see it, thought she was pretty. Maybe they knew it was another death they were watching. Maybe the people watching it were already dead, an army of corpses already shuffling towards the towns, ready to grab the living and shove spores into them. Billions of dead beings, the whole ground swelling with death, the air full of white spores.

Maybe she was falling into that. Good. She'd been to Heaven

and hell, without ever having a choice. Straight out of the womb into the grave, and it was only the TARDIS that had mixed it up, shown her everything in between, all in the wrong order. Without time travel, maybe she could just have had a normal life. It wouldn't have been like she'd seen in the Doctor's head that time. She'd have been a chemist, or an actress, or maybe she'd have chucked the whole thing and gone off to travel herself. 'Course she would.

Those thoughts had taken her out of the despair again. Her eyes had begun to notice the beautiful colours that were blazing past the window. Colours born out of gases being ripped apart.

That was where most elements came from. Out of supernovae, out of the death of stars. One day, the whole universe would probably end, and then everybody who was left would die.

Did anything mean anything at all, then?

Clarity let her exhale, finally, and relax the muscles of her mouth. Ace found that she was tasting blood from where she'd been biting her lip.

The first gesture of his that she'd seen. Biting his lip at her beauty.

Ace closed her eyes as the capsule shuddered. She wanted to remember. It was going to be hard, but they'd been up there together, way up there. They'd been great. Like the universe, like everything, it had come to an end. She wanted to know how.

What goes up –

'Must come down!' The Doctor shouted. Ace jumped, 'cos she thought she'd got her dreams under control now. But she'd heard it. She opened her eyes just in time to see a strange cube drop on to her lap.

Remembering how the muscles worked, hating how the mere act of moving reminded her of him, muscles, moving against her, she reached out and took the cube.

It was silver and transparent. It was like . . . a door, or a crystal ball. She could see things in it. What she wanted to see . . . or . . .

She couldn't stop herself thinking of it now.

His finger hovered over the button.

His other hand was scratching his neck.

He was scratching his neck because he'd been infected, a long time ago. A spore had connected itself to his neck jack, the hole that she'd run a finger around and teased.

With an effort, he seemed to steady himself, and looked down the telescope. That's when he realized, and, in a second, accepted it. She had been watching the creatures making themselves out of human flesh, like it was a dream.

'Can't push the button,' he said. He hadn't given them an inch of victory, hadn't let them see any pain at all.

'I love you,' she said.

'I love you,' he said.

And then something terrible happened.

His body, that beautiful human body, had filled with fungus as the spore in his neck blossomed. His face had gone almost instantly, so there hadn't been any final expression. His head had burst into a bundle of grey nodules.

And then the door slammed shut in front of Ace, and the escape pod blasted out of the ship on explosive bolts.

Ace fell, staring, down towards the planet Heaven.

Ace still fell now, clutching the cube tight to her chest. If she started crying, she thought, she'd never stop.

But she could cry, and she would.

And sometime in the future, she'd be able to start living again. There it was, land on the bloody horizon, far away.

The sky outside the viewport had become blue.

The shooting star fired its retros, and changed course suddenly, leaving a jagged trail in the skies of Heaven.

16:

No Escape From Heaven

The Doctor stared at the screen, and his hand moved to his throat. 'What . . . what do you want me to do?'

'You will go back to the planet Heaven, and you will destroy Operative Miller's communications equipment,' the humanoid Hoothi slave said. 'Then we shall change our location.'

'Are you that afraid of the fleet, to use that much energy?'

'We will be gone before the fleet arrives in three days time. But there is no point in taking chances.'

'If I do this, what then?' The Doctor growled.

'Then you will be allowed to take your TARDIS and leave.'

'I don't believe you. You'd let a Time Lord, a way into Gallifrey, out of your grasp?'

The humanoid attempted its ghastly smile once more. 'We do not care if you believe us. If you do not do as we say, we will detonate the spore, and you will die.'

Benny nodded and took the Doctor's arm. 'Sounds fair enough to me. We'll be off, then.' She started to march the Time Lord back the way they had come, but two slaves stepped forward from the darkness and stopped them.

'Wait,' the humanoid raised a hand. 'We must be safe, Doctor. You know we leave nothing to chance.'

'No. You don't.'

The slaves grabbed Benny by the arms and pulled her forward. The Doctor followed the beckoning finger of the humanoid, and stepped up to one of the puffballs.

A spore extended on the end of a filament, squirming. The Doctor took it between his fingers.

'Oh no . . . oh no . . . ' Benny shook her head, trying to fight free of the creatures that held her. 'Doctor, don't do this.'

The Doctor stepped forward, his gaze finding Benny's. His expression was absolutely neutral. 'I'm sorry,' he said. 'I have to.' Then he smiled, and adopted a cynical tone. 'Here's something for your diary!'

And he slapped the hand containing the spore flat into her neck.

Benny expected pain. There wasn't any. She clenched her teeth and didn't shout. 'I understand,' she hissed. 'But you had a choice, you bastard!'

The Doctor didn't reply.

The humanoid nodded. 'Very good. She is ours.'

The slaves released Benny. She looked at the Doctor for a long moment, as if considering attacking him. Finally, she turned to the Hoothi puffballs. 'You might be able to kill me,' she told them, her voice quiet and steady. 'But I'm not yours.'

There was a motion at the entrance of the cathedral. Through the murk, three slaves were approaching their masters. Patrick, Cathlan and Jan, or their remains, marched into the area.

Benny dropped her hands to her side, and closed her eyes. 'Jan,' she said simply, and didn't speak again.

The Doctor bowed slightly to the puffballs. 'Can I take my companion back to Heaven now?' he asked.

'You may,' the humanoid nodded. 'To do our will.'

'As always,' the Doctor whispered.

The night had passed in whispers, rumours going between the houses of Joycetown, being radioed to remote farms. There was something in the fields. Armies that moved during the night, swinging in great swathes away from the gravelands. Small homesteads ceased contact with the towns, and isolated outposts of troopers reported skirmishes with an enemy that came on, tested their strength, and then vanished once more, leaving no casualties.

Miller spent the night awake, watching reports light up a chart of the planet. Spacefleet was calling every hour, using the Priority Link regardless of expense, and every hour he had just as little to tell them.

The Travellers and Benny's students sang together around a fire, taking turns to guard, as none but children could sleep. Something old and musty was in the autumn air, as if a skeleton had been found under leaves. They had hoped for some word from Jan, or news of Bernice, but as the hours passed, they were losing hope.

At one point, Colm Wylie began a funeral song, but Alec shouted the start of the story over it, and everybody made the effort to listen.

Farmers taking guns out to herd in their animals were glad to see dawn touch the fields near Joycetown, but were fearful at the tracks that had formed across their land.

Whole meadows were scarred with broken earth. And in some, the animals had gone.

From the tower of the Vacuum Church, the sunrise over Heaven was a murky orange. Phaedrus raised his arms to the sky, and considered the moment.

It was at hand. The time he had wished for since his mother had died. Now, every one of them would feel it. The world would know what darkness sat inside him.

He began to bellow, to howl at the dawn. The yell became a kind of melody, a high incantation. As the sunshine began to warm his black robes, bouncing off the roofs of the town, he felt the spore of the Hoothi within him resonate to his song.

The signal was being given. The call had gone out.

Across Joycetown, people looked up from what they were doing and wondered. The call echoed down the alleys, rung out across the fields, rang off the ancient architecture of the Heavenites.

Far way, in the Wasteland, something began to struggle beneath the ground. Fingers kneaded soil, probed for the sky like plants. Fists punched upwards, and bony limbs began to smash aside the ground that covered them.

Whole fields were squirming, the grass rolling like waves. The sky began to darken as soil was flung into the air.

In the oceans, the skeletons of dead sea monsters stirred and thrashed, and the water was suddenly full of fish. Trawlers pulled in full nets, only to find the contents hissing and gnashing at them, a thousand fungoid masses.

In the forests, birds flapped away from their dead cousins. Predators tried to wrestle down thin corpses which wrapped around them and embedded spores in their flesh. The humus carpet warped and the trees creaked as the things dead under their roots stirred to new life.

At the military outpost near Joycetown, a returning patrol of corporate troopers were caught by shadows that rose up at them out of the downlands. Blue blaster fire flickered across the grass as the soldiers retreated, running for the comfort of the enclosure. The dead ran after them, choking them in the dawn, jumping on their backs, pulling them down to the ground. Faces impacted dewy grass, limbs were ripped out, and, time after time, spores were slapped into bare skin. The guards at the gate watched, horrified, as the dead animals and humans ripped the patrol apart. Blaster fire cut through them, severed things from them, but it didn't stop them moving.

A trooper at the gate emptied the powerpack of his weapon into one of the dead figures, a skeletal human, as it walked steadily towards the mesh of the enclosure. The bolts seared straight through its head, splattered away an arm, set the vestiges of cloth afire, but still it came on.

Against the rising sun, it raised its arms, and a cluster of spores launched off its skin into the morning breeze. They wafted into the camp, and the soldiers ran for the safety of the buildings.

The dead being stood there, flesh flapping. Behind it at the fence shambled up many more of its companions, and some of the troopers they'd been fighting.

They were waiting for numbers enough to crush the fence.

In his tower, Phaedrus brought his song to a high shout, and collapsed against the wall.

Joy, he felt joy at the coming of all his hopes. Soon, he too would be part of the great oneness of the legions of death. His part was done, his whole mission completed.

For the first time in his adult life, Phaedrus fully relaxed. From his sitting position, he allowed his gaze to drift upwards into the quiet blue of the sky.

Three points of light had just appeared like stars in the direction of the dawn. They were getting brighter.

Phaedrus tried to interpret this sign. Were his masters trying to tell him something? It took him a moment to realize what the objects were.

Escape pods. Blazing down, now leaving visible trails of brown smoke.

As he contemplated them, Phaedrus saw the retros on one of them fire. It made an abrupt turn. Suddenly, the craft was racing straight for the tower of the church.

For a second, Phaedrus contemplated standing there and waiting.

But then his masters made his legs run, and he went along with them, sprinting down the stairwell.

Benny stood in the TARDIS, hugging herself. She was watching the Doctor delicately adjust controls on the console. His left hand manipulated a tiny device of some kind as he concentrated on setting the coordinates with his right.

'Why did you let them –?' she began.

'Hush,' the Doctor murmured in a gentle voice. 'It had to be done. We must submit to the will of the Hoothi, here, hold this.'

And he handed her the pen that had been in his left hand.

'This is a –'

'It's such hard work, controlling the TARDIS . . . ' the Doctor cut in. 'It takes such concentration. Sometimes my right hand doesn't know what my left hand is doing.'

Benny walked around the console and noticed what he'd written on the surface in biro.

YOU'RE FREE. NOT INFECTED. FIND ACE.

'Would you like to pick up your bags at the dig site, since we're both going to flee this world in terror?' the Doctor asked casually.

'Might be for the best. I'll pick up my diary, so I can rewrite the real world a bit more. Will you drop me off?'

'Certainly.'

'Brothers and sisters!' shouted Phaedrus, bursting into the first floor dining room of the Church.

He stopped. They had all become fungoid creatures, every single one of them. They stood in the remnants of their robes, looking at him almost accusingly. Their tendrils vibrated gently.

Phaedrus slapped at a nervous tic in his cheek. Why not him?

What was there left for him to do? 'We . . . we must –'

The pod turned a moment before it hit the tower, a burst of retros slowing it slightly. For a second, the rocket flames licked the stonework of the church. Then the pod hit the building.

The wall exploded.

The concussion sent mortar flying through the room. Stone blocks slammed out of one wall and into another. Phaedrus was blasted off his feet. The fungoids fell and broke, spinning backwards over furniture.

Somewhere from deep below the church, a great scream of rage erupted.

The TARDIS appeared briefly outside the dig, and Benny ran outside, slamming the door after her. The craft screeched away into hyperspace once more, and she looked around aghast.

Colm Wylie was stumbling up the hill towards her, clutching at the air with his hands. 'I tried . . . ' he said.

And then his head burst open into fungus. Benny grabbed for her gun, but before she could fire, a flaming arrow struck Colm in the back of the head. More followed, setting the body aflame.

The burning creature staggered a few feet forward and then collapsed. Benny ran past it, to see the full picture of what was happening at the dig site.

Travellers were hacking monsters with their swords, setting them aflame with torches, backing them into corners with rakes and forks, and blasting them apart with guns once they'd been isolated. The stone circle had become a battlefield, with ragged tents fluttering in the stiff breeze. Alec was leading archers, blue chemical flame flaring at the ends of their arrows. Many Travellers had fallen in the fight, but, to Benny's astonishment, the creatures were actually losing.

She ran into her tent, ripping open the flap.

Clive lay inside the opening, clutching a gun. Beside him were still-squirming pieces of fungoid, hacked apart by the Travellers.

'Friend!' Benny shouted, putting her hands up. 'What happened?'

'An hour after dawn, they all just erupted.' Clive ran a hand across his face. 'But Alec was prepared. He and some of the others had the arrows ready, and a battle plan. He said that the Doctor had shown him how to use the telescope, to check who was . . . '

'Yes, I can imagine.' Benny reached forward, and grabbed a plasma rifle and a machete from her pack. A horrible thought had come to her, but she was trying to supress it. The Hoothi had been manipulating the great powers into sending their dead to this planet for decades. What if, somewhere out there in the dead armies, her father was stumbling along?

Benny slammed back the loader on the rifle. 'Well Dad, at least I'll know,' she muttered.

'What?' Clive asked.

'Busy day, Clive.' Benny opened the tent flap again and went back outside.

Alec was running between individual battles, raining automatic fire down on a pinned monster, or hacking at one with a blade. The things still kept moving and attacking, whatever happened to them, but if they were reduced to tiny particles, then they could do no more harm, at least. And there had been so many of them, many more than he'd expected.

It was mostly over by the time Benny got there. She fired a few frantic shots into a struggling body, and the others crowded round to join in, reducing the thing to fibres in seconds.

'Where did they come from?' Benny asked.

'From us!' Alec spat on the ground. 'These were Mathilda, and Kerwin, and Grey, and the Mighty Lion! All dead! At least now we're sure of who's infected and who isn't . . . '

From overhead there came a sonic boom, and the Travellers fell to the ground. Benny looked up to see an escape capsule blast across the sky, passing overhead with a screech of retros. It sped over a hill and impacted with an explosion in the forest.

'Ace!' Benny jumped to her feet. 'I'm going to find her. You lot stay here.'

Alex nodded quickly. 'We'll retreat into the dig.'

Benny ran off up the hill, shouldering the rifle. She only glanced back to call once more to Alec. 'Expect me when you see me!'

'These days, that's more of a surprise than an expectation,' murmured the man in the gloves.

Benny crept her way through the forest, brandishing the machete before her. Things were moving all around her, the forest was coming alive in grey and white, but it seemed uncordinated, as if the Hoothi spores needed large neural systems to work well with. Small fungoid animals ran past her feet.

The pod had carved a mile-long avenue of collapsed trees behind it, timber thrown aside by the impact. Benny felt a bit safer walking along this earth. The spores and creatures were obvious, and could be steered clear of. She finally reached the pod itself, a blackened shell, shoved up into the embrace of a solid old oak. It was fizzing with heat in the cool morning air, and the vegetation around was starting to burst into flame.

Benny hopped quickly around to the entrance port and kicked the safety covering aside with her boot. The controls had fused. She cut the release cable with the machete, and the hatch automatically blew out, the door landing a few feet away in the smouldering bushes.

'Come on, Ace –' Benny peered into the capsule.

Tentacles flew up at her face.

The thing wrapped a fibrous rope around her throat, bristling with spores. Benny fell to the ground, trying to bring her rifle up to bear.

Her vision started to fade, the spores ruffling down the tentacle towards her skin. She managed to gasp a word, she wasn't sure what –

And then something silver sliced through the tentacle.

Ace kicked the creature back into the capsule and pulled the tentacle from Benny's shoulders. 'Come on!' she shouted, handing her back her knife.

They sprinted through the forest for ten minutes, until the hissing roars had vanished behind them. 'Who was that?' Benny yelled.

'Fiona!' Ace gasped, slowing down. 'Listen, Benny, Jan is –'

'I know, oh God I know!' Benny pulled Ace to her and held her. 'Christ, are any of us going to get out of this alive?'

'For some of us, that is an absurd question.' Christopher was standing in the forest before them, his black robes and ghostly face shocking against the grey and the green. Benny stared at the figure, amazed.

Ace looked up. She wrenched herself away from Benny, grabbing the machete, and ran at him, yelling something incomprehensible.

The sword caught Christopher in the side, but he showed no pain as it passed through him. No blood was upon it, either.

He caught the second blow between his palms, and looked at Ace for a long moment as their strengths matched.

The anger drained out of the young woman's face. She took a step back, and flung the weapon to the ground.

'It was not my doing,' Christopher told her. 'I, of all people, know that sacrifice is a futile thing. Jan was led into his plan by his own wilfulness, as manifested by the Trickster . . . ' Christopher raised his hand in a gesture of supplication. 'He died because he was free, and he was still free when he died.'

'He's not free now.'

'No. But he was never coerced, never conned. He died out of the expression of his own personality.'

'I don't believe that, but I'm sorry.'

'There is nothing to be sorry about. Now, the Hoothi cannot sense this dead form of mine, but I can sense them. I can guide you around the armies of the dead that are rising this day. There is one more move to make.'

'Take us to Joycetown then,' Ace said before Benny could speak. 'I've got some stuff to take care of there.'

'As you wish.' Christopher pointed out a path and they set off across fields and along muddy tracks, staying as far away from the gravelands as possible. During the journey, Ace was silent, marching fast.

'So, how come you're still with us?' Benny asked Christopher. 'Forgive me, but it is a bit of a surprise.'

'I move this corpse through the power of my will, as once I could move small objects. Now that I have become one with Puterspace –'

'Sorry?'

'The information that is me lives on. I have transplanted it into a programme. The programme is decaying, because dataspace is continually being required by other users. But I have found that I can sometimes tap into – it is so hard to explain – powerful data. Words of power. I have been keeping this body moving using more and more power. Eventually, I will be unable to sustain it.'

'And then you'll just switch off?'

'I shall live on in Puterspace, for a while.'

'I don't know what to feel. Are you . . . content?'

'I have always been content. I have to be. There has been no love for me in years, and without love, you are . . . content.'

'I can sympathize with that, but there are other things –'

'There is the war,' Christopher put a hand on Benny's shoulder, and, astonishingly, touched a pair of cold lips to her cheeks. 'And we are winning that.'

Benny smiled, certain she was blushing.

Ace had marched ahead to see over the brow of a hill.

Benny's gaze followed her. 'You lied to her. I could always tell with you, when you were alive. You didn't do it very often, so you weren't very good at it.'

'I have lied. But only so that her world does not completely collapse. She must have somebody to return to.'

'That's not right. She'll find out. Lies always come to the surface. It's not really up to you to decide what she knows, is it?'

'It is not up to me at all, it's up to –'

'We're here!' Ace shouted down from the hilltop. 'Come on!'

The TARDIS had appeared in front of Operative Miller's desk.

The old lawman stood up, watching the materialization with interest. 'That is absolutely fascinating,' he told the Doctor as he stepped from his time-craft.

'Possibly. But we have important matters to discuss.'

'Indeed we have. This base is under siege, Doctor, by what can only be described as the living dead. Reports are coming in from towns and villages all across the planet. The Draconians are in a state of complete collapse. They venerate their ancestors . . . can't bring themselves to fight them. Doctor, what the hell can I do to stop it?'

'Trust me. Trust me absolutely.'

'I . . . can do that. But give me some hope, at least!'

'The creatures you're encountering won't try to infect the living by force. It's wasteful. They'll get you bottled up, and then release clouds of spores across the large communities. The smaller ones will be already under attack. With the fleet on the way, they'll probably start the last phase of their plan before they attack the towns.'

'And can you save us?'

The Doctor smiled, as if at a complex joke he'd only just thought of. 'Yes, of course I can. I can save nearly everyone. I can wipe this menace from the face of the universe.' He winced at some pain deep inside, and frowned. 'So, take me to your communications equipment.'

Phaedus moved his hand. Still alive. Still moving.

Gravel rustled off his robe as he got to his feet. The roof of the hall had collapsed, and fungoids were twitching under the rubble.

He made his way to the basement door, and nervously called down the stairs. 'Mother? Mother, are you there?'

And then, with a shaky step, he made his way down into the darkness.

In the streets of Joycetown, screams rang out. Townsfolk ran about in the markets, gathering their possessions, arguing with guards who were trying to organize them. A mass of scared people ran past the ruins of the Library, shouting and jostling as they headed for the gates.

The cause of this was something that had been sighted at dawn. A group of strange beings standing on the hill. During the morning, their numbers had steadily grown, but still they stood there, a calm army waiting for battle. Lone horsemen had ridden out and made close passes to the creatures, but those with telescopes could already see what they were.

They were the dead, come back to haunt Joycetown.

There were over three hundred of them by ten o'clock. The townsfolk had been disturbed enough by the apparition, and the continual crack and thump of guards firing mortars at the hill. The bombs had had little effect, anybody could see that.

The destruction of the Vacuum Church by a blazing meteor

was surely some final sign of judgement.

They had rushed for the gate. Guards who had been talking about advancing on the enemy with blasters found themselves holding back a mass of people who wanted to leave the town rather than bar the gates and await a siege.

The blank eyes of the dead watched the confusion, Hoothi tendrils swaying in the wind.

Christopher had taken Ace and Benny to the city walls by means of an old cart track, sunk slightly into the ground. They ran along the walls, Benny staring apprehensively up at the dead on the hill. She didn't like Ace's expression either. It was scarcely more animated than that of the things waiting above the town.

Such a pained frown, like a hurt little girl.

Benny wanted to take her away to some quiet place and make everything fine for her again. But that would mean bringing Jan back, and that she couldn't do.

The group reached the confusion at the gates, a trader with a cart screaming into the face of a guard who was fingering the butt of his blaster. Christopher walked straight through the yelling mob, clearing a path with a wave of his hand.

'Notice something?' Benny asked, grimly. 'No tower. Where's the church gone?'

Ace stared at the ruins of the Vacuum Church when they turned the right corner. 'No!' she shouted angrily. She ran towards the collapsed building.

The Doctor held a tiny module in his hand. 'You can't signal anybody now.'

Miller took a deep breath. 'Can you give me a single reason why I should let you do this?'

'Only that I'm the Doctor. And I know what I'm doing.'

'Do you?'

'Oh yes.' The Doctor seemed to decide to take a risk. 'If I die, replace it!'

Miller raised an eyebrow. 'Good game you're playing?'

'Oh no.' The Doctor smiled. 'The game is over.'

A shadow fell over Heaven.

The Hoothi globe was suddenly in the sky, huge, blotting out the sun. The oceans buckled and blasted, tidal waves sweeping into ports and consuming them. Lightning flickered across the countryside as the atmosphere was whipped into storms.

One second after the sphere appeared, a vast concussion of thunder shook the land.

A cry went up from Joycetown as the shadow fell over it. It was the sound of thousands of people moaning in primitive terror. The moment of harvesting was upon all the animals of Heaven.

Ace looked up at the sky and began to laugh at it. Then she shook her head, and kicked in the door of the Vacuum Church.

Benny stopped in her desperate pursuit of Ace, and gazed at the thing in the sky. You could see the mottled organic hue of the sphere, even as the dark clouds gathered around it. She felt very frightened and very small.

Christopher pointed up. 'Look,' he said.

From the main body of the dark mass, something huge was emerging.

'I wish I could pray,' Benny whispered. 'That's just too big.'

'We do not have to pray,' Christopher told her, putting a cold hand on her shoulder. 'We have to win.'

Ace fell amongst the rubble almost immediately, tripping over a beam.

Crawling to her feet again, she wiped the dust from her gloves, noticing how filaments waved and snatched at the air from under the debris.

'Phaedrus!' she yelled. 'Where are you, you bastard?'

A beam gave way at the sound and fell from the vaulted ceiling. Ace dodged it. She'd heard an echo, some distant cry from inside the building.

She crept towards the basement door.

The shape was unrolling, stretching down towards the ground. It was like a sheet of darkness unfurling.

The screams were echoing across Joycetown now, people falling to their knees in the street and shouting at the sky.

Christopher motioned Benny towards the Church once more. 'What will happen will happen,' he said. 'We must follow the plan.'

'There's a plan?' Benny approached the Church, cranking her plasma rifle.

'With the Doctor,' Christopher murmured, 'I believe there is always a plan.'

Ace threw the basement door aside. It had been leaning against the doorway on its hinges. The stairway was in darkness, but she felt no fear now. She didn't really feel much of anything. Feeling would arrive when she found Phaedrus. Then she'd know what that feeling was.

She had an idea, though.

Ace tiptoed down the stairs, feeling her way against the rough stone walls of the passageway. Total darkness. Like downstairs at night, as a kid. Like those times when she'd been in the house, all alone. There'd be a noise downstairs, and Dorry would take her courage, and her bear, in her hands, and go and see.

That had been good, facing the horror. Turn on the light, and there was nothing bad in the room at all. No monsters. It had taken Julian, and Chad Boyle, and the Doctor, to show her that monsters were real.

There was a faint green light in the basement, the pulse of a Puterspace deck. Ace found a chemical lamp at the bottom of the stairs and twisted it, igniting the billions of protozoa inside into reproduction. By the light of the lamp, she saw Phaedrus, curled up and connected to the deck, his back resting against the big table of the common room.

His lips were moving in some dream. He was half smiling.

Ace pulled the knife from her belt.

She bent over the sleeping figure, and, shivering, pulled his robes from around his neck. The skin there was white, and young-looking.

Ace stayed absolutely still for a moment. She was thinking about all those heroes in stories, most of them blokes, who'd get to somewhere like this, and then say that murder would make them as bad as the villain was.

She'd killed before, of course. Still had dreams about that

Nazi in the castle. But they'd tied her up then, and made her bloody scream, and he'd been a soldier.

Dreaming. In his sleep. Peacefully in his sleep.

'It's not good enough,' Ace whispered.

She found a wire crown on the table, and, without hesitation, plugged herself into the matrix.

Benny and Christopher looked around the rubble of the Vacuum Church.

'Messy,' mused Bernice. 'I always thought these people should get out more. Now they're going to have to.'

'We must wait here for six minutes. Then find our way down to the basement. That is where they will be.'

'What, Ace and Phaedrus? Why can't we go down now?'

'Because the Doctor told us to wait.' And he barred Bernice's way to the door.

'Pawns . . .' Benny sighed, frowning.

The dark shape had almost touched the ground. It was several miles long, and lightning flickered between it and the sky.

The citizens of Joycetown stared up and cried out in fear. A darkness had formed along the horizon, as if a margin had been drawn between Heaven and the sky. The darkness grew greater, until those who were still watching through binoculars, troopers who felt they had to watch, saw what it was.

It was the dead. Millions of them. Coming from all directions.

The dark shape touched the land, and stopped. From the angle at which Joycetown saw it, it was just a wide, dark, band against the sun. But James Miller saw it differently. When the Doctor had left, he'd made sure that the slaves of the Hoothi weren't actually trying to crush the fence. Then he'd put the base on internal life support and run out to the helicopter. He'd refused a pilot. How could you be sure that they weren't going to erupt into fungus? He flew across the fields of Heaven, sobbing sometimes as he saw what was happening. From every graveyard, thousands of corpses were struggling to the surface. Anything with muscles, a rudimentary nervous system, was moving. Some made an attempt to rise and fell apart, there being not enough flesh on their bones. Some were carried along by the weight of others, and some were more fungus than flesh.

Miller realized so many things on his flight. He saw how the ecosytem of Heaven relied on the Earthly, Heavenite and Draconian creatures preying on each other, and not existing parasitically on the remains in the ground. A natural system would tend to do that, with so much raw material around. He saw how strange the composition of the soil was, how different it smelt from the rich loam around his old home on Mandusus.

By the time he got to Joycetown, Miller saw Heaven as a trap, a big box baited for intelligence. It was a fable, a margin where things the great powers didn't like would be sent. Books, anarchists, and the dead. They'd wanted to believe that there was somewhere safe these things could go, somewhere not in their backyard, but still within reach if they needed them. But that wasn't true. When you put what you couldn't face out on the margins, it would putrify and boil like an unfaced fear, and come back to hurt you.

Miller imagined that the dead were carrying burning books and waving black banners. When he got to the stairway, he was ready to believe in it.

A stairway, an unfolded grey mass of fibre and biological remains. It was made of millions of individual steps, and they were fashioned of small bones and bound with muscle.

At the top of it, three figures stood. They were bearlike and tall, covered in thick fur. Sad eyes stared from above their grey muzzles. On their backs, great clusters of Hoothi fibre sat.

The Heavenites had returned to their home.

At the bottom of the stairway, the dead began to push forward. They marched, wave after wave of them, to the first step. And then they began to climb.

James Miller looked down at the people of Joycetown, watching the ascent in terror.

'My God,' he whispered. 'They're leaving them for last.'

Inside the dig, Travellers were shoving boards and equipment up against the entranceway. They had quickly closed the dome of the observatory, and were having some success in blocking the access tunnel. The dead had begun to cluster outside, and then had suddenly decided to advance. Alec had urged the tribe, clutching whatever belongings they could, to run down into the digs, and there they now were going to make their stand.

They wouldn't have as long as Joycetown did, since they were further away from the stairway, but they hammered in planks and shoved in tent pegs, and prepared to die free.

Christopher raised his arm, and let Benny open the door.

'Six minutes?' she asked.

'Time enough to enter Puterspace,' Christopher nodded.

At the bottom of the stairs, they found the comatose forms of Phaedrus and Ace.

'We have to get Ace out of there,' Benny said. 'What does she think she's doing?'

'Taking revenge.' Christopher frowned. 'I can feel them in the matrix. Wait a moment.' He closed his eyes, and Benny watched his body stiffen and tense.

Christ, he'd stopped breathing.

She was just about to do something when Christopher gasped, and opened his eyes. 'Have to . . . remember to keep the lungs going!'

'What did you find out?'

'I exist in Puterspace, I am aware of its backwaters. But the two of them are in . . . an area of their own. They are fighting a private battle. To interfere would take more energy than I possess.'

Benny put a hand to his arm. 'Tell me that what Ace is doing isn't part of the Doctor's plan.'

'It is not.'

'Good.'

'That is what you asked me to tell you. However, the truth is very different.'

Benny turned slowly to Christopher. She'd heard a familiar sound from upstairs. 'This is all part of the game, isn't it?'

'No,' Christopher told her. 'Games involve risk, the chance of winning and losing. The Doctor has told me to say this game is over.'

'Well,' Benny sighed. 'He would say that, wouldn't he?'

The TARDIS appeared amongst the ruins. After a moment, the

door opened and the Doctor got out.

He looked around at the chaos and the rubble, he listened to the screams from outside the building, and smelt the putrification in the air.

And he smiled.

After a moment, he headed for the door to the basement.

17:
The End

Phaedrus stared down at his mother, lying there on her bed. She had pulled the covers over her head, so ashamed of her pain. One wrinkled hand clutched at a corner of the white sheet. When they were fleeing the destruction of Mardal, hiding from Dalek patrols, she'd huddled him in her cloak, and told him old Greek stories.

'I wanted to explain,' the priest began, his hands folded in front of him. 'I had to reset the matrix to get me here. I suppose it's an indulgence of the Hoothi, letting me live this long. I wanted to talk to you. I can now. I've finally done it. Death has come crashing down on them. They can feel what I've always felt. Death is with us all now.'

Audrey threw back the covers and sat up. 'What are you talking about?' she asked the startled Phaedrus.

Behind the priest, a door opened.

Phaedrus turned as Ace ran at him, raised his arm to fend off the blow.

She hit him in the stomach, ramming her bunched fist hard into him.

He fell to his knees, gasping.

Ace looked down at him, and their eyes met. He seemed to be pleading. She kicked at his jaw. The toe of her boot caught the man in the soft flesh of his throat.

He tried to scream as he hit the ground, and it came out as a choked howl.

Ace was trying to feel something. This was what put meaning into Jan's death. This revenge.

Phaedrus had rolled into a foetal ball, an instinctive motion to protect his internal organs. 'Don't!' he gasped. 'Don't . . .' He sounded like a child.

Ace hadn't looked at anything but her enemy since she'd

entered the room. The place had been obvious in Puterspace, beckoning her with an open door. She'd just run straight in and found Phaedrus.

Now she felt a familiar lean strength grab her shoulders. The arms encircled her and pulled her back. It was the action of somebody who wasn't used to violence, who was driven to it by passion.

'Leave him alone!' hissed Audrey, furiously. 'My God, I didn't bring you up to be like this!'

'You didn't bring me up at all!' screamed Ace, smashing her mother up against the wall. 'You didn't! You didn't!' She was yelling into her face now, shaking her by the collar. 'Where were you? Where were you when he died?'

'Oh my poor baby, my poor baby –'

'You're dead! Everybody's dead!' As Ace's attack grew more frenzied, her mother didn't try to protect herself. Instead of putting up her arms to shield herself from her child's blows, Audrey simply let her grip on Ace's shoulders grow tighter. Audrey was wincing as she was shaken, sobs welling up from deep inside her.

'Oh, my poor love,' she sobbed. 'My poor baby, I wanted to do everything for you ... I wanted you to be happy!'

'Everything's so screwed up, and I don't know how anything works anymore, and I'm so ... I'm so alone!' The shouting had broken something, or perhaps it was her mother's tears. Ace burst into wracking sobs, and buried her head in Audrey's shoulder. 'Mum! Oh Mum, make it all okay again!'

'Hush ... hush ...' Audrey smoothed Ace's hair with her hand. 'I'm not just a ghost, am I? Julian remembered me like this, because he used to come and visit me when you weren't there. He told me he was gay. I understood. My Mum had known a few that way, in the Navy. They were always so brave, she said. One night I drank a little too much gin, and he came round and found me crying. I told him how I couldn't talk to you, and how much I loved you. I asked him to tell you. And he wouldn't, because he said I had to. And I never did. I never did.'

Ace looked up at Audrey's face, her own eyes red with tears. 'You bloody well should have ...' she whispered.

There was a noise from behind them. Ace spun round. On the other side of the room, a door was closing. Ace glimpsed Phaedrus limping away, propped up by a little old woman in black.

'I wanted him to know.' Ace told Audrey. 'Know what it's like.'

Audrey pulled her daughter back to her. 'He knows.'

They hung onto each other. After a moment Ace stepped back, patting her mother's forearms. Despite herself, she'd got ashamed at feeling so much with a memory of her Mum. 'We've got stuff to talk about, haven't we, me and him?'

'Yes, I suppose you have. Will you come back here and see me?'

'Yeah,' Ace nodded seriously. ''Course I will. But I've got to find him first. Explain.'

They hugged again, and Ace left the room.

Perhaps when she did, Audrey vanished.

Or perhaps she rang her hands, and went back to bed, and on some Perivale morning woke from a dream. Perhaps she would have thought about the dream over her morning tea. How she'd heard her daughter lie and go away. How, despite this, despite everything, she'd never be able to take her courage in her hands and tell her how she felt.

Because in dreams there are alternatives that don't exist in waking life.

The Doctor walked down the steps into the basement, and nodded to Benny and Christopher. Then he glanced at the Puterspace console. 'Ace!' he muttered urgently. He strode over and knelt by her sleeping form. 'I was meaning to leave this planet. Take her with me. But now I must rescue her. If only I had a Puterspace crown!'

'Doctor . . .' Christopher produced a wire crown and lead from inside his robe. 'They buried me with this. Is it what you require?'

'Yes!' the Doctor jumped up and took the device, plugging it into the deck. 'After I get her back, we will leave here, never to return.'

Bernice's eyebrows had reached their highest possible point.

'Excuse me, but –'

'There's no time to lose!' the Doctor cried. 'We may already be too late!' And he put the crown on his head. His eyes closed.

'Do you think that he is acting strangely?' Christopher asked.

'Not at all,' Benny sighed. 'Just very badly.'

Across the northern continent of Heaven, the meadows were alive with the dead. They scampered through the fields, running towards the summons of the Stairway. In other parts of the planet, pods detached from the Hoothi sphere had released stairways of their own. Everywhere, what was alive was cowering in fear from what had passed. They walked in ranks along the low stone walls, and massed by settlements in the dark of night, making no sound save for the faint clicking and settling of long-unused muscles. In the daylight zones, they marched together in armies, feathering outposts with clouds of spores. There were twenty of them for every living being on the planet.

Operative Miller's helicopter had descended into the market square in Joycetown, and he had swiftly attempted to find his troopers. A few of them were still observing from the walls, training cameras on the Stairway. Most had gone, either into town after loved ones, or simply to hide. Miller could smell it himself. The sweetness in the air was terrifying, what a cow smells in the yard of the slaughterhouse.

He climbed up to the observation post on the town walls, patting a corporal on the back.

'They're not going to get here in time, are they, sir?' the Ellerycorp man whispered. 'The fleet, I mean.'

'We don't need the fleet, lad!' Miller boomed heartily. 'We've got the most dangerous thing in the universe on our side.'

'What's that, sir?'

'The Doctor.' Miller put his binoculars up to his eyes, and stared out at the sea of marching dead. A huge wave of them were halfway up the Stairway now, marching to meet the Heavenites who stood at the top. Miller tried to sound convincing. 'I feel sorry for the poor buggers.'

The Doctor put a foot on to the grass of the Land Under The Hills. He took a slow look around. There was a darkness about the trees, and the sound of birdsong was muted and distant. The place was waiting.

There came a distant crashing sound. Somebody was making their way clumsily through the forest. The Doctor took out his fob watch and peered at it.

'They're doing something, sir!' the trooper handed Miller back the binoculars. The dead were raising their arms to the sky. Along them, hundreds of white spores were sprouting.

'My God, they're about to release their spores! We have to get the people here inside!'

The trooper gazed down at the milling crowd, horror struck. 'How, sir?! How the hell can we do that?!'

At the dig site, the Travellers were crouched, weapons ready, as the rhythmic sound of shoving increased. The dead had appeared outside the dig *en masse*, and were slamming against the barricades, using their bodies as a battering ram.

'Remember who we are,' Alec muttered. 'We'll all see each other again soon, and there'll be Jan there, and Roisa, and Máire.'

The noise stopped. There came a fluttering sound, as if something soft was being released on to the wind.

'Sooner than I thought,' the Traveller sighed. 'Blessed be.'

Ace was running after Phaedrus, through bracken and low bushes. She had been calling out to him, trying to get him to stop. She put a hand to her brow as she ran, trying to sort things out. Christ, what was she doing here? One minute you want to kill somebody, the next you're trying to explain, trying to get some kind of absolution.

'Stop! Listen, I just want to talk!'

Phaedrus was blundering through the forest simulation, unsure of where he was or what he was running from. His mother had been with him for a moment, something for him to lean on. Or was that a dream? Had he found her at all? Whatever had happened, he had to keep running. Something terrible was pursuing him. If he stopped running, then –

He dashed between two trees, glanced over his shoulder, and

tripped into a clearing, tumbling.

A dark shadow fell over him. An awful figure was standing between the priest and the sun.

The Doctor bent low over Phaedrus, and snapped a finger into his chin. 'You,' he growled, 'are responsible for all that has happened here. When did the Hoothi contact you?'

'When I was an initiate! Many years, many years . . .'

'You called out to them! You offered up this world for sacrifice! For your mistakes!'

'Yes! Yes, I did, but –'

'Do you feel alone, now? Are you afraid, Phaedrus?' The Doctor's finger jabbed into the injured man's neck. 'There's nobody to save you from me, and now you want to be saved, now you've seen something you want to live for, haven't you?!' The Doctor grabbed the priest by the collar and snarled into his face. 'Haven't you?!'

'Yes, mother, I, I –'

'Call your protectors! Call them!'

Phaedrus blinked, trying to concentrate. His mind focused on the spore inside him, and he felt the familiar answer to his call. They'd take this pain away, they'd give him the time to see his mother again. Just a little time.

The graphic of the Hoothi sphere appeared over the grove, and the air turned solid once more. The Doctor's face creased in pain, and he dropped Phaedrus.

Ace grabbed the trees at the edge of the grove, and swayed against the impact of the sound and compression. A hand clasped her shoulder, and she gasped to see Christopher, in his matrix form, beside her, his eyes closed in concentration. Ace could almost see what the two of them were concentrating on, a familiar feeling was rising about the clearing, like they were thinking of somebody she knew. She turned back to see the Doctor raise his hands to his chest, the nails biting into his palms.

He sucked in a deep breath, and bellowed.

'ARADRATH!'

The word echoed across the council chamber of the Hoothi ship.

'What does that . . . mean?' one of the puffballs hissed.

'It is . . . familiar. It is . . . in the group . . . mind.'

A strange emotion fluttered across the mind of the Hoothi Consciousness. Perhaps it was some kind of elation. For the first time time in centuries, the thousands of souls held captive in the group mind felt their masters . . . falter.

Beside a thin membrane, the thing that had been Jan had been watching the dead creatures march up the stairway into the belly of the sphere.

The creature was swaying slightly. The tattoo of the snake, consuming its own head, was visible across the puffy layers of fungus. The being was mindless, of course. But its eyeless head was turned to the world below, and its stumpy hands were raised in some half-formed emotion.

And then it remembered.

For a brief second, it was pulled out of the group mind. It was an individual. It . . . he . . . was important. Special.

'Time to repay the debt,' Christopher told him.

'Change the world!' the Doctor cried.

They were talking to him through the Puterspace link in his fungoid neck, through the Hoothi Consciousness itself, and through an ancient friendship, as yet left unsettled.

Jan remembered Heaven, and the Travellers, and his love for Ace.

He remembered that his secret name was Aradrath.

'Aradrath,' the Doctor said to Jan. 'Make fire!'

So he did.

The first small blast took the Hoothi by surprise.

'What . . . has . . . happened?' one hissed.

'We have . . . been . . .'

The Hoothi sphere exploded.

The fireball erupted across the sky, blasted in the roofs and toppled the towers of Joycetown, sent the dead flying from the stairway, which buckled and folded and burst into fragments of bone and flying cinders. The blast scorched walls, and set timbers alight, and threw troopers from their platforms. It set afire clothes, and burst eardrums, echoing across the valley, thundering between the hillsides.

When the dead fell into the square they were just dead. Poor corpses, with nothing alive still about them. A fine grey powder was all that showed what they had been part of.

The debris crashed down on the town, bones and bones, a collapsing rain of animal leftovers. Scapulae bounced off tiles, and knuckles clattered into the gutters. A hard shower of joints and femurs shattered down across the landscape.

The heat cloud rose in a mushroom of roaring mist, water beginning to condense and spatter down on to the fires that had sprung up everywhere.

James Miller took a hand away from his blackened face, and yelled up at the sky. 'We're alive! We're alive!'

All across Heaven, the Hoothi pods had toppled and swayed, with no mind left to control them. Some of them crashed into mountains, some lumbered into the earth. A few spontaneously exploded. Whatever happened, bodies fell from the stairways, no longer animated. Thousands of skeletons and corpses plummeted from the sky, or rolled back down into the lifeless heaps that had fallen all around the pods.

At the dig site, Alec stuck his head out between the barricades.

Across the meadow lay a hundred bodies. Some of them were piled, leaning, on the planks that had shielded the Travellers from attack. One had its bony hand stuck through a tiny gap.

All were covered in a fine dust.

Alec threw aside the timbers, and stepped out into the sunlight. He fell to his knees amongst the bodies, and soon he was joined by the rest of the Travellers, who kissed the ground, held each other, and sobbed in relief.

They were alive.

18:
Afterwards

All Christopher had said was 'now'. His eyes had been closed, and Benny hadn't actually had the impression that this was an instruction to get undercover because the alien spacecraft was about to explode overhead.

However, when it had done, she managed to do just that.

Now she stood up, shakily, from the alcove where she'd dived. Christopher still had his eyes closed, half in the matrix. She looked down at the three bodies. Phaedrus, gasping and weeping. The Doctor, a stern look of contentment on his face.

And Ace. Ace had her eyes open.

Benny quickly pulled the wire crown from her head, and helped her into a sitting position.

'Jan . . .' Ace whispered.

'Ace, listen to me –'

'Jan was in the sphere. Because the Doctor knew he was infected. And he didn't tell me.'

'What do you mean?'

'The only firemaker on the planet. And he goes and takes a spaceship. Gets into the sphere before anybody else. Because of Roisa. Because of the Doctor. He saved the whole bloody universe again, right? You see that? Except the man I was in love with.' She looked down at the Doctor. 'Oh god, oh god, get me away from him!' She started to shake, and put a hand to her mouth. 'Get me away from him!'

Bernice hauled Ace to her feet, and bundled her up the stairs. 'It's all right,' she told her.

But she knew that it wasn't. It was never going to be all right again.

When the Doctor awoke, the first face he saw was Christopher's.

The tall being pulled him to his feet with one hand. 'You did a good thing,' he said.

'I destroyed the Hoothi,' the Doctor replied. 'One sphere of them, anyway. Where's Ace?'

Benny appeared at the top of the stairs. 'You're not seeing her. I've found her a bed at the military base. She'll just . . . It really isn't a good idea, right?'

The Doctor looked anguished. 'There was no other way. I couldn't tell her, I –'

'Tell me later.' Benny turned once more. 'If I want to talk to you then, which I may not.' And she left.

'You saved thousands of lives.' Christopher rested his hand on the Doctor's shoulder. 'Billions, on a galactic scale.'

The Doctor shrugged the hand aside. 'Not important. They won't know. They won't care. Dodo, or whatever her name is . . . She cares.'

Phaedrus groaned, and opened his eyes. 'Let me go back,' he pleaded.

The Doctor gently removed the lead from the Puterspace deck. 'I have no reason to harm you,' he muttered. 'Go and find a life, find something to do. Go out and live!'

Phaedrus stood, and looked around the room like a lost little boy. 'But what shall I do? Who can help me now?'

The Doctor turned his head, and waited until Phaedrus had climbed the stairs from the basement.

'You have saved them. But I see that you are as misplaced in the aftermath as Phaedrus is,' Christopher said to the Doctor. 'Where will you go now?'

'Away.' The Time Lord stuffed his hat back on his head. 'Alone.'

'Please return to us.' Christopher paused. 'I should like to see you once more before I also leave.'

The Doctor frowned and nodded. 'You will,' he said, and climbed the stairs.

A moment later, Christopher heard the powerful rushing and grinding of temporal engines.

The dead man shook his head.

Operative Miller wandered along the central street of Joycetown, checking on a clipboard where fire-fighting teams had been sent.

Everything was rubble. The Library, the Vacuum Church, many other buildings. Miller refused to be awestruck by the destruction around him. A minute after the sphere had exploded, he'd been roaring orders at this troopers. Even with the fires and the casualties, a hysterical atmosphere of celebration was starting to seize the town. People, realizing that the threat was over, had begun to cluster in the streets, and, with so much rescue work to do, that was a danger in itself.

Bernice had made his troubles worse by running up to him with the girl, Ace. Miller had been supervising the landing of a large ambulance helicopter, and Benny had insisted, almost to the point of violence, that Ace get a place on it. The girl herself was in shock, Miller recognized it from his days on the front. She was staring at everything, not speaking, fascinated by tiny details.

When he'd asked why she should get a place over the wounded and dying, Benny had said: 'She was with the Doctor. Her sacrifice saved your planet.'

He'd believed her expression instantly.

After the helicopter had taken off, Benny had run off back to the Vacuum Church.

Now she caught up with the lawman once more, and slapped his shoulder. 'Thanks for your help. How did we do?'

'Badly, lass. In Joycetown alone, over one hundred civilians dead, fifteen troopers, three hundred or so injuries. Large-scale damage to property. Personally, I don't think the place is fit to live in anymore. When Spacefleet arrives, I'll be advising them that we evacuate the colony. The Draconians had it worse than we did. They're already packing their bags.'

'It could have been far worse.'

'Aye, it could have been the whole human race, from what I heard. We're bloody lucky to be alive. We've got the Doctor to thank, I suppose.'

'If you can find him. I went back to the church, and he seems to have vanished, which is probably just as well for Ace. Incidentally, if I wanted two passes out of human space . . .'

'Taking her with you?'

'Somebody's got to do it,' Benny shrugged. 'I can't just leave her here, and I'm not going to be shipped back to Central.'

'I don't think you'll find you have any problems.'

'Good.'

Miller stopped writing. 'Do you think things'll get any better when they close the frontier here? When all's divided between us and the Draconians?'

'No,' Benny shook her head decisively. 'It never does. Civilization just happens. It makes people all behave one way, and when they don't, it kills them. You have to keep moving I suppose, keep making up new ways to read things, and keep the old books safe. When the frontier closes, the mincer opens.'

'Well then, I've had enough of war.' Miller theatrically dropped the clipboard and looked down at it. 'I'm going to vanish somewhere and write a book. A good one. Put some love back into the world.'

'Good.'

'You can't leave things undone though,' Miller picked up the clipboard again. 'So I'm resigning when we're finished here.'

'I'm glad,' Benny smiled. 'Anyway, now I can go and check out the dig.' She strode off back down the street, slapping the dust from her chinos. 'You're not so bad, you know, for a soldier!'

For the first time in days, James Miller grinned. 'See how I am for a novelist!' he shouted back. 'Don't count your chickens!'

Ace was propped up on her pillow in the blue glow. The military sick bay was sparse, and full of wounded. She felt like she was in the way.

They'd got to her last, after the more serious cases had been dealt with. Things had speeded up once the staff had ascertained that any spores which had been ingested or externally attached to people had dissolved. When he came to Ace, the medic had diagnosed shock, and had given her a gentle sedative and a hot drink.

She had taken the strange cube that had appeared in the escape pod from out of her jacket. Now she tossed it from hand to hand, gazing into it. It was full of Jan. Pictures, sounds, even the hint of touches, like a ghostly radio receiver. The surfaces reflected him, told her about him. Ace was sure that nobody else could see. And it was cool, too, because this was the real stuff, just like he had been. There was nothing maudlin or naff about it. This could really help her . . . heal. Yeah, maybe one day she could do that. Still a long way off, though. Still some times when she didn't want to think about him.

And absolutely not about the Doctor.

It wasn't like she was crazy, not like she was going to kick him about or anything, but . . .

She didn't want to see him. Ever again. It was complex, but she saw it. How the Doctor must have known about Jan's spore, had manoeuvred him into making a futile attempt at attacking the Hoothi. He'd even made sure that he was told about the Heavenite telescope.

Mum, the Doctor, Jan . . . it was all really complicated. And she'd always hated hospitals. Yeah.

Ace hopped out of bed, pulled on her leggings, and slipped the cube into her jacket pocket. 'Going for a walk,' she told the intern as she laced her boots.

Nobody was worried about stopping her.

It was a long walk, across the fields from the emergency medical centre. It took most of a drug-slowed afternoon. The meadows were littered with the dead, the earth furrowed. Ace stopped to rest in woodlands, and slept under a tree, until a nightmare brought her upright again, sweating.

By the time she got there, night was falling over the remains of Joycetown. Columns of smoke were obscuring the stars. The gates were swinging open, clusters of people made homeless sheltering in military tents by them. The streets were littered with human remains. A plague of insects and scavengers had already descended on the town. Ace heard troopers talking about environmental collapse.

The moon was rising above the hills, and it was blood red.

All the dust, Ace told herself. Not funny at all.

But she laughed at it. Bit sour, that laugh. She nearly cried as she laughed it, and her smile was nearly a snarl.

The remains of the Vacuum Church were being gradually scattered, people stealing stones to shore up their own homes. The tower was spread over the street, and the tail of an escape pod was pointed at the sky.

Máire, Ace remembered. Sacrificed, like they'd all been. Not just Jan. The Doctor had opened up the mincing machine of war, and beckoned them all in.

He'd never been like that. Never hurt her so badly before. There had been times of such tremendous love, walks and great talks and evenings toasting muffins.

And then he turns and kills everything. Time's Champion. Nothing like a person at all.

Ace wandered towards the door of the Church, and paused on the threshold. She could find Máire, maybe. Yeah, like another body wasn't going to freak her, was it?'

Something inside her told her that this was all just waiting around, waiting for whatever was inside to break. The sedative, the wandering, it was all just holding off the reckoning.

Ace shrugged and entered the building.

It was dark, and it took a while to step carefully over the fallen beams. Moonlight was turning the whole mess red, and Ace's imagination wandered into the idea that she was picking her way through a mass of bodies.

From the basement, there came a low moan.

'Máire?' Ace whispered, and made her way towards the door.

Down the stairs, the basement was empty, just a Puterspace deck on a table. No sign of anybody.

But there was another door. The door to the cellar.

Ace opened it and called down. 'Anybody about?'

There was no answer. The glow of chemical light was filtering up the stairwell. Somebody had ignited a lamp.

She made her way slowly down the stairs. The steps creaked slightly beneath her feet.

Ace peered around the corner of the stairwell. 'If you can hear me, call –'

She only had a second to take in what she saw.

Phaedrus was standing in the middle of the room, his knife poised at his own throat.

'It's for the best,' told Ace. 'For Piers.'

The blood sprayed, in that second when she didn't act. It sprayed on to a fungoid mass that was supported by a metal frame.

'Meat!' the grey blob hissed. Phaedrus fell.

A tentacle lashed up from the ground and slapped into the wall near Ace's throat.

Ace dived aside, rolled, stood, and found herself looking down the barrel of a gun.

Roisa stood there, her muscles shaking. She no longer wore the pack of explosives, and a patch of grey fungus had sprouted from her empty arm socket. Her pistol was aimed straight at Ace.

'We . . . leave nothing . . . to chance . . .' hissed the Hoothi. 'We kept Phaedrus . . . fresh for this moment. I have only . . . the strength . . . to control one slave. But now you will add to my . . . nutrition. I will grow spores . . . I will bloom . . . I will infest this world . . . again! And when we are . . . powerful . . . we will signal my species. They . . . will . . . win!'

Roisa took a step forward.

Ace realized that she was going to be marched back into the thing's embrace. Over Phaedrus' body, the blood being sucked up by tentacles, she would be made to stumble. For a moment, she felt like diving at Roisa. She'd just be blown away. Let the damn thing find some other meat.

But then her eyes met Roisa's. There was a desperate pain in the woman's face. 'Oh, yeah, right!' Ace found herself shouting. 'You're the great manipulators, aren't you, the ones who play games!'

The slow walk backwards continued.

'You got all those people inside you, Jan and Jules and all of them? They still aren't free?'

'I . . . contain . . . the group mind for this . . . portion . . . of my species.' The filaments of the creature were thrashing in anticipation. Phaedrus' blood was already making the thing bigger. The tentacles were reaching out for Ace.

'I hope you bloody well choke on them!' Ace spat, getting ready to grab for Roisa. Maybe she'd hesitate, maybe Ace could get the gun, maybe –

'Roisa!' The choked yell came from the other side of the room.

From out of a great crack in the wall, a head and an arm were protruding, both covered in blood.

Máire was aiming her Dalek gun at Roisa. 'Drop it!' she croaked.

Roisa's expression grew more desperate. 'Couldn't help it!' she croaked. 'Spore went through my boot. Led the sphere to the Great Wheel. Goddess, and I'm paying for it!' She closed her eyes. Ace moved a shoulder, tensing to escape, but the gun followed her centre of gravity. Roisa was seeing through the senses of the Hoothi now.

They continued to slowly back towards the mass of tentacles.

'For the Lady's sake!' Máire shouted. 'Can't you drop the gun? Can't you stop?'

A choked sob broke from Roisa, and Ace saw Máire grit her teeth. 'Can't, love.'

'In that case, my love . . . open your eyes.'

Roisa concentrated, her arm shaking. With a huge effort of will, her eyes opened.

'That's the way,' Máire whispered. 'Like a Traveller.'

And she squeezed the trigger.

The hard light blasted Roisa across the room. She slammed into the opposite wall, but her arm still snapped up, about to kill Ace.

Máire fired again.

Roisa's body tensed against the wall, negative in the blast.

This time when she fell, she lay still.

Ace had been thrown off her feet too, and as she scrambled to get up, a tentacle caught her ankle. A heave backwards, one snagged her shoulder, a bundle of them closed around her waist.

'No!' she bellowed. 'I won't go! Not now!'

Máire fired again, at the Hoothi, but the pack had expired, as she'd expected. The blast was just a thin beam of light. It made no impact on the monster.

'Wouldn't have worked . . . anyway . . .' Máire slumped unconscious.

Ace was encircled by tentacles. They were pulling against her muscles as she strained forward, her boots about to slip off the floor.

'Julian!' she shouted. 'Jules! Are you going to stand up against that thing?' Ace knew that she was losing the battle, and a fierce sadness shook her. 'There's millions of them in there, but you're the special one! Stand up! For God's sake, stand up and shout against them!'

Her feet left the floor, and she felt the warm embrace of the Hoothi constrict around her. A sharp wet tentacle slid towards her face. 'Remember Scrane End? Remember the lights! It wasn't a spaceship, out there where the maps stopped, it was a prison! Loads of lights and guards running about, and you were so upset, you said that if that was what was out there on the edge you didn't want to go there, but there was something else wasn't there?! Tell me what was there!'

The tentacle slowed, and wavered.

Ace gasped as a tentacle began, almost reluctantly, to constrict about her neck. 'You turned the Allegro, and skidded past the prison gates, and we shot up off a side road. You were driving like a madman, because you hadn't wanted to find that, you'd wanted to find nowhere. We raced along this little road, and bounced straight out on to the sand. A beach, the edge of a marsh that lead to the sea!' Ace was freely weeping, shouting and not caring about dying or anything else except finishing the story. 'You jumped out of the car, and rolled in the sand under the moon, and you shouted, you said – tell me what you said!'

The Hoothi quivered. Something strong had risen up inside it. From the horrible recesses of its mouth, a powerful voice forced its way out.

'I said . . . we're okay. We've found it! There's something on the other side!' The voice broke out into peals of laughter, and the Hoothi shivered. 'Ace . . .' The voice waited for a second, grasping for something to say. 'Goodbye!'

' 'Bye, Jules!' Ace whispered.

The core of the Hoothi blasted apart, strands whipping across the room and spattering on the walls. Tentacles and filaments were sent spinning, as the mucoid mass at the creature's heart exploded.

Ace spun out herself, thrown over Phaedrus's body and hitting the wall.

The hurricane of destruction only stopped when there was nothing left of the creature, just a fungal paste that dripped off everything in the cellar.

Ace stood, swaying, crawling her way up the wall, She stared at the mucus that was splattered around the cellar. 'You're all free,' she whispered. Then she staggered over to Máire.

The Traveller woman was semi-conscious. She blinked up at Ace. 'Did we win?'

Ace smoothed back a hair from the woman's bloodied face. 'Yes . . .' she said. 'I suppose we did.'

Máire smiled grimly. 'Dalek gun'll kill anything,' she whispered. 'Even love.'

And then she fell unconscious once more.

'No.' Ace held her, gazing at the bodies of Roisa and Phaedrus. 'No, Máire. It doesn't kill that.'

Epilogues:
Deaths And Other Lives

The funeral was in an undamaged place. It took some time to find, Traveller scouts riding far out into the fields to look for an area that wasn't ripped and hummocked by the rise of the dead.

They found a meadow, drained by a farmer to give her cattle grazing land. She'd cleared the ground beforehand, and it seemed that nothing large had died there since.

A pyre was built, as there were no bodies to be buried. A body would have been some sort of insult, anyhow. There were so many now, and so many pieces. The religious authorities of Heaven (not including the Vacuum Church, which had been dissolved, its assets seized), had been speculating on what to do with the corpses.

The planet was going to be evacuated. It would be blessed from space. The ecology of the place would go into a meat-fuelled frenzy. Species would battle for natural niches, evolution would step up a pace. But finally, some natural balance would be found.

The world wouldn't be as beautiful then, but it would at least be real. Only then would the prohibitions over Heaven be lifted.

The name would also be changed. Nobody had any ideas about what to call it.

Ace watched, calm, as each Traveller threw a log on to the pyre. It had been lit by Alec, who had thrown his gloves into the blaze. When he'd first seen Ace, as she walked into camp with the injured Máire, he'd told her that he wanted to touch real things more often now.

Above the bonfire, another night was falling, one of the last nights for humans on Heaven. The stars were coming out.

Christopher threw his log, his face blank. He had wandered back into the camp at twilight, each step now seeming an effort.

He had spent an hour instructing Cook William, the new Priest of the Travellers. The man had said that he and Máire would retake the Great Wheel, and that the Travellers would take the Land Under The Hills with them wherever they went. In some other place, a new white horse would be built.

Then Christopher had talked to Máire about the history and future of the tribe. His features seemed flaccid now, his eyes growing milky. When he had made his contribution to the bonfire, he paused for a moment, and then turned to walk away into the night.

Ace wanted to call to him, and then she didn't.

Benny stood beside her, a bit too close. She'd been looking after the woman from Perivale ever since she and Máire had returned to the camp, and Ace hated it. She couldn't talk to her anymore, like she couldn't talk to Christopher, 'cos she didn't know how much she'd done to trick her, or how much she'd known about Jan's death.

Máire had her arm in a sling, and a patch over her eye. She stood by Ace's other shoulder, and her closeness was fine. She'd been down to the wire with death too, had lost just as much as Ace had.

Benny closed her eyes and threw her log. It bounced off the summit of the bonfire, flaring up. She'd been trying to find out what had happened to her students. Six dead. Paul Magrs had left for the equatorial docks already, declaring that he 'bloody ought to have said something different'. Kyla and Clive were packing. She felt that they, as well as Ace, were accusing her of something. ''Bye, Jan, take care . . .' she whispered.

Ace thought that was . . . she would have thought that was obscene. But there was no room in her for anger. There was no room for anything really except an expression, and that expression was one of empty pain.

It was her turn. She weighed the log in her hand, and thought about nothing. The wood was quite solid, it hadn't rotted. It was knotted into some interesting shapes.

She swung back her arm, and hurled the branch as hard as she could into the fire. It hit the pyre straight on, and erupted, causing all the branches around it to burn more brightly.

'Jan,' Ace said, and turned away.

On a distant hilltop, Time's Champion was watching the blaze too.

The Doctor's eyes were narrowed as he observed the bonfire. He'd been a long time in the vortex, visited some worlds, drifted past others.

His expression was dark as the clouds rolled up over the downs behind him.

Suddenly, Christopher was at his shoulder.

'I have come to say goodbye.'

'Goodbye.' The Time Lord frowned, as if considering the concept. 'And thank you. You understood what I was doing.'

'I understood, yes. But that does not mean that I approved. The dead can help the living, Doctor, but only as symbols. I wish to become a symbol. That is why I want to show you something.'

Christopher took a step forward, fixed the Doctor's eyes with his, and collapsed into the Time Lord's arms.

The small man staggered under the weight, wrestled with Christopher's limp form, finally had to let go.

Christopher fell to the ground.

The Doctor knelt down, and turned over the body. A lifeless face. No last breath, no final words. Just death.

He stood up, and looked down at the corpse.

'Dodo . . .' he murmured. 'No. Not Dodo. Ace. What have I done?'

Ace was walking the path back to the dig site alone, not thinking. The Travellers on their horses had passed her, and she'd shook her head to every offer of a ride. She'd already wrapped Jan's tent up, having given the useful stuff to other Travellers. Now there was just the business of getting the camp dismantled. The Travellers wanted to head on out to some new world, the archaeologists wanted to go back to their universities. Benny wanted to go on right out of human space. And she wanted to take Ace with her.

Well, that wasn't going to happen.

Ace was kicking tiny stones on the chalk track, trying to ignore the churned grass in the great plains. The thought of that just took her on a long low plunge to nothing.

There was a figure running across the grass.

Ace saw who it was, and was seized by a terrible fear. She turned and sprinted into the woods.

The figure came after her.

She dived through the trees, not really looking where she was going, tripping over roots and branches, The figure followed, scampering across the bracken and hopping neatly over the obstacles. It was calling her name.

'Leave me alone!' Ace shouted as she ran.

'I can't! I won't!' it shouted back.

Ace fell, went sprawling, and the thing was on top of her, trying to hold her face, to touch her hair.

'Get off!' she shrieked, lashing out. A finger fastened on her wrist, and suddenly she couldn't move.

'You can speak,' the Doctor told her.

'Leave me alone.'

'I . . . I just realized. I was only half there, like in a dream. I had to be, they'd have understood me otherwise, read my mind. That's why I did this now, while I'm all mixed up. I'm . . . strange at the moment. Changed.'

'Yeah.' Ace had to look at him, but there was nothing in her gaze.

The Doctor grew frantic, waving his free hand in the air. 'I should have told you that I could see Jan was infected from his retinal patterns, right at the start. I didn't expect you to –'

'You weren't jealous, then?'

'No! I'm a Time Lord, I don't –'

'You were.'

'I saved the lives of millions of people. Isn't one person –?' The Doctor stopped himself.

'What?! You think that's a good deal?' Ace shivered convulsively. 'If you let go my wrist, I'll kill you now, you know that? I'll kill you. You wanted me to leave him, just 'cos you told me to!'

'That may have . . . that might –'

Ace closed her eyes, disgusted. 'Leave me alone.'

'But I'm not me any more! I'm not –'

'Leave me alone!'

'Leave her alone.' Bernice was standing over them both. 'I

told you that you shouldn't meet. Look at you, you're afraid she'll attack you! Let her go, for God's sake!'

The Doctor released Ace's wrist.

She looked between the two of them. 'Fake Mum and Dad!' she spat. 'Bit worse, though. Thanks, but no thanks!' She stood up. 'Were we ever mates?'

'Yes!' the Doctor shouted, his voice like that of an aggrieved little boy.

'We can't have been.' Ace took a few steps away. 'You're not human, right, Professor? You're so clever, you little shit.' A few more, confident, steps backward. She took the cube from her pocket, and tossed it from hand to hand. 'I'm never gonna play your games again . . . never get manipulated again. Know what? You can have this too!'

Ace grabbed the jacket off her shoulders and slammed it on to the ground. Then she walked quickly away, clutching the cube to her chest.

Some way off, Máire met her and put an arm around her shoulders. The two women vanished into the depths of the forest. They seemed to be trying to speak to each other, as if Ace was having trouble understanding Máire's language. Just before she was gone, Benny thought that Ace had taken a quick glance over her shoulder.

But she couldn't be sure.

Benny wandered over to the jacket, and picked it up. 'Do you think she'll ever need this again?' she asked the Doctor.

'Oh yes . . .' the Time Lord muttered, gazing after his lost companion. 'But it doesn't make it any better.'

The Doctor and Benny trudged up the hill to where the TARDIS was standing, just above the dig site. The great arch had returned, and was somehow shining silver in the red moonlight.

Students were packing up their kit bags, and taking down tents.

'What do you think of me?' the Doctor asked.

'Oh,' Benny looked aside and then back to him, raising an eyebrow. 'You're like most men, aren't you? You think the end justifies the means, which isn't a very pretty attitude. Do you know, I half expected my old Dad to appear this week, as a zombie. He'd turn out to be part of one of your plans, and you'd expect me, of course, to go along with it. Rather than have a sort of breakdown, or just stop in my tracks. Which I suppose I would. Anybody would. Except you.'

'I haven't any buts left.' The Doctor looked down at his shoes, the TARDIS key in his hand. He whirled it around with his finger on the end of its chord. 'I do my best. I fight evil. I win.'

'Why did you treat her so badly?'

'Because I had to.'

'That isn't good enough.'

'It'll have to do.'

Benny pursed her lips. 'Well, I'll be off then, I've got a shuttle to catch in the morning. It was very nice to meet you.' She offered the Doctor her hand. He took it.

'This isn't supposed to happen.'

'Oh? And you know that, do you?' Benny let go, and wandered off in the direction of her tent. 'Has it occurred to you that you might actually be wrong?'

The Doctor watched her go. 'Yes,' he muttered. 'But not this time.'

Benny slid her diary into a rucksack, sighing. 'No,' she told herself. 'No, we will lay all that history, all those other worlds, aside. We shall not use this wonderful opportunity to find Dad, because the man who offers it is not charming, but is actually a bit of a git. Besides, he hasn't offered it.'

The Doctor's head poked through the tent flaps. 'I thought you could help. I went back into the TARDIS, and, taped to the console, I found another note to myself . . .'

'Really? Was it abusive?'

'Yes. Shall I read it?'

'Liberty hall, Professor.'

'Thank you, Professor.'

Benny lowered the Japanese fan she'd been about to insert into her pack. 'Tell you what. You call me Benny, and I'll call you Doctor. Professor isn't true for either of us.'

'Fine, fine. This is what the note says. "He is never cruel or cowardly. Although he is caught up in violent events, he is a man of peace." It goes on for a while. Do you recognize who this person is? I don't know if I do.'

'I presume it's talking about you. Obviously you don't know yourself very well. This is the person who presumably could have given the fleet details of where the Hoothi were earlier, but took time out to visit a graveyard.'

'No, it was a bluff. They would never have got here in time. The Hoothi were just waiting until the spores had buried deep enough into the soil. And when they changed position, it was just to appear above Joycetown. I thought for a while that perhaps ... I don't know what I thought. We were both just playing for time. But I had to confront them, for my own peace of mind. I had to know that there was no other way. I'm the Doctor ...' The Doctor shook himself by the hand.

'And I will obey you? Or are you going to have a little ... er, phrase to introduce me with?'

'I'm the Doctor, and this is my friend Benny?'

'Sounds bloody awful. How about "partner"?'

'Can't we be friends?'

'I don't know you well enough.'

The Doctor put a hand on Benny's shoulder.

She took it away again. 'Please don't touch me. You're very tactile and I'm not, really. I'd prefer it if you didn't.

'I'm the Doctor.' The Doctor frowned, looking round for inspiration. 'I know that I am ... I'm just confused. I need your help ...'

'No, wait, I remember you putting a Hoothi fibre to my neck. There is, as they say, just one thing I don't understand. How the hell did you manage to convince them that I was infected?'

'If I remember, and I'm not sure I do, I took the fibre into my own palm. My strange biology at the moment. And then I convinced them that they'd got you in the group mind.'

'How?'

'By letting them access the image of you that I held in my own mind. We touched minds. Over chess. In your tent. I was trying to hint that to you, by mentioning your diary. It can be rewritten.'

'So there is a corner of the Doctor's head that is forever Benny?'

'Yes!'

'You asked for my help.'

'For two things. Do you know "Puff the Magic Dragon?" '

'We went out a few times, he was very immature.'

'Do you know the bit where Jacky Piper leaves him, leaves him all alone?'

'I really don't want to hear this . . .' Benny zipped up her bag purposefully.

'The dragon can't be brave without the little boy. He doesn't have anything to be brave for. He might as well go, might as well drift off into myth, and just be something in old stories.'

'What would happen then?' Benny put down her belongings and folded her arms. 'There are other monsters . . . other terrible things out there, besides the Hoothi?'

'Many of them, yes.'

'Well, they must be fought. Because, and this is important, you can't just be alone. That's a childish thing to be. You can't just isolate yourself from everything, no matter what terrible things have happened. You have to help other people.'

'That's what Jacky Piper would have said.'

Bernice Summerfield sighed, and pulled on her rucksack. She considered the Doctor for a moment. 'You'll never play games with my life?'

'Never. I don't have to. You have my word.'

'So what's the other thing you wanted help with?'

The Doctor grinned, a beautiful seven-year-old grin. 'Ah . . .' he murmured. 'That's about the owls.'

The TARDIS door was open, where it stood atop a sandy bank. The low winds of autumn blew across the grass, and the strange inner light of the police box was a white triangle against the grey ridge.

Bernice Summerfield breathed in the air of a different century, and looked around. She had an owl tethered on her arm. 'Why,' she asked the Doctor, 'are we doing this? Is it part of a plan?'

'No . . .' The Doctor shook his head. He had an owl too. 'The species would have died out on Heaven. It wouldn't have survived the change in the ecosystem. We're doing it because . . . because it's poetic. Perhaps I believe in reincarnation. Perhaps I should.'

Benny looked back to the TARDIS. One journey, she had said. She'd hung Ace's jacket on a hatstand in the console room. When she'd come back after depositing her bags, it had vanished. 'Shall we let them go, then?'

'Yes.' The Doctor removed the small bag from the owl's head, and quickly pulled the cords that released its talons. Benny did likewise. The two birds of prey burst into the air like small fireworks, and circled higher and higher, up against the silver moon.

The owls in love looked down at the two tiny figures. The woman had taken the man's arm, and they were heading back to the TARDIS, him telling her that Scrane End wasn't the best place on twentieth-century Earth. There was a prison here. Ah, Benny was saying, but beyond the prison there's –

The door of the time craft closed, and a noise roared into the night, and then it was gone.

The owls circled, wingtips nearly touching. They were in love, and were making new owl poetry every moment with their flight. They would prepare a nest soon, and put eggs in it. It would never occur to them not to, even in the face of certain death, the same certainty that all life shared.

Their poetry told them that they were different to other life. It was difference, not length, that made their lives what they were. It was a good poem, and this is where it came to an end, when the owls headed inland on the warm air currents of Lincolnshire.

Beneath them, an old Allegro took a corner far too fast.

Long ago in an English autumn.